Pow

Power, Jo-Ann

Missing member

DUE DATE

10\06

missing

member

Also by Jo-Ann Power

Allure
Never Say Never
Never Again
Never Before
The Nightingale's Song
Gifts
Treasures
Remembrance
Angel of Midnight
You and No Other
The Last Duchess of Wolff's Lair
The Mark of the Chadwicks

missing

member

Jo-Ann Power

THOMAS DUNNE BOOKS   ST. MARTIN'S MINOTAUR   🐚   NEW YORK

This is a work of fiction. All of the characters, organizations, and events portrayed in this novel are either products of the author's imagination or are used fictitiously.

THOMAS DUNNE BOOKS.
An imprint of St. Martin's Press.

www.thomasdunnebooks.com
www.minotaurbooks.com

Library of Congress Cataloging-in-Publication Data

Power, Jo-Ann.
    Missing member : a me & Mr. Jones mystery / Jo-Ann Power.—1st ed.
        p. cm.
    ISBN-13: 978-0-312-35799-3
    ISBN-10: 0-312-35799-0
    1. Women legislators—United States—Fiction.   2. Washington (D.C.)—Fiction.   3. Texas—Fiction.   4. Political fiction.   I. Title.
    PS3616.O883M57 2006
    813'.54—dc22

                                                            2006044494

First Edition: September 2006

10   9   8   7   6   5   4   3   2   1

For Steve
With love

Acknowledgments

T hanking those who contributed to the appearance of this book is a bit like charting stars in the sky, but I will try.

Eliza Sunneland, radio talk-show host in San Antonio, who allowed me to be a ghost in her studio.

Steve and Vicki Schmidt, who shared stories of Texas ranching, childhood experiences, plus the finer points of how to ride a horse—and a longhorn.

To my many wonderful friends, new and old, in Texas and Washington, who gave of their time and expertise to help make Carly a living, breathing woman of substance.

My friends in San Antonio Romance Authors, who read rough drafts and encouraged me, and our Saturday morning critique group, Deloris Lynders, Mary Fechter, Mary Jernigan, and Miriam Minger, who helped me iron out lots of wrinkles in the manuscript.

My love and thanks to my family, Ann and Jason, who encouraged me, and Steve, who chuckled over Carly and told me to finish the story.

To my agent, Jay Poynor, who believed this could sell, and to my editor, Marcia Markland, who believed it deserved a place on bookshelves, this has been a wonderful experience.

Thank you all.

Cast of Characters

Aaron Blumfeld—Carly's chief of staff in her Washington office.

Barbara—Zachary Dunhill's governess, no last name.

Sarge Brown—detective with Capitol Police, Homicide Division.

"Big John" Casey—Carly's granddaddy and mentor, a former judge; deceased.

Alistair Dunhill—minority whip, murder victim.

Zachary (Zack) Dunhill—Alistair Dunhill's son, Jordan Underwood's friend.

Rayanne Ferrer—Carly's receptionist in her Washington office.

George Freiburger—congressman from Minneapolis.

Bubba Gardener—head of Southwest Texas Ranchers Association from Fort Davis, Texas.

Mickey ("Mickey G.") Gonzales—reporter for *San Antonio Express-News*.

Anna Harlan—Dez's wife, who went to school with Carly and Dez.

Desmond (Dez) Harlan—State Department official in charge of intelligence; Carly's high school friend.

Jimmy Jeff Holden—congressman from Thirteenth Congressional District of Texas (adjacent to Carly's district).

Holly Ireland—lobbyist for Senior Citizens United; former congresswoman.

Glenna Iverson—wife of Tommy Iverson, chairman of Carly's political party.

Tommy Iverson—chairman of Carly's political party; aka The Voice or The Money; wife is Glenna.

Abe Lincoln—Carly and Jordan's pet chimp.

Esme Navarro—Carly's constituent office manager in Uvalde regional office.

Sadie O'Neill—Carly's mother; widow; Texas rancher.

Ted O'Neill—Carly's father, who disappeared when she was sixteen; presumed dead.

Mirinda Pace—congresswoman in her first term; widow.

Louise (Lou) Rawlings—senior senator from Texas; aka "Grandma" Lou from Dallas, Texas.

Renard (no last name)—maître d' at La Colline.

William Preston Scott—minority leader of the House, congressman from Georgia.

Sally Sonderberg—congresswoman from Minnesota.

Patricia Tipton—Washington doyenne.

Jordan Underwood—Carly's daughter and only child, age twelve; father is Leonard Underwood.

Leonard (Len) Underwood—Carly's ex-husband; father of Jordan; lobbyist in the defense industry.

Krystal Vaughn—Alistair's receptionist.

Carly Wagner (née O'Neill)—"Legs" or "Red" to some in her Texas hometown; congresswoman from the Twenty-third Congressional District of Texas.

Frank Wagner—deceased, first husband of Carly.

Frank Wagner II—"Short-stuff," Frank II, Frank senior's son.

Woodruff—currently chairman of opposing political party (no first name).

Harry Woznowski—guard at front door of Rayburn Building.

Ming Yu-Bao—Carly's Chinese housekeeper; currently law student at Georgetown University.

missing

member

one

It's easy to wish the womanizer with a zipper problem would one day wind up with his dick in his hand. But when the guy is one you've dated, with news-hour name recognition, and he's gracing your office chair one morning with a bloody hole in his chest, your letter opener in one hand, and his severed penis in the other, you wish you'd never been so bold.

You ask yourself, calmly, while your mind does the whirling dervish thing before you call the guard at the front desk, *Did I ever say out loud I wanted this guy on a slab?*

Did I ever voice this to a friend? No, I shake my head, doubtful mostly because my closest friend died in '96 and I don't take time to make new ones.

Would I ever say this to a colleague? No. I would have to have downed half a dozen body shots of Herradura Silver to rage on someone like that. True, anyone on my staff might imprudently blurt out I could kill a man at twenty yards with my stare, but no, I don't do straight shots of tequila like I used to when I was young, loco, and unknown, with nothing to lose but my virginity.

I take a step closer to the body. Whoa, there. Death definitely smells like stale fish. And it doesn't provide a flattering photo op, either. Alistair Dunhill, once a six-foot-nine black-haired powerhouse with a year-round tan and blinding Brite Smile teeth, slumps without pride or dignity in my overstuffed, old oak chair. With head sloping over to one shoulder, his skin the color of paste, he'd be horrified to see himself, perfectionist that he once was. His mouth lies slack, with pink froth drooling out one side onto his crisp white shirt collar. His Armani suit coat is open. A dark red splotch marks his shirt on the right above his belly, the only flaccid part of him. His shirttails frame his open fly, gaping wide to reveal pale skin and a few short and curlies. Blood, dark and dry, encrusts the zipper.

I slap a hand over my mouth and gag, but, ghoul that I am, I move in for a closer look. His big onyx eyes are wide open, milky in death, and gazing . . . or rather, *not*, but pointing toward the skyline.

I get down to his level, something I repeatedly refused to do when he was living, and face the way he is, squinting at the detail. The view is the office building across the street. Its gray gaping windows stare back, most of the blinds still down. At five forty-five A.M. in this nose-to-the-grindstone town, the worker bees have not yet begun to swarm into their hives.

Thanking God, Buddha, and Allah (I pray at the altar of political correctness), I stride to the window. Lower the shade. On the second yank of the cord, I lift my hands, splay my fingers, then curl them like a burn victim. I shouldn't have touched that and left my prints and perspiration and whatever else forensics pros collect from scenes like this.

I wipe my hands on my skirt while my blood pressure climbs the charts. Dizzy does not become me. *Get it together, Carly. You need to be centered when the police start to ask questions—and you will need to be firmly in command of your army when Katie Couric tries to break this story like morning eggs all over the seven o'clock news.*

I take two steps to my briefcase, still standing like a soldier where my fingers dropped it to the carpet upon discovering Alistair in my chair. I dig out my cell phone. Punch in the number for the front desk. And breathe.

The guard picks up. I identify myself. What do I say? *Look,*

Harry. Small problemo. I have a dead man in my office. In my office chair, my inner office, Harry.

Who the hell knows what I say, but it must be something like that because Harry at first is speechless. I envision him, groping like a guppy. Good. I am not alone. Always have allies.

He mutters something that sounds like a curse and then enunciates so slowly that he implies my IQ logs in at cretin. "Don't touch anything. Don't *do* anything. And do not make or take any phone calls."

Oh, don't worry. I'd prefer to do the Three Monkeys on this one: See, hear, and definitely speak no evil. My personal fave would be to turn around, drive home, and crawl back between the sheets. I could pull them over my head and tell myself that the day has not begun. Dunhill is not clutching his cigar-sized penis, not holding the shiny silver murder weapon tipped with blood, not soaking my chair with his bodily fluids. I am not involved. I could even call in and declare I am just working from home today!

In a rat's eye, I could.

Denial is one psychological trait I used to get into big-time. Like a bubble bath. But I reformed years ago in the interest of keeping my job—and excelling at it. Wallowing now during the daylight only in projections, budget numbers, and press releases, I do tai chi to relieve tension. But when fatigue sets in, I turn on my patio lights and dig at night in the dirt of my backyard garden, burying seeds and bulbs along with any remaining frustrations. The result is I tend a disgustingly overcrowded English garden. Surveying Alistair, I predict that tonight I'll be planting enough seeds to regrow the Amazon jungle.

I curse. Then clamp the phone closed, drop it back in my briefcase.

I study Alistair.

What the hell is he doing in my inner office, in my chair? Why not outside in my receptionist's?

I circle my desk.

Alistair could have picked any one of the other offices on this hall to die in. Or how about in his own office chair?

But he did not pick, did he?

Someone did it for him.

They chose the place. Mine. The weapon. Mine, too. They'd also chosen the time—clearly, after I had gone home, maybe nine-thirtyish. I had been here alone most of the evening, except for Alistair's ten-minute visit to me around nine. Chances are, whoever killed him and left him here might have known that.

Crossing my arms, I shiver as I recall my actions after he'd left. I had pushed my chair into the desk, flicked off the overheads, then traipsed down into the garage, revved up my trusty Chevy Tahoe, and toddled on home alone to an empty house. No alibi, no corroborating witnesses in sight. Then, with no one at home to confirm my story there, either, I had planted chrysanthemums in the backyard until my energy and my desire for gin ran out a little past midnight.

I stoop to examine Alistair's body more closely—and this time I ignore his twanger, just like I did when he was alive. His hair is ruffled. His suit is a shambles, wrinkled as if he'd slept in it. His left lapel is torn or ripped—maybe by my letter opener. His left eyelid seems cut with a line of blood as if someone poked him good. Did his killer attack him, beat him up first? Makes sense to me. Weaken your foe before you move in for the final blow. I haven't risen this far up in the world without practicing Sun Tzu's *Art of War*. Of course, my mother's five rules formed my character first. Tempt 'em, tell 'em, order 'em, love 'em, leave 'em wanting more. Sadie O'Neill didn't raise no fool.

I jam my hands in my skirt pockets and devote myself to wearing a circular path in my carpet while I absorb details of the crime scene. My desktop is bare, except for the two items that should be there. The photo of my pride and joy, my twelve-year-old daughter, Jordan, and the small marble trophy I won at age fifteen for Texas State Rodeo Barrel-Racing Champion. Definitely the desk is the way I left it, but what about all the drawers? All appear neatly closed, the way they should be. But are they locked? I wince. My heart picks up a salsa beat. They better be. I try to remember and, for the life of me, can't recall if I did turn the lock with my key before I left for home! But at least the center drawer had to have been open, right? Otherwise, how could Alistair be holding my letter opener? I reach to open that drawer and think better of that little maneuver. I'm not into implicating myself or covering up anyone else's prints . . . if indeed there are any, other than Alistair's.

I bend over, scrutinizing the keyholes and edges. None appears to be tampered with. The desk, due to its advanced age, is secure as a vault, the previous owner told me when I purchased it from him as he left this office. The four-foot-by-six-foot expanse is early Johnson (Andrew, not Lyndon), and coveting it as I had for years, I was thrilled to find it for sale when I moved into this building last year. The building, like the desk, was supposed to be unbreachable, an inner sanctum, holy of holies, that no one could just enter at will. After all, the doors to each of our offices are key coded. No one passes through the metal-detector gates down at the front entrance or the garage or even the press entrance without presenting a badge with photo ID. Briefcases are wanded. All packages, too. Bomb-sniffing dogs as feral as those patrolling death row at Huntsville roam the halls and the grounds, receiving one solid square meal a day for their 24/7 devotion. Security is the highest priority here. No need to worry.

Unless you are Alistair Dunhill and someone wants to cut off your life and your dick.

And that same someone wants to frame the little lady who works in Rayburn Office Building Room 2336, Carly Wagner, five-time elected congresswoman from the Twenty-third District of Texas.

I have often thought I might be bipolar. With a mother like mine, you would, too. Sadie O'Neill's usually an Irish angel in snakeskin boots. Unless you cross her. Then, before you can turn tail to run, she'll sink her fangs into you and swallow you whole. This day when a dead man lies in my office, I note my mood swings from red-haired viper to cool fish with a career to save.

To Harry Woznowski, who mans the front desk and is the guy I broke the news to about Alistair—I am calm. He enters my office now, approximately four minutes after I called him, and he's huffing and puffing, two hundred pounds of Polish sausage stuffed into five-foot-five, tops. And on him, I smile down, grateful for his speed. I remain cooperative. Personable.

While he does a silent and lengthy perusal of Alistair, I tell him that, yes, this is how I found the fourth most powerful man in the House of Representatives, the minority whip. My party's number-two honcho here. No, I have not touched anything in the office—except the cord of the window blinds. I also did touch my phone, my briefcase, my skirt, but that is irrelevant to the crime scene since all those things were with me or on me before I walked in. Yes, I am blathering, and I know it, so finally I just shut up. But when Harry moves in for a close-up of Alistair's shriveled little wiener and says, "Wow. Not too big, was it?" I show the other side of my nature—and bare my teeth at him. "Harry, forget his penis."

"He never did." Harry does a salacious chuckle, but clears his throat and repents. "Sorry. Any ideas how he got in here?"

I roll my eyeballs.

But he smacks his thick lips like a dog over a bone and offers, "Someone let him in or he had a key."

Here, I go over to my Sadie O'Neill suffer-no-idiots pole and hiss, "No one let him in and he did not have a key." The words tumble out, but I realize I have reason to wonder if they're true. Couldn't someone have come in after I left or given him a key?

Skeptical, too, Harry grunts at me as he bends to examine the bloody spot on Alistair's shirt. "We gotta ask your staff."

"By all means. But I was the last one in here last night." I shift from one foot to the other, antsy with my growing suspicions.

"Congressman Dunhill had been here to visit me a few minutes earlier but left maybe ten minutes before I did."

"And?"

I level my gaze at Harry and stare.

Most men—even an impartial, erudite newsman like Jim Lehrer—can go goofy over my eyes. For those I wish to warm, my big brown babies can melt a man. For others who try to walk on the hot sands of my disapproval and live to tell the tale, my stare can mean many things. Get lost. Get to work. Get the answer. Get a life.

For Harry, this morning's message is, *Get real.* But realizing how this will play out in police records and in the press, I strive for serenity. "When I left, the congressman was not in the hall. No one was," I recall with clarity.

"So the congressman did not leave with you?" Harry could really be a testy little bugger.

"He did not go with me, nor did I leave him here." I conclude that is all I will say to Harry. I'll save myself for the big boys. For certain, this is kind of like saving yourself for your wedding night, knowing you have given the goods away but lying to yourself that the groom won't notice because he is so eager to get on with the main event.

"I'm going to take my briefcase and sit in my legislative aides' office." I know I can watch from that vantage point who comes in and out of my suite's main door and my inner office. Plus, I can sit there and try to read this slew of statistics before this morning's committee meeting on military base closings.

Sure, I tell myself that the prospect of dealing with murder and the police could put the fear of god in me. But I'm a big girl. I can weather that.

I snort. Recognizing I'm serving myself a load of prime bull, I know if I stop to think too hard, I'll wind up in the john with my head over the toilet.

And I am nothing if not brave. You can't fix stupid, but brave you are either born with or not. No acquiring it.

Me, I now vow to keep the lid on my nerves by focusing on the possibility that the committee chairman would postpone this morning's session because of Alistair's murder. That I can't have. This morning's hearings are to discuss Air Force bases the President wants to close down in my district. These bases bring in more than three billion dollars a year to my district's economy and delaying the hearings would only prolong the agony of impending layoffs for folks who counted on me to ensure the federal budget gave them their daily bread.

So I focus on money. Money that soothes and money that heals. Like money from alimony—and money from child support. I like any kind of money.

My head clears, my stomach stops flipping. I'm going to be fine. Alistair is gone, but there is nothing I can do about that. I repeat that to myself as I commandeer a desk in the main room, sit down, and dig my cell phone out of my briefcase. I'm calling in my cavalry, speed-dialing my chief administrative aide at home. Why? Because in this political town, when something goes awry in a politician's day, the man to call is the one who knows more about the politician than god. In my case, that was my AA of nine years, Aaron Blumfeld. And this morning, ol' Aaron is not answering his phone very quickly. So when I get voice mail, I end the call and hit the number pad again. He'll know who it is. I listen to the ring begin and take the phone from my ear to read the face clock . . . 6:08 A.M. April 4. Tuesday.

Springtime in the nation's capital. Pink cherry blossoms. Lady Bird's psychedelic-colored tulips. A dead man in my inner office. Just another day, right?

I tap my fingernails on the desktop. Where, oh, where is Aaron? To fail to answer his phone means he is doing one of two things. Either walking from his D Street townhouse to Rayburn (because he loathes talking on the horn on the street)—or he is still in the sack humping his newest romantic interest. Another guy. Aaron changes lovers like laundry.

At the next ring, he picks up and shouts, "Hello?" He's out of breath, like he's been running.

"Aaron!" He knows my voice, understands my tones. "What took you so long?"

"Good morning, ma'am. I apologize." He's fumbling with the phone. As if he's jumping into his pants. "What can I help you with?"

"Are you on your way in?"

"Yes, ma'am. I will be there in about . . . twenty minutes."

"Speed it up, will you?"

When he asks why, I deliver the news.

He pauses, processing for maybe half a second. "Media there yet?" Aaron always thinks of first things first.

"No."

"Good. I'll be there in . . . fifteen."

"Ten."

"I'll hail a cab."

It's tough to find a cab in the residential areas east of the Capitol at any time of the day, especially this early on a midweek morning. Nonetheless, within his own time frame, Aaron blows through the door. He is dressed in a dapper dark gray suit, appropriate for someone who needs to appear bereaved. Holding aloft a necktie of an even grimmer charcoal in his hand, he's trying to squeeze past one recently arrived uniformed Capitol policeman, another with a giant camera bag, and one plainclothesman, all of whom are chatting each other up like women at a baby shower.

Aaron is lithe, quick, but he can't elude the reflexes of the tall one in plainclothes, a dour-faced black man.

"Hold on a minute there, sir!" He grabs Aaron by the sleeve, a faux pas of the highest order to Aaron the Fashion Plate, who irons every item of clothing, probably even his silk thongs.

Aaron is definitely affronted and lets his eyes slowly ascend from the man's hand up into this guy's very long, very broad face.

"Excuse me," he tells his captor. The policeman releases Aaron's elbow. "I work here. I am Congresswoman Wagner's chief aide and she needs me."

A set of onyx eyes fly to mine. "Guard." The plainclothesman beckons Harry from his roost in front of my office door and nods at me. "Now is good for introductions."

Harry walks him over, so I get to take my time examining him. He reminds me oddly of Columbo because of his wild and woolly hair and his wrinkled raincoat. But any resemblance ends there. This man is young, maybe late thirties, and therefore surprisingly young for a Capitol policeman, most of whom are retired from the D.C. police force and looking for less stressful duty. With shoulders like a quarterhorse and tall as an NBA all-star, he is one supple hunk of flesh I don't want to wrestle with.

"Ma'am," Harry does his duty when they get in front of me, "this is Capitol Police Detective Brown. Sarge Brown." Detective Brown takes stock of me, from my natural wine-red hair to my sensible black pumps—and I know he's matching the woman he's seen on TV to the one in this chair. I get no read on what he concludes, so I play to both of my advantages—power and sex appeal, in that order.

I do not rise from my chair, though I do—with Miss Manners my constant guide—stick out my hand to shake his. Wrong move.

He shoots his white palms up in the air. "Ma'am, if you would please not touch anything until we get our crime inspection crew here. We want to process your hands. I'm sure you understand." One point to the detective.

"I do, but the only things I touched this morning were the window shade cord, my cell phone, this pen, these papers, and my suit." One point to me.

His jaw tightens, unhappy with my snap. "We'll process those, too."

"When?" I'm determined that if he's got his sights set on being a star, he can't cast me as his stairway to heaven. "I am happy to cooperate, Detective. But let's do it quickly. I have hearings beginning soon." Purposely, I do not say when. "If you need my clothes, that's no problem, just say so. I can change into another set I keep in my inner office closet, but let me get on with my work."

Shouts interrupt us.

We both turn to my inner office door, where Harry is barring the door with hands out across the jamb. He and Aaron are nose-to-nose.

Detective Brown lurches toward them. "Sir!"

His outrage makes me grimace. I hustle over to catch Aaron before he goes into his version of "This Land Is My Land," but I don't quite make it.

"Officer, we need to be in this office," Aaron objects to Harry, but turns to Sarge.

I step forward. "Sergeant—"

"Detective," he corrects me. "My given name is Sarge."

"Sorry," I reply, but he's not listening.

He's leaning down, nearly pressing his broad flat nose against my Aaron's beak. "Now, as for you, sir—"

Aaron remains unruffled. "Detective, my job is to see that the congresswoman moves through her day quickly and efficiently. If you bar us from her office—"

Soon these two guys are gonna bite each other. But the only one I can control is Aaron. I reach out to him, but the detective inches closer.

"Your name, Mr. . . . ?"

"Blumfeld. Aaron Blumfeld."

"Mr. Aaron Flowerfield."

"You know German?" Aaron is mildly impressed.

"Yiddish. My grandmother cleaned house for thirty-two years for the rabbi over at Temple Sinai. Mr. Blumfeld, hear me. You will not go into that room. No one does, not even you, ma'am." He pins me with his fathomless black eyes. "We will start processing the crime scene with my photographer there." He nods to the guy he'd been talking to. "More of my technicians will soon get here."

"Detective," I press him, "I have to be able to get in there. I have a lot of papers locked in my desk"—*or I hope they are*—"that I'll need today." Like my notes on how job losses in San Antonio will affect local health care if the Air Force medical facility there closes. "I cannot allow you to keep me out indefinitely."

"Depending on what we find," he insists, "you can probably get in sometime tomorrow or the next day."

"That's too long, Detective." I like giving suggestions that make folks pivot. "What if you supervise me, can't I get into my desk? Certainly, if you want me to change clothes, I'll have to go in there to get them."

"No, I'm sorry you can't do that, either. Have someone on your staff get clothes from your home. We'll do our best to give you access as quickly as we can, but I have no idea what we'll need to process when I haven't even been in there myself yet." A group of officers in jumpsuits appears at the door. "Here they are. I'll get them started and then come back to talk to you, Congresswoman. Until then"—Sarge directs his heavy-lidded gaze toward the chair where I had been sitting when he came in—"please sit down."

I glance at my watch and try for whatever concession to power I can grab. "I hope this means within the next twenty minutes." I'm not due to the committee hearing room for another three hours, but I'm not going to cool my heels waiting for Sarge to decide how I manage my day.

"I'll do my best," he says without convincing me.

Aaron hovers at my side, sizing up what I really think of Detective Sarge Brown.

He knows what I think of policemen in general.

I don't venture any words, but lift my chin toward him, our signal that I am able to handle this situation on my own. Detective Sarge Brown is the first law enforcement type I have dealt with for a personal reason since my father stomped out of the family ranch house one morning twenty-six years ago and never came back. We never found him, not hide nor hair, and nearly everyone in the county suspected Sadie had shot him and buried him somewhere in the high, hot South Texas desert. And for a good long while, so did I.

But that was old news. Past as prelude, crisis as character development, and motivation to wash yourself white as snow.

Which I had.

Which I would do here, too.

So I walk over and settle myself into my old chair, filling my lungs with fresh oxygen, inventing this new form of stress reduction for murder suspects. At the tender age of sixteen when my dad disappeared, I didn't have any such exotic techniques to cope with disaster. I just had nerves of steel, taut and sharp as our barbed-wire fence. Back then I developed a distrust of sheriffs and the white-hatted do-good Texas Rangers. They didn't listen well, didn't know how to write well or read, and years later, I cut my teeth in Texas politics by standing up for better schools and better law enforcement.

I vow Sarge is getting nothing out of me that I do not want to give.

But I know I better get Aaron to send our receptionist over to Georgetown to get another suit of clothes for me—and while she's out she should swing into Johnson's to buy a dozen or more flats of seedlings for me. Better to fill my day anticipating planting impatiens than brooding over how this murder might put me in an early political grave.

two

The media circus is about to pitch its first big top over me.
I spot the white Channel 11 TV news van stuck near the Rayburn Building checkpoint out on Independence Ave. and bet
that means their news producer is sending in a bigger crew to
cover this story about Alistair.

I've got one hip perched on the window ledge, having given
up memorizing the Air Force stats in favor of watching the sun
come up. In the interval since my introduction to Detective
Brown, I have had my fill of postmortem police activities. A
forensic techie has inked my fingerprints. Aaron sent our receptionist, Rayanne, to fetch another suit, blouse, and pair of shoes
from home and I've handed over to Sarge's pathologist the navy
duds I wore into work. He's had his man bag everything, except
for my underwear and hose. Now I'm wearing what Rayanne
chose from my closet for me—my neon-bright emerald suit.
Twice before in the year since Aaron hired this curvy Barbie
doll, I have questioned Rayanne's discretion in choosing attire
for events. Today, the image she will have me projecting later, appearing on nationwide news discussing murder, will be that of a
leprechaun. I grind my teeth, but there's nothing I can do except let my grief for Alistair's loss show through the TV lens.
Meanwhile, until someone assures me that Alistair's only remaining family—his young twelve-year-old son—has been notified

of his father's death, I am not feeding the media by making any formal statement.

I fret about that a lot because I know Alistair's boy and like him tremendously. And so does my daughter.

While I stare out at nothing and try to figure how to maneuver my day like the *Titanic* through ice floes, three of my legislative aides plus my press secretary have arrived for work. They are the only folks who can get past the policeman at the hall door. The place is buzzing, what with a dozen police traipsing in and out of my office, the phones ringing, printers whirring—and my paranoia screaming at me like some bad old dog.

I hear Aaron objecting to someone coming in and I peek around a corner of the bookcase. Suddenly I am face-to-face with Mickey Gonzales, my most unfavorite newspaperman.

"Good morning, Congresswoman Wagner," Mickey G. lisps in a voice that gives eerie evidence of his life as a scorpion. He's the Washington correspondent for the San Antonio *Express-News* and my numero uno nemesis. "I see Aaron's got a replacement for his Cerberus-at-the-gate act this morning." He nods at the policeman.

I don't spar with this guy. Ever. Without being certain I can win. "How can I help you, Mr. Gonzales?"

Aaron has hustled over to try to extricate me from the reporter whose words had stung me on more than one occasion. Mickey G. hails from a Rio Grande border town, meaning he has sprung out of one of the most impoverished areas of the country. Yes, he'd done it with hard work, a scholarship to UT in Austin, and a hard-wired connection to two South Texas political bosses who work well with the mostly Hispanic population—and, lately, with me. My district stretches for eight hundred miles along the border and these folks are my constituents. Keeping them happy, safe, and sound is my top priority. But lest we forget, I am Anglo and female. Two minority designations where I come from, amigos. That means I have to prove my worth almost daily to Mickey G. and his buddies. Today, that is going to be tough. Cuz if I can't talk myself out of this locked-room murder mystery, my girlish Anglo ass is going to be grass. And that, so rare in the high desert of South Texas, means I can die for want of support from Mickey G.'s readers.

"Thank you, Aaron." I try to dismiss my AA with a small smile.

"Mr. Gonzales is breaking the police line, ma'am," Aaron fumes, giving the evil eye to our culprit. "I promised the policeman on the door I wouldn't let anyone in while he went to the bathroom. I turned my back and Mr. Gonzales squeezed through."

"Aaron, it's okay." As long as Mickey G. is here, I might as well try to use him to my advantage. "I will speak with Mr. Gonzales for a minute."

"Want to tell me what's going on here, ma'am? We've got rumors that Congressman Alistair Dunhill was found dead in your inner office."

"Yes, I am very sad to tell you that is true."

"Who found him?"

"I did."

"What time?"

I think slowly, speak more slowly, but this is necessary so that Mickey G. can't ride roughshod over me. "Approximately five forty-five. I was stunned to see him there."

"I bet you were."

I move not one muscle. How I hate this guy's lack of tact. How I hunger for the day when I catch him in some misstatement or breach of ethics, anything so that I can watch him die a slow death.

He reads my expression and asks a more prudent question. "Want to give me a formal statement?"

"Not right now."

"Why's that?"

"I am hoping that Congressman Dunhill's family learns about this first before the media begin to discuss it."

"Word's leaking out. You should do what you can. Damage control."

Political advice from Mickey G. is like taking candy from a baby. It's easy and you feel like crap afterward. "I mean it, Mr. Gonzales." *Do not mess with me on this,* my look warns him.

He withers, but only a hair. "So?"

"I don't want my words splashed across papers on the same headline level as the announcement of the congressman's death."

"Right. Agreed. But you're sad, yes?" His stinger comes up over his head to strike.

Damn him. I get closer, adamant. "I want you to print these words exactly as I say them, but not as a direct quote, agreed?"

He hesitates.

"Those are my terms."

"But—"

"Agree or I take this up with Manuel in Del Rio." Hector Manuel is a border lord, a *jefe* no one messes with. And Hector happens to be a big supporter of mine.

Mickey G. nods. He retracts his stinger.

I refrain from smiling and collect my thoughts. "I am saddened by the loss of a man who was a noted statesman and a friend. I will miss him, his help, his advice, and his leadership. I know all our colleagues in the House and the Senate join me in giving our sincerest condolences to his family."

My sentiment is no crock, either. Alistair was a deft politico, with the knowledge and finesse to corral the most stubborn of our colleagues and drive them in the right direction on many issues. If he'd been losing his touch lately, many in the party figured it was a temporary condition.

Mickey is scribbling down my words but facing the window, so he can't see that they are about to be all he'll have from me. Detective Brown is frowning down on Mickey G.'s dark head and clearly wants to say a few choice words of his own to him.

"Pardon me!" The detective uses his bass voice like a club, making Mickey lurch around. "Who are you?"

Mickey stands a bit straighter facing the law. "I'm the Washington correspondent for the San Antonio *Express-News.*" He digs in his jacket pocket for his press ID and holds it up to Sarge's nose.

The detective doesn't read it, but pushes it down with one clawlike hand. "Put that away. We're in the midst of a crime scene investigation and you are in here without my authorization . . . so frankly, Mr. . . . ?"

"Gonzales."

"Right. You, Mr. Gonzales, are . . . out of here."

"But I just—"

"We will issue formal statements for the press after we have finished. This means that you, sir, are gone. Now."

Mickey throws me a pleading look, though why he thinks I'd save him beats me. He has to trudge off.

I'm tempted to gloat and say, *Toodles,* but stuff it because I'm a diplomat, don't you see, and because Sarge is training his eyes on me. "No more interviews, please, ma'am, until you and I can talk."

"I'd be happy to comply. But in the meantime, I think you need another patrolman on that door, Detective." I nod toward the street below. "We've got more company headed this way."

He leans over me and grunts at the sight of the TV van. "I'll call for assistance. Thanks." He whips out his cell phone as he marches back into my inner office.

I watch the flurry around me for a minute or two but can't sit still. I peek around the bookcase again, note that Detective Brown and his band of renown are behind my closed office door. My briefcase and my cell phone are within grabbing distance. I convince myself that I'll be following Sarge's orders if I talk to someone who will not technically "interview" me. So what's a girl to do when she's dying to talk to the only person who can give her some objective advice?

I reach for my phone and snuggle back into the blind spot between bookcase and window. The phone rings and on the count of two, I get a real live person. "Good morning, this is Senator Louise Rawlings's office. How may I help you?"

"Good morning, this is Congresswoman Wagner. Is the senator in yet this morning?"

"Yes, ma'am, she is."

"Is she able to take my call?" I am speaking softly, not interested in letting my staff know who I'm talking to. It's not that I'm not proud of my friendship with Lou. Oh, boy, am I. But, here in these halls and out on these streets, you mustn't ever let anyone see you sweat—or let anyone know who your best friends are. Not even the folks you pay to do your work.

"If you could please hold on, ma'am, while I buzz her and ask?"

"Yes, thank you, I will."

I hear the click off and then on.

"Carly."

"Hi, Lou."

"How are you?" From her no-nonsense tone, I can tell that the senior senator from my home state has heard of the tragedy in my office. She's held her seat for thirty-five years, swimming with the current along the Potomac since Nixon churned and burned. She's one of my party's stars, a compassionate woman, wife and mother of five, with a heart of gold and a stranglehold on the female vote in the Lone Star State. If anyone understands a woman's challenges, the press say, it's got to be Grandma Lou from Dallas. I figure she'll understand mine this morning.

"Holding my own. It gets tougher by the minute, however."

"I hear rumors that Alistair was dismembered."

"Gee, that news is faster than a speeding bullet."

"So it's true. My God. Sensationalism above and beyond 'I did not have sex with that woman.' We will become the next political party living in Animal House. How do we survive this one." This last is really no question.

I lick my lips and blurt out the other fact that rocks my world this morning. "They used my letter opener to kill him."

Louise makes an agonized sound. "Any ideas how Alistair got into your office?"

"None." I could tell her later how he had come and gone before I left last night. Right now I need an opinion on something else. "Should I call a lawyer?"

"Not unless you need one." Half a diplomatic second ticks by. "Do you?"

I appreciate where she's coming from, why she has to ask to satisfy herself. After all, she's running in presidential primaries this spring and she has to be careful what she says and does. Nonetheless, Lou has always been good to me as my friend and also my mentor. I admire her; she relies on me. We're Texas cowgirls, born and raised to ride herd on cattle and men, taught to act fast, think last, especially if shooting a varmint seems like the right thing to do. "No, Lou, lawyers aren't my favorite folks, but I'm not familiar with technicalities of this kind of thing." I have never gone to law school, but earned my spurs hosting the morning drive-time talk show at KTSA radio in San Antonio. "I can watch a thousand police shows, but who knows when the best time is to call for help? Really?"

"Just tell them exactly what they ask for. No more or less. And don't let them smell your fear."

I clear my throat. "I know, but—"

"What?"

She's alarmed and impatient. Hey, I get it. So am I. "I've dealt with police before when my father disappeared in 'eighty."

"You probably didn't do so well then, darlin', because you were a kid."

"Right."

"You're wiser now. Show it. I have got to go, but you call me back, hear me?"

"Yes. Much later, it looks like."

"For me, too. I have back-to-backs all day. We'll talk after four or so. Call me on my cell, not this. Who knows where I'll be— but I will leave it on for your call."

"Thanks, Lou."

We say good-bye and I feel a bit stronger. Like a flu patient who's downed a dose of chicken soup.

I make a beeline to the office coffeepot.

I'm sitting at one of my LAs' desks giving one more go at those Air Force stats when I notice Sarge walking toward me. Finally.

Almost two hours have passed since he and his team shut me out of my office to secure the crime scene. Minutes ago, the pathologist, looking as ashen and bereaved as a funeral mourner, walked behind four of his technicians as they carried out a slate-gray body bag. Alistair was zipped up inside. Rigor had set in, so that he was in a sitting position inside the bag, making a zigzag shape as they toted him out. Close behind him, a score of Capitol Police filed out. Now one patrolman secures yellow crime scene tape across my office door. So Sarge is ready for me.

He hooks a hand under the top of an old ladder-back chair and pulls it forward. "Ma'am, excuse me."

I put down my papers, take off my reading glasses, and sit back.

"Let's go through the events of last night and this morning in more detail, shall we?" He fans out his wrinkled raincoat kind of like Superman coming in for a landing. Then he straddles the chair.

I nod, but I've had too much coffee and too much time to mull over just how much damage control I'm going to have to do. I'm edgy. I can't circle my wagons. I have nibbled on my lips until I need a gob of Vaseline. I wonder if the FBI gets involved in the violent deaths of congressmen, and if so, when. I worry that I can't tell my daughter about this before it hits the airwaves because she's with her father in-flight to Tokyo. I haven't had a callback from the minority leader, who is my party chieftain here in the House. The Channel 11 team has so far not sent up a request to see me and neither have any other media since

Mickey G. broke the barrier. But soon they will. And so will their friends. By the droves.

To boot, I have rejected four edits of a press release written by my new and very green press aide. I've gotten a run in my stocking from when I changed clothes. We haven't heard from the Defense Appropriations Subcommittee chairman's office notifying us whether he'll hold the hearings this morning. And the chair, who presides over this subcommittee like Sherman marching through Georgia, is a TV hound dog. I can just picture him salivating at the prospect of laying postponement of the hearings on my doorstep.

I want to talk, give Sarge the facts, and get out of his gun sights. I cross my arms, but undo them in a flash when I realize the defensive body lingo it portrays. I try to look congenial. "I'm happy to help, Detective."

He extracts a skinny green steno pad and pen from inside his coat. "Why don't you start by describing what happened here last night?"

"Certainly." That question is about as wide open as the Texas sky. "What would you like to know?"

"You say you were here late last night. Until what time?" He clicks his pen and examines me—I swear—pore by facial pore. From the mouth up.

"About nine-thirty."

"How do you know?"

"I checked the clock as I was clearing my desk."

"Do you always?"

"Check the clock? No. Clear the desk? Yes."

"Why?"

"Habit." I shrug, trying to stay calm, but he is examining my eyebrows and I wonder if he thinks assessing my wax job will give him clues to my character. "I like to think I have a tabula rasa each morning." I smile, hard, then drop it. "Why?"

I get the distinct impression he does not appreciate the challenge to his control of the conversation, but he tilts his head in a little boy's way. "I'm a messy desktop person myself."

I relax enough to show some of my usual sass. "Whatever gets you through the night, right?" He gives me a glimpse of his pearly whites and I see his tactic is to confuse his suspects into dropping their guard. Be kind, be cruel, be indifferent. Big *problemo* for me, because no matter how hard I'd like to change it, my guard begins to show all the qualities of Saran Wrap—see-through, tight, and thin.

He leans forward, as if he's sharing bedroom secrets. "I like to see all the projects I need to keep up with."

"I can remember mine."

"Good for you."

Is that last comment a compliment or just repartee to catch me in his web? I can't decide because I'm too busy doing a mental two-step around the room. He can't be out to nail me for a murder I didn't commit. Why would he be? Mistakes like that don't look good on a personnel record, much less the annual salary review. Plus, chances are superb his yummy bone structure and dark chocolate skin are going to have exposure on every major news channel in the country, so he'd better get his facts right from the git-go.

"Back to your contact with the deceased yesterday."

"Yes. Last night around nine, he came here." I wait.

So does he.

I don't bat an eye.

He tries for the endurance award in our Mexican standoff but gives up, probably in the interest of saving time. "Were you surprised at his visit? Why had he come?"

"Alistair called me earlier in the day. He wanted to talk about—"

Sarge held up a finger.

I cocked my head. What was wrong?

"You called the congressman by his first name?"

"Yes." Damn. I'm not thinking before I speak. This is a bad, bad thing. "I have known him for ten years, Detective. Since the day I arrived on Capitol Hill, Congressman Dunhill"—I refer to

Alistair the way Sarge thinks I should—"has been the minority whip. He and I talk often, work together often, especially this last term when I gained more seniority, especially in Appropriations, where we decide how all the money is spent. If you want me to be formal, I can do that and call him by his last name or even his title. However, if you want to do this interview quickly—and naturally—then you'd best let me speak as I wish to tell my story."

Sarge looks only vaguely apologetic. "Please, continue."

I shove out a breath. "Alistair called me because he wanted to meet, talk. We have a vote coming up on the floor for the administration's Medicare bill. I didn't have much time to talk when he called, so I told him I was going to work late here, I could come see him when I got finished."

"What time was your phone discussion?"

"Around two or so."

"And did you go see him?"

"No."

"Why not?"

"I was working on these numbers for this morning's hearings and time slipped away." I tap my fingers on the pile of Air Force documents. "But Alistair gave me a ring around six, said he was hungry, and asked if I wanted to join him and a friend for dinner. I begged off and he suggested that when he returned, he could come see me. I told him he could. I would be here."

Sarge is one of those folks who puts the tip of his tongue between his lips when he concentrates and writes. From the way his hand moves in little jerks and dots, I get the impression he uses old-fashioned Gregg shorthand to take his notes. "Ahhnn-ha. Okaaay. . . . Any idea who the friend was he went to dinner with?"

"None." Sarge is back to being too casual for a policeman, setting all kinds of traps I have to find.

"Any idea where they went to eat?"

I shake my head. "I can't recall if he said La Colline over on

North Capitol Street or if he had a reservation. I'm sorry, I'm just not sure. You might ask his AA or his receptionist. Someone in his office makes appointments and keeps track of receipts."

"I'll check it out. Now . . ." He flips a page in his notebook and examines my pores again. This time, he takes to measuring my cheekbones. "Tell me about when he arrived. Do you remember the time?"

Why isn't he looking me in the eye? That's where police discover whether a person is lying or not. "Approximately nine. Like I told you before."

"All right. Now . . ." He is scribbling. "Tell me everything you remember about him and what you talked about."

"He wanted to talk about wording in a new Medicaid bill that changes eligibility rules for the elderly and disabled."

"And . . ." Sarge circles a hand in the air, like a team coach looking for some speed. "Was he for? Against?"

"He wanted my support on the bill. I told him again, as I have a few times before, I would vote against the bill if the wording remained the way it was because millions of people would be cut off from adequate funding for long-term care. He was unhappy I clung to that view, because it's opposite to our party's position."

Sarge leans forward. I don't think it's an attempt to look friendly. Three phones are ringing off the hook, Aaron's having a heated debate with Rayanne, our receptionist, not twenty paces behind Sarge, and one of our legislative aides is muttering at the stalled printer on his desk off to my right.

Sarge scans the room, scowling at the bustle of the place, and scrapes his chair closer. "So you disagreed on the bill's wording. How badly?"

"We debated the matter." Actually, Alistair was pretty unhappy with me and yelled until he realized we were going nowhere fast.

"Did you argue with him?"

"On a few points, yes." This is true, but a bit of a dress-down of the hot rhetoric he threw at me.

Brown raises a brow, skeptical at my brevity. "I see. And how long did your debate take?"

I shrug. "A few minutes."

"Five? Ten? Fifteen?"

"Maybe ten to fifteen." I press my lips together. "What more could I tell you except the exact words?" *Do you want me to?*

"It would help if you can recount what you said, what you did, what you touched, yes."

I frown at Sarge. He's not letting me off the hook easily. Was there something about my office I had missed this morning? I mentally rewind the videotape of my predawn arrival—and recall nothing new. Resigned, careful of my words, I begin to moderate the scene of the night before for him.

"Okay." I close my eyes a second. "Alistair walks in. I'm surprised because I have not heard his footsteps approaching. He startles me when he steps into my doorway there." I tip my head toward the entry near my receptionist's desk. "The door was open. I had left it open because I knew he was coming eventually. He says hello. I'm sitting at my desk working and I say hello to him. He comes in. 'Hi, Carly, how are you, long day, good dinner, too bad you missed it . . .' et cetera, et cetera, I don't know exactly what he says, but it's small talk."

"Good. And then what? Does the congressman remain standing, sit down—if so, where?"

I direct my attention to the yellow tape across my office, reliving a scene that, like most in life, seemed ordinary and, at the time, forgettable. "He walks in, shakes my hand across the desk, and I indicate he should sit in the chair facing me. He does. I ask him if he wants a drink. He says yes and I move to my wall cabinet to get it out. I pour. I hand it to him and sit in my chair again."

"Did you drink with him?"

"No."

"Why not?"

"I didn't want one."

"Because?"

"I ration my carbs for weight control." Why is he pursuing this issue?

"You seem to be able to handle that."

"Thanks." I take the compliment for what it is—not so much praise as a way to wear down my defenses. "At my age, one drink equals ten minutes on the treadmill." Last night's quota meant I should be doing forty minutes today. Fat chance. "Besides, scotch is not my favorite."

"Really. What is?"

Had he looked inside my liquor cabinet to see what I stock? I'm answering, "Gin. Tanqueray. With tonic. Two limes. Six ice cubes." But all the while, I'm wondering if he has access to everything in that room because it is a crime scene. Or does he need a warrant to open every drawer, every nook and cranny? I don't care so much about my liquor cabinet, but I do care about the files in my desk drawers. Some of them are classified documents—and access to them bothers me. But when it comes to the liquor cabinet, he can have at it, because, after all, I did not kill Alistair.

"No one else joined you?"

I shake my head. Had there been another glass out? Not on my desktop. Where, then? I'm recalling my office as I saw it this morning. Everything, seemingly, in its rightful place, except Alistair and my letter opener, of course. "Why do you ask?"

"Because it's my job to ask, ma'am." He stretches his lips in a smile that back home we'd call, *Eat dirt.*

I'm leveling one of my Code Red glares at him. But I keep my thoughts to myself. Manners, I hold dear, even for policemen—especially for policemen—interviewing me about a crime.

Sarge seems unfazed, cuz he's staring at me. "So then, your conversation proceeded as he drank?"

I nod.

"Was it all a discussion of Medicaid eligibility?"

Thrilled he left the issue that had Alistair and I at each other's throats, I cross my arms again and this time I don't care what image I project. "A mixed bag. Some party politics. Some personal." I recall how forlorn Alistair became last night as he revealed that he discovered his twelve-year-old son is smoking weed.

"And what were the personal issues?"

My cue to cough up unsavory facts. "He has a son the same age as my daughter. They go to the same school and are close friends. Alistair has recently had some challenges with Zachary and wondered if my daughter had hinted at any problems Zachary might have confided to her."

"What kind of problems?"

"You'll have to ask Alistair's governess." I was certainly not going to squeal on Zack.

The sarcastic look on Sarge's face said he had not run into a lot of governesses in his lifetime. "And her name is?"

"Her first name is Barbara, but I don't recall her last."

"Describe your daughter and Zachary Dunhill's relationship."

Sarge doesn't want to leave any stone unturned, does he? "Pals," I tell him. "Since age three when they went to Montessori together up in Potomac. Last September, they started going to the same private school in Georgetown. They're getting older, becoming more gender-oriented, but they still relate as easily as when they were younger." That, I decided, would be the end of my revelations about Jordan and Zack.

Sarge moved his mouth around his face a minute. "How old are they?"

"My Jordan is twelve. Zack is almost thirteen."

"Strange, isn't it, that Congressman Dunhill would come to you for information about his son's behavior?"

"Not really." I note that Sarge has no wedding band around his finger, so I am left to wonder if he has any experience with a wife or a lover or kids.

"So then explain to me why that's so."

He asks that question, I decide, not because he's stupid, but because he needs to record my response to it. "Kids can be inscrutable. I'd want to seek out anyone who might help me if I had a challenge with my daughter."

Aaron appears in my line of vision, directly behind Sarge. He's pulling on his left earlobe with such force that I'm certain he'll extend it to his knees. This is our signal that something urgent has come up. I'm about to respond and incur Sarge's wrath when Aaron's left eye begins to twitch. Ahh, so it's not news from the subcommittee chair on whether the hearings were canceled. Nothing so simple. My mother's on the phone.

Sarge turns to follow my line of vision.

"I apologize, Detective. Multitasking is a job my staff performs quite well."

Sarge spins around to me, fire in his eyes. "Mr. Blumfeld can perform his tasking somewhere else." Sarge could tolerate changes in dialogue, but interruptions drove him bananas. I would remember this. In Washington, and in murder investigations, one survived by many means—or any means.

"Aaron, please tell my mother I will call her from home this evening." Aaron, never happy to spar with Sadie O'Neill, flaps his arms but strides away, shoulders lax. Mama was going to have to cool her heels until I had presence of mind to handle her in such a way that ensured she would not meddle in this mess.

But Sarge shoots to his feet and examines my staffers milling about at their jobs. "I'm going to ask all of you to step outside into the hall for a few minutes." As they file out with careful glances at me for approval to go, I nod and he takes a seat. "Let's continue, shall we?" He moves his chair in closer to me and frowns like a bulldog. "Describe to me how Congressman Dunhill looked, acted, if he said anything unusual."

Right. I settle in, determined to get this nasty business over with and get on with my day. "Alistair was agitated, that I knew right off. He looked . . . almost as if he'd been . . ." I glance at Sarge and figure he's a big boy, he can take this. "Having an argument or . . ."

"Having an argument with someone before he came in and argued with you?"

"Well, yes"—I am miffed he injected that, but eager to finish my thought—"but I was about to say he looked like he was either having an argument . . . or sex."

"Hav . . . ing sex." Bata-bah, bata-bing with the pen on the paper. Sarge looks up at me as naively as if we're talkin' about kissing babies. "Did he tell you that?"

"No." Of course not.

"Then how do you know?"

"I don't. You asked me. I told you what I thought."

"Why sex?"

Because the man could be *a tenorio!* A rooster who screwed any woman he could get his hands on. Call it widower's fever, call it excess of hubris, call it nuts. Alistair had *cojones* and he used 'em. My instinct said he did it for recreation. But I came from a land where adding notches to your gun gained you enemies—and only Alistair knew how many of those he had. "I feel awkward talking about this."

"I'm sure you do."

"It's a delicate issue."

"Just tell me what you thought when he walked in here."

"All right, Sarge."

"Detective."

"Sorry, I get the name confused with the title."

"Imagine my distress."

"I do, Detective." I shift, crossing one leg over the other and smoothing my skirt. Sarge's eyes drift to the limbs that won me the title of Miss Texas and a nickname that at age forty-two I need to ditch. Alistair had called me 'Legs' only once, when I shot him down the first time he put his hands on my thighs. "The congressman had a flirtatious way with women."

"Are you being diplomatic?"

Now, that was the silliest statement he'd made all morning. He worked in this town. In these hallowed halls. Was he new to this job? Or trying to make me say things I would regret? I might be nervous, but I was not dumb. "I am well aware my words to you are not by any stretch of the imagination off the record, Detective."

"Yes, ma'am." His eyes lock on mine. We had finally come to a gentleman's agreement.

"Congressman Dunhill appeared in my office last night dressed not quite as neatly as normal for him. His shirt collar was slightly askew and his face very red—beet-red, in fact—when he came in here. I asked him if he wanted a drink and he accepted. He drank it rather quickly and I asked if he'd care for another. He did. That was unusual for him. He likes his scotch straight, but in a moderate dose. So to me, he was emotionally upset. If you are a loyal and interested member of his party—or even if you just curry his favor—you have on hand in your wall liquor cabinet his favorite, Macallan's, a single-malt from Scotland. He usually savors it."

"Did he accept another round because he was upset about his son—or overexerted from an argument or physical activities?"

"I really don't know. And I didn't ask. He was concerned about Zack, but at the time I thought he accepted a second round because he was overwrought about something else before he came in here. In any case, he was going home right after we talked."

"Is that what he said? He was going home?"

"Yes, he was tired and looked it. Weary. Worried about his boy."

"Did you take his glass from him when he left?"

"I picked it up, yes. Washed it out in my little sink in my private bathroom in my office." Why?

"How many glasses do you keep in your office, ma'am?"

"Six." Was one missing? "What relevance has that to do with anything?"

"Just asking."

"Are you?" I still cannot recall if I saw a glass out anywhere this morning. "Or just trying to make me wonder what your next move is?"

"I have an investigation to run."

"And I have a district to run, Detective." *And I am tired of playing word games.* "If we are finished, I need to get ready for this hearing." I put a hand on top of my briefing papers.

"A few more questions."

I raise my brows at him.

"Your relationship."

I give him another fiery stare—and bull-nosed guy that he is, he does not flinch. "Detective, our relationship was purely professional."

His expression says, *Is that so.* But his words are, "Describe it for me."

"We were colleagues in one sense. Equals. Representatives of congressional districts. He represented a ranching district in Montana and he had many of the same interests I did. Farm subsidies, gun control, border control issues, saving wild animals about to become extinct. He and I have voted the same way on many bills—and differently on many others. But Alistair was more than my peer. He was the minority whip. A man of power and seniority, responsible for keeping the party together on voting. Alistair and I worked together often on all bills that came through the Congress. I often voted the way the party recommends not because I must, but because I believe in the programs we espouse. I knew that what I helped him and the party with, I could expect to come back to me at some future date."

"Okay, okay." He nods a few times, clearly bored with politics, then looks me in the eye. "Let's explore a different kind of date."

Ahh. He wonders if Alistair and I had a thing going on. He has thin cause to ask, but I'll give him the dope. "You mean my personal relationship with him."

Sarge just waits.

"I am single."

Sarge cocks his head, brows going up.

Okay. He's heard the fuller bio, so I add, "Divorced."

He frowns. "I thought you were a widow."

"I was. My first husband died."

"So then your daughter is—"

"By my second husband, from whom I am divorced."

Sarge scratches his cheek and waves his pencil in the air. "Then your relationship with Congressman Dunhill is—what?"

"Platonic. Alistair is a widower. He and I were often invited to the same events, public and private. Occasionally, it was appropriate that we go together." After that first date when Alistair wound up with his hands in his lap, he kept them to himself when we were out together. All totaled, we went to dinner parties or fundraisers maybe once a year over the past nine. "We belong to the same party and we had things in common. Ideas. Agendas." It looked good in *The Washington Post* Style section for me to be seen with the minority whip. It looked better in the *San Antonio Express-News*. Folks back home understand a politician's need to trade horses—and they expect it. They also know that I am easy to look at and if they like to do it often, who am I to object? The exposure helps keep me in office.

I'm on a roll now. "Congressman Dunhill was an expert politician, Detective. I learned a few things from him that were useful to me, like which congressmen are likely to vote against a new spy plane funding bill that I strongly endorse." Of course, I had also learned a few other facts that did me no political good, but had me gasping. Like which senator's wife Alistair had slept with recently.

"Have you ever had a sexual relationship with Congressman Dunhill?"

"No."

"Were you interested in one?"

"No."

"Why not?"

"Congressman Dunhill was an intelligent man, an influential one. He had many admirers and many friends. I enjoyed his wit and his largesse, but he was not a man in whom I had any personal interest."

"Other than the relationship between his son and your daughter."

"That's correct."

"Congressman Dunhill was a powerful man. That can be very appealing to a woman with a career to build."

If his implication is the old-fashioned one that the only way up for a woman in any job is to spread her legs, I choose to ignore it. "It can. But not to me."

"Why? Do you currently have a personal relationship with someone else?"

"I find that intrusive, Detective."

"You are deeply involved in a murder investigation, Congresswoman Wagner. Everything about you is now my business. Including any aspects of your personal life that may help us paint a picture of how and why Alistair Dunhill died here."

"I have no idea why that is."

He brushes his mouth with a forefinger, looks away and then comes back to me, slowly rephrasing his point. "Ma'am, you are an attractive woman. You are assertive, funny, articulate, and increasingly well-known outside your home state."

"Thank you, Detective. I can only hope that means I'll have an easy time running my reelection campaign come September."

"You are changing the subject."

"And rightfully so, sir. The subject you wish to pursue is pure fantasy."

"They look like facts to me."

"Not from where I sit."

Sarge jots that in his little green book. Then lays down his pen. Folds his hands and stares me in the eye. "Any ideas, then, why he sits in your chair dead with his fly down and his penis severed?"

"None."

"If the two of you had no affair and you didn't kill him . . ."

I glower at him.

". . . and no one did it out of jealousy over an affair between you, then—"

Geez, what yarns this man could spin. "That is such a crock," I say, immediately regret it, but note, appreciatively, that Sarge is not writing it down.

"Then Dunhill's death is a political statement."

In this town, how you dispose of your garbage is a political statement.

I'm intrigued that a man who dealt in facts would introduce a topic full of conjecture, so I say, "Describe it for me." Damned if I am going to walk down some garden path Sarge has only pointed toward.

"You are becoming increasingly visible in this town. I'm certain that in your district this is true, too. A lot of people all over have trouble with powerful women gaining more power."

"If Alistair's death is an attempt to suppress all women by framing one—and on circumstantial evidence at that—the act is not only antediluvian but short-sighted."

"It is possible."

"But not probable."

"The way Congressman Dunhill was murdered may indicate the perpetrator had a political motive."

"Detective, the key word there is 'may.'"

"Isn't sex the ultimate weapon of mass destruction in this town?"

Wasn't that the God's honest truth? Selling arms to rogue nations got a government official two to four years in a cushy federal prison. Consensual sexual activity got you scandal, finger-pointing by every self-righteous do-gooder from Oshkosh to Ozona, impeachment hearings, and a one-way ticket to obscurity for you and your party. "You forget that I was not intimately involved with Congressman Dunhill."

"Does that matter?"

"I hope, to you, it does."

"But to the world this morning, what will matter?"

Oh, I know, all right. It's not what you are, but what they think you are that counts. I have always used that principle to get where I am.

"The media will show a female politician who is a beautiful, articulate redhead with humor, brains, and soul."

I shift in my chair, panic mixing in my stomach with all the acid from the coffee I consumed. "I'm flattered by your words, Detective, but not your logic."

"Don't think it could happen, huh?"

I am scared as a cornered jackrabbit. So I come out, fast and hopping mad. "Drink with Congresswoman Wagner and she'll cut your dick off?" I snort. "Detective, I am in my fifth term, my tenth year. Some of my colleagues have been here for thirty, forty years. I am one of four hundred and thirty-five people. My biggest claim to fame and power is that I am the second-ranking minority member of the subcommittee that approves of all money spent on the military. In the realms of power, I rank far behind the leader of the pack—and closer to dead last. Who would be out to get little old me?"

"You," he says slow as molasses, "tell me."

I am out of my chair. Fighting the urge to upchuck at the prospect that someone could have purposely maimed and killed a man in my office for political gain—and my political demise.

I had to get practical. Fast. I also needed to be cooperative so that I could get this man out of my office and think. "You are going to come back. Right?" He nods. "When?"

"Maybe later today, but definitely by early tomorrow. Whenever we have more results from forensics and the autopsy and I know more."

"I'm here. In town. Call me at home if you want." I grab a piece of my stationery and jot down my unlisted phone number. My brain is racing, listing anyone who'd hate me enough to set me up for murder.

"I'd like to go over these facts again," he's saying in a solemn tone. "After I have those reports, I'm going to ask you to come to my office."

"Sure. Not a problem."

"Promise me that when we meet again, you will have thought about who would follow the congressman here and kill him."

"Right, right." What else *could* I think about? I fold my arms across my chest and squeeze my eyes shut a minute. "I will."

That means enemies of Alistair's and mine.

Good god. How many could that be?

In this town, in any given second, that could be a party of one—or a cast of thousands.

three

At six, I hang up the phone after Detective Brown tells me to meet him at Capitol Police headquarters at nine-thirty the next morning.

With me in the main room with my staff, we are all cramped and cranky. None of us has accomplished much today with police in and out—and all of us are weary. I rub my eyes and decide I am really done here for the day.

Within minutes, I'm down out of my office, into my Tahoe, barreling west toward home along M Street in the new American position—my cell phone receiver cord stuck in my ear. I'm trying to reach Lou, and okay, it is not legal to drive this way in D.C., but I'm chancing it just so I can feel the love of talking to one person I trust. Except Lou's not answering her private line and I leave her a message to call me.

Ticked, I click off and hit the brake, genuflecting to a D.C. police cruiser that's monitoring rush hour. He doesn't care to follow and that is really fine by me. Two more blocks and I get to Wisconsin Avenue and hang a right, gleeful as a puppy when I see that the traffic is not bumper-to-bumper and I'll make the next half a dozen blocks to home in a jiffy.

From the second I round the corner from Wisconsin into Q Street, I zero in on my three-story Federal townhouse that's my sanctuary every night. I love the rough red brick and the creamy wood trim. I like the huge black front door with tiny lead glass inserts. Tonight, one thing I do not like about the house is the throng of reporters loitering on the sidewalk.

Why Aaron thought this welcome-home party would not occur beats me. I didn't think these types could find you if you are unlisted. Apparently, however, I am listed somewhere and these ten dudes deserve Sherlock Holmes awards.

Times like these, I wish I had a horse. I could ride away. Instead, I give the gas a goose, climbing to a spectacular fifteen miles per hour as I scoot around the Mercedes and Porsches lining both sides of the road. Half a block away, I'm impatient and hit the garage door opener above my head.

I hear the whir of the doors going up and pull in the driveway. Here I wait for a minute on my own private property. And the journalists who surround me—pen or cameras or lights in hand—cannot touch my car or me. They call to me, gesture, wave.

I stare straight ahead at my house. It's tall, it's skinny, it's older than the state of Texas. A right nice piece of property, as my mama likes to brag, it's in WASPy Georgetown next to the homes of those who also like to retreat after the day's battles behind the gentility of the tree-lined three-hundred-year-old neighborhood. As zealous of my privacy as my neighbors, I pull into the garage and listen to the door grind down and shut out the world.

On my own, I never would have swung the mortgage on this house. But five years ago, a terrific thing happened to me on a scale of winning the Texas Lotto. With a five-figure inheritance from Great-Aunt Priscilla, God bless her thrifty old soul, and a whopping six-figure life insurance benefit I got when my first husband Frank bit the dust, I paid for this house, lock, stock, and barrel. Frank's son, Frank II, or Short Stuff, as his father nicknamed him, was a mite riled over that bequest, but hey, I was not the one who forgot to change the beneficiary, was I? Besides, what would Short Stuff go and do with any more money he inherited from his daddy? You could bet your shorts he'd live up to his name and down to his shoe size and just piss it down another dry hole in West Texas, where few have struck a major line since James Dean whooped it up with Rock and Liz in '55. Me, I put my money—his daddy's, rather—to good use and bought a fine place for my daughter to grow up in and bring her friends home to.

Smug at my choice—and feeling more secure separated from the horde—I reach for my purse. Then my phone rings and has me digging past my wallet and lipstick to answer it. "Hello?"

"Tell me what is going on, Carly." The static makes me wince, but I know who it is. My ex.

"Hi, Len." I turn off the ignition, pull the key out, and sit straighter in my seat cuz Len is a bear when he's riled. And with me, even when he's not. "Glad you called me back. I need to tell you about something here—"

"I got a newspaper with my morning coffee a few minutes ago. Shocked the hell out of me because I read it before I got your voice mail message. What is this about Alistair Dunhill murdered in your office?"

"True. All true. Listen, Len, I am concerned about Jordan."

"Damn right, you'd better be. She and I were going to have fun here, Carly, and now you've ruined that—"

"Whoa, there, Len. I did nothing except walk into my office this morning."

"You didn't kill him?"

"Jesus Christ, Len." I grab my purse, climb out of my Tahoe, and slam my fanny against the car door to shut it. "That's low."

Well, what did I expect from him? Let's face it, Len is the type of ex-husband about whom Stephen King would write. Len's self-righteous, rich, and vindictive. Not the kind you want to meet in divorce court. But, considering I was his second wife (and he is currently making whoopee with Number Four), Len is skilled at the characterization. He is smooth and sensual as a forties leading man. But the dark kind. What did they call them?

Noir. Len is so very noir, he has a job to match. A lawyer for a defense contractor, Len could, when sufficiently inspired by money, sweet-talk a wild boar into his gun sights. Trouble is, tonight, no money reared its pretty green head. Instead, he has to break the news of Alistair's death to our daughter—and that requires compassion. Let me say that when it comes to compassion, General Patton regularly displayed more than Len Underwood.

I put my house key in the kitchen door lock and turn, only to find I have locked it. "How could that be?" I murmur, and try again.

"All right, all right, Carly, stop fuming and tell me what happened."

I step into my bright white kitchen and sitting in front of me in his crate is Abe. I wave. He waves back, jumps up and down in greeting inside his metal crate. Our family pet is a seven-year-old, one-eyed chimpanzee named Abe. Lincoln, natch. And a finer gentleman I have not yet met in this town.

"I told you, Len, I walked into my inner office and there he was, sitting in the chair. Stabbed and . . . emasculated."

Len must be drinking his coffee, because he sounds like he's choking and asks me to repeat that.

"His penis was severed."

It is now Len's turn to curse. "Serves him right."

"Len, the poor man is dead."

"If you didn't cut it off, then some other woman did."

I take note of his certainty. "Anyone I should know about?"

"His receptionist."

"Is that right?" I drop my purse and my keys on the kitchen island. "Who else knows about that?"

"Anyone who has been to a 'Skins game last season."

"That was months ago. Are you sure they are still dating now?"

"Dating? Carly. Come into the newest century. Alistair was not *dating* Krystal."

Len knows her name. Her first name. Why is that? "She's a real beauty, then, if you know her."

"Yeah, only by reputation. And her looks."

I try to picture this woman, walk myself mentally through Alistair's outer office—and I draw a total blank. This isn't surprising, because I just don't take note of other women. "Fill me in."

"Tall. Brunette. Legs almost as long as yours."

Len is a leg man. Mine—or any other woman's whose legs reach her armpits without destroying her cup size. "And her reputation?"

"Let's just say that she used to work for Yancy Delacroix and before that, Jared Quinn."

Oh, boy. Krystal, don't let your mama know your true self, because you are far, far from fragile. She is, in fact, a true rough rider—and maybe I am not far off in my metaphor, either, because the two retired representatives Len just named were alley cats, if ever there were two. Some whispered that in their heyday, they had even prowled together.

"None of that matters, though," Len interjects, "because you seem to be the recipient of the booby prize."

Smart-ass. "I'll take care of that detail." I revert to my original agenda in talking to him. "I am concerned about how Jordan hears about this. I want you to talk to her this morning. Wake her up if you have to, especially since you have a newspaper there. I don't want her reading it before you tell her."

"Carly, I hate to wake her up now. Christ. It's eight-thirty A.M. here and we didn't get into the hotel room until midnight. I was going to let her sleep while I left for my meeting."

"Okay." I heave a big sigh of relief. Len could be the world's biggest jerk with his divorced wives, but with his only child, he tried very hard to act like an angel. "If she wants to talk to me, have her call me. I'm at home. Just got here." I'm shrugging out of my jacket and enjoying the welcome-home grin on Abe's hairy little face.

"But Carly, I'm warning you, if she tells you she wants to fly back to be with that boy, I am dead set against it. She already cut this trip short so that she could be there for his birthday party."

"Two days early she wanted you both to come home, Len. That's not a huge cut in your trip."

"Yeah, but this is my vacation, too, you know. Our vacation." He corrects himself to make himself sound more appealing.

Leave it to Len to wedge his own interests into the tragedy of murder. "Let's see what Jordan wants to do. She has a good head on her shoulders and she'll feel sorrow for her friend. You have got to honor that."

"I do not have to do anything, Carly."

"Len!"

"I will break the news gently, I promise you that. She'll get all the consolation she needs, but I will not put her on a plane home, and that is final."

"Look, Len, I know you don't like Zack—"

"Last time I saw him, he had another ring in his lip."

"Well, now he has no father." Bonehead.

"Not my concern."

"Precisely. Yours is Jordan. She'll worry about Zack, especially if he has to endure a public funeral alone." Tears come to my eyes—and I freeze with the memory of me consoling Alistair the other night about his son—and how I touched him. Cupped his cheek. Oh, god. I touched Alistair—and he kissed my palm.

"He'll get through it," Len is chiming on.

I'm gulping at my memory. Is that evidence to put me on death row?

"But Carly, Jordan can worry about him here—and a tour of Tokyo and Kyoto will be just what she needs to take her mind off a murder in her mother's office."

I want to yell at him that I did not kill Alistair, that he should wake her up and let me break the news. But I calm down, knowing I can't force him, only play on his love for her. "I hope you don't lead off with that, Len. I know nothing about this and it would not be fair to her, nor in her best interests, for you to imply that I do."

He grunts. "I want to know what more there is to this before I talk to her. When did you see him last? Why the hell was he in your office? How did he get in?"

I discover I have another card in my hand and I play it. "Len, you of all people ought to know that I cannot discuss this."

"You can talk to me, Carly."

Len's con game is, *You can trust me.* Fool me once, shame on you. Fool me twice, shame on me. "I am not discussing this over the phone." *Or any other way.*

"You can," he crooned in such a way that I couldn't tell if he implied I could if I wanted to, or I could because I could trust him. Both were putting lipstick on a pig. Leonard's relationship and mine had gone to hell in a handbasket eight years ago when I caught him in an affair. But beneath that betrayal was another I found no proof for. I suspected he had shared information he learned from me about Defense Department budget numbers to influence his way to the top of his law firm. I had decided then I wasn't even sharing toilet paper with him—and now I certainly wasn't sharing the details of a murder that occurred in my inner office.

"Leonard, get a grip. My major concern and yours, too, should be how Jordan takes this. So either agree to focus on her psychological needs or go wake her up so that I can do it."

My dare to wake her up hints that he is incapable of proper affection and bangs the most sensitive nail in his toolbox. It could make him screwy or compliant.

"I'll do it, don't worry. It's better to have her hear it from me."

That I did not agree with, but for now, he was there and capable of compassion, if he wanted to be. "Good. Call me when she's got a handle on it so that I can talk to her, too."

"Will do. So do the police have any ideas who . . . ?"

Len, always the coyote after a kill. "No." *Truth be told, Len, you probably have more ideas, if you know this Krystal is a player.* "Goodbye, Len. Call me. I'll be waiting."

My fingers itch for a cigarette. Sure, I quit more than ten years ago, but every once in a while, I crave one. I don't buy them but bum one now and again off a friend when the mood hits me.

That thought drifts away as I consider Abe. His crate, a four-by-four black steel one meant for large dogs, seems out of place. As if he has maneuvered it across the kitchen floor. I step closer and note the black scuff marks on the tile. My housekeeper Ming keeps my floors polished to a mirror shine, so these marks are new since yesterday when she was last here . . . and I'm mystified about why Abe would rattle his cage like this. He is usually a calm fellow, unless he is afraid or protective.

I let him out and scratch his head. "How are you doing, buddy?"

He nods, up and down, up and down. Translation: *Good, now that you are home.*

"Want to go out and play?" I grin at him and he imitates me.

He chitters and moves his head again, up and down, up and down. Translation: *You bet.*

As I kick off my pumps and head over to the French doors to my garden, Abe scampers over to the drapes and peeks out back. I hate for him to touch the drapes because he loves the feel of the thick satin. He loves them so much that he has swung from them, using them too often like a jungle tree branch and shredding them. That's why he's confined to a cage when no one is home with him.

"Come on, Abe, out you go." I unlatch the door and beckon him to smell the flowers.

But he leaves one window for another, peering out with his little face swathed in fabric, like a kid plastering the sheets around his face, fearful of some monster. "What's your bag, Abe? Go, go." I pull open the door and sweep my hand for him to leave, but he doesn't move. Now, Abe adores my garden and he is well housebroken and complies with the priority I place on his sanitary habits. Slowly, he emerges from the drapes and when he stares at me, I know he was definitely searching for something. A trill shimmies up my back as Abe trundles over to me and exits to the back yard. I'm gazing at his cage, trying to piece together this odd behavior with the evidence that he has been jumping around in his cage so violently that the metal has made marks on the tile. Going nowhere fast with this puzzle, I gear up to perform my most pressing duty—calling my mother.

Fortifying myself, I walk to my bar and pull out the Tanqueray, dig in the fridge for my lime, and hit the glass against the ice dispenser. The click, click, clunk helps me focus on what I will say to Sadie. Truth is, it won't be much different tactically than talking to Len. Both can be mean buzzards.

Someday, I promise myself, I am going to have a relationship with someone I do not have to maneuver. Someone, please god, I can just enjoy.

Yeah, right. I stir my drink with my finger, bend over, and inhale the aroma of a flat of petunias that Rayanne must have bought at Johnson's floral shop this morning. They are bright and happy, but for sure, Rayanne knows nada about gardening because these babies are gonna die if I plant them tonight in this fifty-degree weather. Besides, I'm not crazy about petunias. Too frilly-dilly for me. Ah, well, I pick up my cell phone and hit the speed-dial number for Sadie.

"Hi, Ma, how are you?"

In a voice roughed over by too many Marlboros and too much Texas dust, Sadie O'Neill answers me. "Bigger question is, how the hell are you?"

"Look, I have to change for a dinner party." I'm lying, because I've decided I'm not braving my scheduled dinner with the Style editor of the *Post*, much less going out to fight off that pack of dogs out front. "But I wanted you to know that I am fine. The headlines will die down after a while and I am certain the police will find—"

"Who are you kidding, girl?"

"No, Ma. Really, I think that—"

"You didn't work this hard, come this far, to have your future ruined by Alistair Dunhill's murderer."

"Yeah, that's my thought, too, but at the moment there is not much I can do about it."

"You'd better get your shapely ass down here this weekend to shake some hands. That's what you'd better do about it."

"I was just there ten days ago."

"That is no never mind."

I squeeze my eyes shut. "Ma, I can't come."

"Why the hell not?"

"It's a murder investigation, Ma. And I am a principal."

"Suspect, you mean."

"No." I fear she is right, but I will not admit it. Not to her. Not to myself.

"I was in the Mercantile this afternoon and folks are askin' about this."

"I figured they would be." I take another sip of my G&T. "I'm making a plan about how to handle this." Soon as I have two minutes to call my own. But I'm buying time cuz I hate to fly, and the trip from Dulles to Dallas is four hours of rockin' and rollin'. On top of that comes another hour in the air to San Antonio. Then the drive south or west. Hell, you have to be Superwoman to do it more than once a month. "But I am swamped. I have paperwork piling up here."

"Your constituents can't see how high your paperwork is, baby girl. They just know how high the bullshit stacks. Now you just get yourself situated and get down here."

"Soon as I can, I will. But you buy me some time." I'm sipping and looking down into my trash can. And if I am not mistaken, the aluminum foil from last night's dinner is sitting at the top of the heap. Not the bottom.

"I will," my mama's saying as I reach in and peel the foil back. "You know I will."

The remains of my oatmeal breakfast sit underneath the foil.

"Carly?"

"Yes, Ma."

"What would you like me to say to the locals?"

"Ah, let me think." But I'm thinking, *Did someone look through my kitchen trash?*

"Yes. So?"

"Ah. Anyone specific I should know about who called you to complain?"

"Grace Wilkins and Cody Mainnerd."

Grace is the wife of the most prosperous preacher in South Texas, the busiest body in an eight-hundred-mile stretch. Cody is sheriff of my home county. And a man who knows every secret in town. "Okay. Just call and buzz 'em a bit. Tell them I would love to do a town hall meeting in two weeks." Please God, let this murder be solved before that. "Make it a Friday night, and afterward you and I will go dancin' at the Two Step. Shake a few hands."

Sadie loved having her only daughter as a congresswoman. Gave her braggin' rights. Also gave her power. "I will also tell them that you know nothing about this murder."

"And you'd be right, Ma."

"Alrighty, then. Sleep tight."

Love to. Doubt I will, though, because I'm staring at my key to my garden shed that happens to hang on the hook nearest the fridge. And it is hanging by the hole in its top, not by the macramé loop Jordan wove at Girl Scouts.

So I know that what I am looking at is evidence that someone has been in my home today, snooping around. Frightening my chimp, rummaging through my trash, and even taking a gander at the contents of my backyard shed.

Sure, Rayanne had been inside. Brought the petunias, fetched my leprechaun green suit. Maybe she had been the one who had not locked the kitchen door as she departed. She could, on rare occasions, screw up a two-car funeral. And all morning, she had looked rather piqued. Hell, who hadn't? But she was not a snoop. Or, she hadn't been in the year she'd worked for me. Why start now? There surely was nothing in my oatmeal that would give her—or anyone else, for that matter—any indication of what had occurred in my inner office after nine-thirty last night.

Or so logic would tell me.

But I stand there, sipping and opening my junk drawer, blindly reaching for my SIG-Sauer. There, still there. I wrap my fingers around the cold hard weapon that had been my granddaddy's.

I listen to my home. Silent. Very totally silent.

Yes, the intruder is no longer here. I glance at Abe poking around the roses in the garden. He would still be going ape if someone remained in the house. He wouldn't have gone to the window and peered out, searching for whomever had obviously left by way of the garden.

I take another drink of gin, crunch on the ice cubes. Frowning, I ask myself, who am I going to talk to about this?

No one. Not yet. Because I don't want the notoriety. Not in the press, not in the House. Not in my district.

I swallow more gin and tonic. Who broke into my home?

Detective Sarge Brown and his merry men? That didn't make any sense at all. Brown and his boys would come with a warrant, if they came at all. But who else would break and enter, and why? What have I got, that someone wants to poke around in my things? How did they get in?

And if they are talented enough to get inside, how come they are such dickweeds at covering their tracks?

four

Detective Brown scratches his temple and grumbles to himself about how faulty my memory is. I wish I could be as blunt. He's asked me the same questions as yesterday and I've had to repeat my answers like some wooden Indian.

He's hunting for something, has been since I came in over an hour ago. If he expects me to blurt out the one thing that might incriminate me, he's wrong. I haven't gotten the guts to say it out loud yet.

Instead I look congenial and say, "I wish I could tell you more."

Hey, wasn't that exactly what my receptionist Rayanne told me this morning in my office when I asked her if she recalled locking my kitchen door yesterday? She looked so honestly surprised when I asked that I didn't continue to probe her about snooping in my trash can or shed. Such an inquiry would have sounded silly, I thought, especially when she declared she was certain she'd locked the door. Nah, someone else was interested in what I was doing, and their search—as far as I could tell by a tour of the rest of the house—had included my desk, where they had opened my private journal. Clumsy buggers had once again botched their cover and not been so careful how they replaced it inside the top left drawer.

What kind of second-story men were so inept?

I sit straighter with my next thought. Unless they intended to be.

Wow, that's a scarier idea than any. Have I been living in this town for so long that I am now doing the double-triple-think thingie? Geez, I need to be rational here and get some quick answers.

"Did you just remember something new?" Brown invades my reverie.

I frown.

"You sat up like you thought of something you should tell me."

"How long have you been a detective?"

Now he frowns. "Almost two years with the Capitol Police. Twelve years with D.C. force before that." He shifts and his metal chair squeaks. No surprise there—the olive drab metal looks older than government-issue circa 1944 and is the same bile color as the walls and ceiling of the Capitol Police headquarters. "Why?" He thinks I'm questioning his competence.

Maybe in one way, I am. "You like your job?"

"Love it."

"I like mine, too. So much, I wouldn't break the rules to stay where I am. Let alone kill a man who was, to some extent, my mentor and my boss."

"That's a nice statement of innocence."

"It's more than a statement, Detective. It's the truth."

"What else is it?"

"A question."

He crosses his arms. "About?"

"How innocent you are."

He gets grim now. "Of what?"

"Going out of your way to get information about me."

"I don't have to. I have all the access I need to learn anything at all about you." He is now alarmed, at his personal Code Red. "But who has stepped over the line?"

"Good question, Detective."

"How'd it happen?"

I describe what was disturbed in my home, aside from me.

"When was this?"

"Yesterday before dark. I don't have a precise time. I wish I did."

Good old Sarge is letting his fingers do the dialing. "Marie, get Williams in here," he barks into his phone, and drops it in its cradle. "You should have called me when you discovered this."

"I thought of it, but last night—after the day I had yesterday— I just wanted to be alone."

"If what you're saying is for real, then you shouldn't be alone," he scolds me. "Ever. Plus, if you had called, we might have been able to lift some prints."

"That I doubt. They were careful about what they did, what clues they left, and they just wanted me to know they'd been there." As I say that, I am convinced I am right. Call it my gut instinct. "No fingerprints exist. Whoever got in was skilled enough not to break any locks."

"Pick."

"Pardon me?"

"Locks are picked." He makes a twisting motion with one hand.

"Ah. Right. Well, whoever it was rummaged in my trash and my garden shed, then took a tour of my personal journal."

"Maybe I should look there, too."

"Sarge, you need a really good reason plus a warrant to peek into anything in my house, especially my journal. And my thinking is that right now you have no viable reason to ask for a warrant. Maybe my fingerprints are on my letter opener, but that's to be expected because it was mine. But there must be other prints. Got to be. You just need to have your forensics find them. Plus, I have no motive to hurt Alistair. I am no lawyer, but I do know you have no cause to really be looking at me for this murder."

"Except where the congressman was attacked and died," Brown retorts.

A couple of staccato raps on the door and a short, dapper black man enters Brown's office. "Sir, you wanted to see me?"

Detective Brown introduces us and tells me that this man will put a detail on my home. "You see any evidence of anything suspicious, all you have to do is summon the man outside your front door."

"Wonderful," I tell Brown when his man leaves.

"You're not happy. Well, I am sorry, but that's the way it'll be. You are a public person and if I let things like this happen, this investigation will suffer. I cannot have that."

"Any thoughts on who the culprit really is?"

"At this point, you still look good."

"Why?" I'm thinking of obvious evidence he could have. "My fingerprints on my letter opener and my desk? They should be there. My hair on the carpet? My hair either falls out or I pull it out on a regular basis right there."

His mouth twitches. "According to your statement, you left at approximately nine-thirty Monday evening. At the time we arrived yesterday morning, the deceased's body temperature told us that he died between nine and ten the previous night."

"That does not make me the murderer."

"You argued with the deceased," he insists.

"About a professional matter."

"It does make you the obvious choice."

"Well, there have to be other obvious choices." I tantalize him, poor man.

He bites. "Who?"

"I don't cast aspersions, Detective. I just know it was not me."

His chocolate eyes light up with fireworks. "You are not to be investigating this yourself. No talking to anyone about this; what we say here, stays here."

I nod. "Fair enough." I was an expert at subtleties. Hadn't I lived with Sadie O'Neill and survived all these years?

"I mean it. I find you talking to people about this, I will be very happy to deprive you of your immunity from prosecution. You might be exempt from traffic tickets, but not criminal charges."

"I know that, Detective." But I have my skin to save, don't I?

Brown warns me with stern eyes. "All right, then. We are

clear." He gets up from his chair. "Thank you, ma'am." He is dismissing me like a schoolgirl. The rudeness rankles. We congressional types get high on the deference we normally get, but Brown is handing out none.

His change of mood, I suspect, is meant to put me off balance, but I am awake and aware and don't move. "You are telling me we are finished for today?"

"Yes, but you might be back."

"I will." I rise, pulling up dignity and using it as my shield and sword. "Until you catch who did this, you will want to talk to me again and again. I will cooperate where I can."

"And where can you not cooperate, ma'am?"

"Anything you may ask that is classified information." I don't say how or by whom, but let the impression linger.

He puts a finger to his chin, rubbing it as he ponders. "I do have one more question before you go."

No, really? Wait, wait. I bet it's the biggest one he has wanted me to answer since I walked in this morning at nine. I try to get my lips to form the words that might save me from the electric chair, but I chicken out and ask, "What can I tell you, Detective?"

"How many glasses did you keep in your liquor cabinet?"

Do I look relieved? "Six," I blurt, and add, "The same number I told you I had yesterday."

"You didn't break any?"

"No."

"Give any away?"

"No."

"What did you wear to work on Monday?"

The pause that does not refresh. I am stumped. "Damn if I can remember."

"Do."

I struggle for a minute or more, come up with my gray suit, dove gray with white silk blouse, green pin, gold earrings.

"Shoes?"

"Pardon me?"

"What shoes did you have on Monday?"

"That's easy. The ones I had on yesterday morning. The ones you have in your crime scene lab along with my clothes." Is he going to tell me why he wants to explore my wardrobe selections?

He scratches his temple again, then looks me in the eye with no mercy. "We found glass fragments in the sole of the left shoe you had on yesterday."

Ah. His pursuit of the issue of the number of glasses is based on—perhaps—one broken? "Do they match the kind of glass in my set?"

A corner of his lips rises in the barest of smiles. "Should they?"

"I don't recall crunching into any glass as I stepped around yesterday in my office, Detective."

He frowns. "Why do you suppose that is?"

I shrug. "Beats me."

"Try a few on for size."

"Isn't that your job?"

"Humor me."

He wants to hear my logic—shoot holes in any he can. Alrighty, I'll play. "The carpet is thick. I was shocked and not thinking about how or where I was walking around."

"Makes sense." He nods, turns away, then whirls back. Boy, the maneuvers they teach these guys are worthy of the choreography of the Four Tops. "I'd like to examine your car."

"Examine away. You won't find any glass inside." A lipstick, two Tampax, my repair records, but no broken glass.

"You are sure?"

"Positive. It seems rather outrageous to me, if a glass were broken in my office while I was there with Alistair, that fragments would have remained embedded in my shoe until I left the second floor, traveled the hall, stepped into the elevator, down into the garage and climbed into my car—went home and came back again the next day."

His turn to shrug. "The shards were very deeply embedded."

See Carly get thrilled. "Terrific. But I'm gonna tell you no glass was broken while I was there with him."

"That's your statement?"

"And I'm stickin' to it."

"All right, then." He spreads his hands wide. "We are done here."

I reach for my purse. "When do you think you'll let me into my inner office again?"

"Now that we've found glass, I have to comb the entire carpet. That'll take a day or two."

See Carly take gas. Swell. I was going to have to request temporary quarters. I'd get some banged-up glorified closet over in the old Cannon or Longworth office buildings. Akin to working in a feed barn, both were terrible. In contrast with a congressman's regular digs, temporary offices seemed like gray, drafty rooms with twenty-foot ceilings and two two-watt bulbs to light your dreary day. "As fast as you could make it, Detective, the more appreciative I'll be."

"Right. We'll talk soon."

Just my fantasy. I thank him and turn for the door when I think better of it. "I need to ask you a question."

"I'll see if I can answer."

"I suppose you are doing an autopsy."

"You'd be right. All violent deaths require one be done."

"Right. How long will this one take?"

He cocks his head. "Why?"

"The funeral. I'd like to have an idea so that I can tell my daughter, who is friends with Congressman Dunhill's son."

"The coroner is performing it now. If all goes without a hitch, he might be finished sometime later today or tomorrow. A funeral date is entirely up to the family and the efficiency of the undertaker they choose."

I nod. "Thanks."

I'm ready to make tracks out of there when he stops me.

"One more thought, Ms. Wagner. Did you think up that list of people who might wish you ill?"

And who'd kill somebody in my office? "The list I began last night is rather long, Detective. I conclude that's because I'm a bit paranoid at the moment. So I need some time to give you a list that might have some value to it, other than my worst nightmare."

"Tomorrow?"

I inhale. "I'll try," I promise him. But as I forgo the elevator for the exercise of the stairs, I'm drafting instead a mental list of what I can and cannot do to help myself survive the next few days. It's a short list, beginning with a recognition that I'm going to need a few more ways to blow off steam than just this jog down these steps and my contemplative tai chi in the mornings. Maybe I could go to Darnestown this afternoon to the stables and rent a horse. There's a stallion there that understands me— and gallops like he has Comanches on his tail.

I hit the sidewalk before I realize that Brown has shared only one new fact with me about what he's got or where he's going with this. Glass. Broken. In my carpet. In my goddamn shoe. But how many glasses remain? How can I find out?

I am breathing in the cool spring air, mulling numbers of glasses, and opt for walking instead of trying to hail a cab back to Rayburn. While I chew up about ten blocks at a pace that revs my blood pressure I fear I may just destroy my deodorant. How I smell depends less on chemicals at this point than on how long I let my reputation rot in this cesspool of implication.

We know that Alistair came to see me. Looked like he'd been yelling at the top of his lungs or doing the nasty. He took a drink. Downed it. Left his glass on my desk. When I poured him his scotch, were there six glasses in my cabinet? I cannot recall. I curse and stop. Looking up, I'm a block from the Dirksen Senate Office Building. Lou has her office there. Resentment pours through me because she never called me back last night. I could stop in, ask to see her, but if she doesn't want to be associated with me, she could easily leave me outside to dangle in the wind. By lunchtime, the Texas press corps knows I am frozen out—and Mickey G. emails a story down to the San Antonio *Express-News* about me being persona non grata.

Remedial action is wiser. I fish out my cell phone and call. Her receptionist tells me Lou is not available. I leave a message. If she doesn't call me back today, I can rest assured I gotta survive all by my lonesome until something, someone takes suspicion off me.

"Or, Carly, my dear," I say to myself, "you take control and track down who killed Alistair."

I get a wild-eyed look from a passerby that indicates either she knows me—or fears I'm some kook. I wink. Her eyes pop. She scuttles away.

I'm feeling feisty. Standing by a lamppost, I lean against it, watching the midmorning pedestrians on their way to meetings, meetings, meetings. I'm across from one Senate office building, looking at another, and down the street I can see the Supreme Court, and beyond it the dome of the Library of Congress. Inside that huge and comfy repository of all the nation's publications, I like to go and sit in the main reading room. All libraries make me feel solid, informed. Intelligent. Like I can discover anything if I dig long enough and hard enough.

Just like I can figure out who hurt Alistair. Or I can come close to it. I'd better, because no one else seems as devoted.

First stop, re-create his day. Meet who he met. Go where he went. Think like he did.

The first person who can help me is my own AA, Aaron. Aaron, who had made friends among his staffer colleagues eight years before I even arrived in D.C. Aaron, who made his living trading information and whose loyalty to me I never had reason to question.

A gust of crisp air blows through my hair—and my mind.

I can do this.

And then my cell phone rings and I fish it from my purse.

The originating number reads "Unknown." Silly me, I freeze. Always do at unknowns. "Hello?"

"Mom?" The static is ear-piercing, but I can hear that Jordan is crying. "Mom?"

I pause in the street, one finger to my eardrum. "Hi, honey, yes. You're breaking up." What time is it in Tokyo? Twelve hours or more ahead of me, she's calling at midnight or more. Why isn't she in bed?

"Mom, you . . . help me. Zack . . . and he told me . . . his fa-ther's funeral."

Damn. "Okay, sweetie, listen to me."

"Got to come home. Dad won't let me. . . ."

"Look, sweetie, start over and go slowly. I can't hear you." Well, hell, I know what this conversation is about, don't I? Why torture my daughter with unnecessary repetition?

She's getting louder and more angry as she talks. "Dad says we are . . ."

I squeeze my eyes shut. "Listen, honey, don't worry. I will talk to your father."

"You've got to! He is being such an ass!"

Oh, boy. For my shy, calm little girl to utter one three-letter word about her dad tells me more about her state of mind than an encyclopedia. "You will be coming home, Jordan. Do you hear me?"

"Yes."

"Calm down. And put your father on the line."

"Can't."

"Why not?"

"I'm in the business office of the hotel. I made them prom-ise I could call and pay for it in cash so that Dad wouldn't know."

Another indication that my sweet little girl is determined to come home to be with her best friend in his hour of grief. An-other indication that Len has just lost Jordan's good house-keeping seal of approval. "All right, sweetie. Not to worry. I will make it happen. Go back to your rooms—and for god's sake, stay there and get some rest."

Len, Len, how is it you schmooze deals with the biggest, brightest brass in this town, but you cannot negotiate with the people who care for you?

I snap my phone closed. And stare at the one truth I see before me. Len and Alistair were very much alike. Self-centered. Irrational, if driven. Charming when necessary. Controlling always. Even over their nearest and dearest, their children. For Len, this set of traits made him a dynamite negotiator, a man who could nail billions of dollars' worth of defense contracts. For Alistair, this made him a bulldozer in his party and among 434 other congressmen. It made them successful in their work.

And failures with those who loved them.

Within minutes, I arrive in my own outer office. Rayanne greets me with a wide azalea-pink-gloss smile. "Where's Aaron?" I ask her.

"On the phone in his office. Shall I get him?"

"No, not necessary. But order a rental car for me, please." I begin to turn away because I am not going to reveal why I need one. Let her guess. Even if she is my staff. The less everyone knows of my business, the less negative buzz will leak out to the press. But a thought occurs to me and I face her. "Yesterday, when you were in my house, Rayanne, did you perhaps talk to Abe?"

She tilts her head and thinks a spell. "No, ma'am. He wanted me to, doing his monkey-talk thing at me, but I didn't stop, no."

"Did he seem upset when you saw him?"

"Ah, no." She looks confused now. "Just his usual self. You know, grinnin' at me and chattin' away."

So she did not incite him to move his cage.

Aaron comes out of his office and heads toward us.

Rayanne is thinking hard and says, "I think he was taking a nap, actually, when I got there. All tucked up nice inside."

If this is true, then whoever broke in, did it after she left. And if she is wrong about locking the door behind her, then an open door certainly made their entry easier. "Okay, thanks, Rayanne, that helps me." With a smile to her, I face Aaron and we walk toward my nook in the main room.

"How did it go with Brown?"

I lower my voice, settling into the old, hard wooden chair I worked in yesterday. "Not bad. Not good." Now I'm wondering what I can tell Aaron. Geez, is this murder going to make me question everyone I know? "I told Rayanne to order a rental car for me. The police want to go over my Tahoe." There I stop short, damn it all, figuring the less Aaron knows about why they need it, the better off he will be, too. God, I am paranoid. "Call the Admin Office, too, and get me into some temporary digs. I can't continue to work at this desk because I need some privacy." He's nodding. "Also, I need a little info about Dunhill's activities day before yesterday."

"Not a problem. His chief of staff and I just happened to see each other in the cafeteria this morning." He smacks his lips, indicating he planned that accidental meeting. "He and I are having coffee at eleven. Outside," he adds with a grin, "assuming the weather holds. Otherwise"—Aaron checks his watch—"I find something as private. Anything in particular I need to ask?"

"Dunhill's schedule day before yesterday. Who he saw, didn't. Who he dined with, especially dinner. Where he went. What was on his mind that day. Absolutely anything."

"Right." Aaron straightens his spine and his jacket. "I'm off."

"One more thing—"

He turns back.

I lower my voice. "See what you can learn about his relationship with his receptionist."

Aaron cocks his head and our eyes communicate the reason he should ask. "Is that right." *Son of a bitch,* he mouths.

I purse my lips. And my cell phone rings. With one finger in the air to Aaron, I dig it out of my purse and recognize the number. "Hello?"

"Carly. Lou."

I'm so ecstatic I'm grinning probably from my butt to my eyebrows. "Hi, how are you?"

"Sorry I have taken so long to get back to you. How's it going?"

"Interesting." I am not ready to share any details with her about the investigation or about the break-in to my home and garden shed. Her delay might be just normal pressures of time, but I can't take the chance it might have been orders from party honchos to let me hang high.

"I want you to know that help is on the way."

"Oh?" I go still as stone—pleased, shocked, scared to death. I don't know whether to spit or go blind.

"I had a conversation last night with Iverson."

Tommy Iverson is chairman of my party's national committee. The Money. The Voice. Depending on how he feels about you, he can be your Luke Skywalker or your Darth Vader.

"He wants you to have protection."

"Pro—" I bite my lip. Two of my legislative aides pivot to peer at me and Aaron's eyes have widened in alarm. I must have been at high decibel. "What does that mean, specifically?"

"Public support. Affirmation that we believe in you."

A statement by Iverson to the press? A press release? What kind of protection am I being given? I face the wall, lower my voice to a wisp. "He has no reason to believe in my innocence." Does he? What does he know that I don't? Might he have ordered someone to read my journal and the remains of my oatmeal?

"I did not ask him for his rationale, Carly."

"Right, right." I'm running a hand across my brow. Rule

Number One with your party gifts: Accept them. Ask no questions. The assumption is that you need the help—and, like a dutiful member of the Family, you will return the favor when called upon sometime in the future. I believe in give and take in politics—in most of life situations, in fact. But here, the favor may be more than I am willing to repay. Still, can I look a gift horse in the mouth? "Any idea when he gave the order for this?"

"After I talked to him."

"Which was when?"

"Eight, eight-fifteen. Why?"

I'm looking down, examining the people hustling up and down South Capitol Street. They're fighting headlong into a stiff wind. The sun has disappeared behind thickening clouds and the sky is turning to an iridescent gray of coming doom. At eight o'clock last night, I was tucked into my bed, making lists of what I knew about Alistair, when I knew it—and anyone who might want to hurt him and frame me for his murder. At eight o'clock last night, my home and garden shed had already been broken into. At eight o'clock last night, I might have gained one advocate in Iverson and my party, but I already had one foe. One snoop doggie dog who was not hunting at my command or my party's. Or so logic would say.

"Carly? What else is going on?"

I am quaking in my boots, that's what. "Double-think is not something I am good at, Lou."

"This is a straight deal, Carly."

You may be sure, but I am not. "I know you have the best intentions." Hold your friends close, but your enemies closer. "But I am going to refuse."

"You can't."

"I must."

"Carly. You shouldn't."

"I hear you—and I appreciate the advice." Thunder crackles overhead. A black mushroom cloud slithers across the skyline.

The line crackles. "Carly, don't be foolish."

"Trying not to be. Give him my regards and my thanks, but I will not be needing his aid."

"Carly—?"

Static breaks up her words. I pretend my line has gone dead and click off the call, then power down my phone. Aaron and I are facing each other.

"Anything else I can do for you before I go?" he probes.

I nod. "Go have your coffee, ask the right questions, then come back and do me a favor."

He waits.

I am collecting all my *cojones* into both fists.

"Get me Scott on the phone."

"Yeah?" Aaron yelps, impressed.

So am I. "No foolin'." William Preston Scott is no mere mortal. He's the minority leader and so little ol' me dialing him up is akin to calling god. You don't do it every day—and you must go with an offering. This morning I have nothing to give—and nothing to fear but fear itself. But I must know how deep and wide this interest is in saving my hide. "Ask for soon. This morning, preferably, before we have any more requests for TV interviews." At eight this morning, I had refused CNN and the evening host of NBC in San Antonio. "I don't want to have to do that again without some indication of how well he thinks I am doing here. And Aaron—"

"Yes, ma'am?"

"You probably want to make it clear that this is a nonevent."

For Scott, a nonevent is a real special occasion. Sure, it's only one of his signature ways that he has managed to ride herd on his congressmen for more than two decades. His quiet little meetings never occur in public, but in scenic spots like closets (walk-ins or stand-ups), cars (tinted glass required), hotel rooms (five stars necessary because you are paying for the ultra-confidentiality), and steam or boiler rooms (foggier the better). Among newly minted representatives, these tête-à-têtes are the stuff of guffaws until you are summoned to one. Then, like a soldier in the Mob, you never fail to take the meeting. I've taken exactly three in my ten years. I deserve to call one now.

Screw protocol. A dead man in my office means I can be presumptuous, can't I? "I'm going down to the hearing room." I could bet it was quiet down there and I could sit and think. "Let me know when you have a time and place."

Turning on my heel, I head down the hall, passing two staffers and the congresswoman who has the office next door to mine. Mirinda Pace gives me a piteous smile and says hello, but her staffers don't even blink. Clearly, to some, I suffer from leprosy.

Well, what could I expect? Chocolates and roses for the murder suspect? Wouldn't they drop their teeth to know that the head of my national committee thinks I'm worth protecting?

"Hey, Carly, tough blow." I am frowning up into the hound dog face of Jimmy Jeff Holden. The congressman from the Thirteenth District of Texas that borders mine has always been a pal. Not a friend, exactly. But a sweet ol' guy who runs his campaigns and his staff in the time-honored tradition of gentlemanly behavior. He and I are from the same class, as they say here when folks get elected in the same year. We are also from the same party, even if his style is as different from mine as a coon dog from a setter.

We enter the elevator together, both facing forward, because neither one of us wants this chat to look like a planned activity, should anyone along the hall be examining this scene.

"Thanks, Jimmy Jeff." The doors whisk closed.

"Bet you were shook up yesterday morning."

"Something fierce," I admit.

"It'll get better soon."

I restrain myself from looking into his baggy, kindly eyes. "You think?"

"Got to. You didn't slice him up."

I wince. "No, sir. I appreciate the vote of confidence."

"You're welcome. Now, you call me, you hear, if you need a shoulder."

"I will." I won't. We both know it. But I sure do appreciate his belief that I haven't hurt Alistair. I need all the reassurance I can get. But that's all I want, for now, maybe forever. Because I do not want to owe my soul to the company store.

The doors whoosh open and I step out, heading left for the committee rooms.

In the Rayburn Building, committee rooms are on the first floor and not too far from the main entrance. The noise filling the hall tells me that folks are lined up to get into some hearing or other. I'd bet the ranch that the masses would love to catch a glimpse of headliner Carly Wagner in her natural habitat, so I turn the other way and duck into one committee room, which has no one queing in front of it.

The huge room is hushed, dim, and just what I need. I sit in the audience, a treat for me. Looking at issues from the other side of the table is one task I do well. It is why my constituents put me here. Why I stay here. Why I try to stay within my party's line, but not to the detriment of the folks who brung me to this dance in the first place.

So what are the reasons I am in big trouble here? There are the visible reasons. I am bright, photogenic, younger than most, and articulate. The TV cameras like me. I know how to use them. That kind of expertise breeds jealousy. Contempt. But it's hard to replace.

I cross my arms. Let them try.

Outside, I hear thunderclaps. Washington weather is gearing up to match my troubles.

And they are many. My long list of woes is really a litany that I developed last night in my bed—and sadist that I am, I bring them out like bags of old garbage to reexamine. I favor an increase in spending for Border Patrol and harbor cargo container inspections—and that opposes the budget cuts of the President. I don't go along with my party's desire to increase Social Security paycheck deductions. Plus, I want to overhaul the Medicare program and that makes me a radical to my own party as well as the opposing one.

That equals three strikes against me in policy. Three groups of enemies—the first at 1600 Pennsylvania, another in the opposite party—and many among my own, headed by Tommy Iverson. He, of the protection offer.

And we haven't even gotten to the social issues, like who dislikes me as a dinner speaker (too funny for a woman), a scout leader (too sexy to be a young girls' role model), or a single mother (Alistair and other shakers in town who were horned toads over anything celibate in a skirt).

I'm getting wildly depressed at the numbers of people who surely wish me dead when the door opens, light streams in, and Aaron calls to me.

He trundles over, happy as a small dog with a big bone. "Two home runs. You are right on the after-hours issue." He means Alistair and Krystal were partying together.

"Interesting." One suspect confirmed. "And the other?"

Aaron beams. Scott and I must have a date. "He took my call immediately. He wants this now."

Omigod. "Where?"

"You and he are going to take a walk."

"You are pulling my leg." Taking a walk was one of Scott's other methods of control. Because it was public, he declared openly whose ear he had—and who had his. It was private, because Scott, a six-time finalist of the Marine Corps marathon, walked faster than any cowboy with fire ants in his undies. But it also carried a huge risk. If you didn't get the verbiage right, if you promised more than you delivered, if you failed to repay the favor, soon your tail was worth less than a flat beer on Saturday night.

"No, ma'am, we are going for a stroll." Aaron offers me a hand up from my chair. "I am dead-on honest."

I lead us toward the doors. "Where do we meet?"

"At the nurses' station."

"Seems appropriate," I mutter, "for the walking wounded."

"Now, now," Aaron cajoles, "if the man thought that, you'd be doing a stand-up in some broom closet."

"You got that right." We're turning down the hall, away from the entrance and the crowds. We get to the stairway where I need to go on alone. I stop short, pull my suit coat down my hips, and fluff my hair. Scott likes women. Especially those with curves, sass, and power. Trying to get in a girl's pants, he's been known to eat her alive. This morning, he can look at the menu, but he will not be nibbling on the goods. "All right. How do I look?"

"Lick your lips."

I roll my eyes, do as I'm told—and charge through the door.

I'm chugging down the stairs, searching for some clarity of mind, and trying to do a mental Cosmic Consciousness to relieve tension. But I'm outta time and open the hall door to see Scott laughing with one of the nurses on duty.

"Thank you so much, Miz Harley," he is cooing in his Georgia drawl. "I shall take your advice, my dear, about the aspirin. Only four little ones a day." His lime-green eyes widen at my appearance. "Why, here is the next best thing for my constitution, a beautiful woman from Texas. Congresswoman Wagner, have you had the pleasure of meeting Miz Annette Harley?"

"No, sir, I have not." I put out my hand and we do the friendly thing and shake. "Wonderful to meet you. Have you been with us long?"

"No, ma'am. Only a few months."

"A welcome addition, I am sure," Scott is booming, but pivoting to take my arm. "Shall we walk together a bit, Congresswoman?"

"I welcome the opportunity, sir."

We bid our nurse a good day and turn with the blank expressions of two sprinters going to their mark.

"Good day for you, Carly?" *No Mr. Nice Guy till we have the measure of your worth, Miz Wagner.*

"I've had better."

He snorts. Mr. Sensitive. My immediate boss, William Preston Scott, the minority leader of the House of Representatives. Two hundred and thirty-plus pounds packed into six sleek feet of muscle, Scott walks these hallowed halls like the physical and political giant he is. He first won election the year I was born, so that makes him almost as big an enchilada as his counterpart, the majority leader, and on par with the man down at 1600 Pennsylvania.

But he better get out his diplomacy because I'm not showing him mine unless he wises up—and shows me his.

"I must know all of it, Carly." He's picking up his pace, eyes never venturing my way. "We have a stake in your successful extrication from any misrepresentation by the press."

Consecutive translation: *We—the party and I—want to make sure we are all distanced from any scandal.* "I hear you, sir. I want distance myself."

"Alistair came to see you Monday night."

"He did, yes." I'm huffing and puffing like one of the three little piggies to keep up with him.

"What can you share with me about his visit?"

"I did not kill him."

"Did you convince that nice Detective Brown of that this morning?"

Ah, Scott had known I was at headquarters. Why am I not surprised? Scott has held on to his seat through scandals from Watergate to Iran-Contra to Whitewater. He's on a first-name basis with Cronkite and Woodward. He does lunch with Larry King and cocktails with whomever the hell he chooses. He knows where almost every body is buried in this town—and why. And as for the body of Alistair Dunhill, he wants to know that story from the horse's mouth—and I can't blame him.

But I do not look good in Naïve. Never did. So as Scott holds open the door to the stairwell for me, I smile up at him like a tipsy sorority girl at a calf fry and ask, "Who was Alistair screwing?"

His green eyes drift to mine and remind me of a lizard's. "You know?"

"A few. Not the latest ones." *Do share,* I am praying as we take the stairs like we're both twenty.

"His receptionist."

Bingo. Our girl Krystal. "And?"

He purses his mouth.

I encourage him. "He never had just one."

"And not just one at a time."

I stop in my tracks. This was kinky news to me.

"There were questions, too . . ." He drifts off, suddenly and uncharacteristically embarrassed, searching for words. "About their gender."

I swallow. Hard. Suddenly Scott is way ahead of me and I hustle up to keep up.

He blinks, recovering from what he just revealed to me. "He was concerned about his son."

"True." It was now my turn to share goodies with him. "Since his wife died, he has tried to be a good father to Zack."

"But the boy is into drugs."

"Pot. Big difference."

"Not if the press learns." We reach the top of the stairwell and he pulls open the door to the first floor. I am stunned. He wants to take a turn with me around the most public floor of the building?

My courage hits new lows, but I pretend I'm brave as a bull. "He went to dinner with someone that night. He invited me to go, but I refused. Should I have gone?" *Do you know who he dined with?*

"No idea." Now Scott is frowning.

Meanwhile, I am hoping Aaron is having more success than I am learning the answer to that. "When did you last see him?"

"That afternoon. It was not an agreeable meeting. He left in a snit."

"Not like him." *Not with you.* "Is it important for my own defense that I know why you argued?" I know it is not diplomatic to press Scott for this answer, but my neck is in the noose at the moment.

"Legislation. The Medicaid bill. But . . . well, there, look who it is. . . ." Scott pulls to a halt to shake hands with a congressman from Ohio. He does the polite *you know Ms. Wagner from Texas* intro, they slap each other's back, chew the fat, say so-long, and Scott and I are off on our trek again. "Alistair has money problems. Personal, he swears, all personal. I told him to clean them up. Borrow money if he had to. I said I would stand behind him while he did."

Lawzy, Miss Scarlett. Money. The root of all evil. And in this city, the root of many a dead political career. The more frightening part of Scott's statement, however, was his last one that he would support him in his efforts. The only reason Scott might have to was if Alistair was suspected of taking money he shouldn't. Bribes or PAC money.

Scott stops abruptly, before we begin to pass a throng waiting for admission to a hearing room. "How friendly were you two?"

"Never as close as our children are."

Scott fixes me with the eerie green vision that makes you think he can look right through your skin into your gray matter. Then he croons, slow and deep, "I can see that you did not kill him."

I breathe deeply.

"I had to know."

I nod.

"Otherwise, I couldn't protect you."

That word again. Poison to my ears. I get my gumption out again. "You don't have to, sir."

"Thank you for saying so, my dear." We start to walk again—and he says, warm and soft as a baby's butt, "But I do need to."

"No, sir. No, you don't, sir."

"This August we are going to Chicago."

Chicago. My heart goes thunk, right down to the pit of my stomach—and my instincts sit up and wag their tails eager as a passel of newborn puppies. Chicago is this year's site of our party's national convention to nominate a president.

"In Chicago, Carly, you are going to be front and center."

I am? Since when?

"We need you."

Yeah? Ambition makes me salivate. "I—I would—" I would give my eyeteeth.

"I know you're thrilled."

Can you hear my knees knock?

He grins. "We're planning your nationwide debut. Say, opening night keynote speech." It's no question.

This is great, cuz I've got no answer.

"You look good, Carly. You sound good. You will *do* good." He runs his eyes over my hair, my eyes, my mouth, and yes, my tits. Well, hell's bells. What did I expect? He was gonna love me for my brains? That is not why he's putting me on nationwide TV. No, siree. Sex sells. Even politics.

And I oughta know. I have never been bashful about using my looks to help me gain a vote. How far would I have come wearing sackcloth and ashes?

"So you understand where we're going here?"

Up. We're going up. "Yes, indeed, I do."

Facing me, he smiles like Colonel Sanders in a chicken coop. "Good, we're all so pleased, Carly." I am here to tell you he is now dripping sugar so badly all over me that, if we were in private, he would reach over and pinch my cheeks like a fond uncle. "Got to run. You be good, now, hear?"

Faster than a roadrunner on skates, zoom, that man is gone.

And I am left standing here, my mouth open like a fish with a hook in her mouth.

five

A super hunk at your front door with a gun in his pocket is always a welcome sight, if you're single and lonely. Tonight, I am conflicted big-time that this huge, very Terminator-looking type guy serves only as a reminder that I am guarded. Correction, I am *protected* by the police and some other guys—nameless and, so far, faceless—hired by my political party. What fun, to be a murder suspect, a victim of breaking and entering, and a woman who now owes her soul to her party—a creature of her own ambition. All rolled into one.

This tall, dark-looking man on point atop my neat little porch spots me at the same time as I do him, just as I turn the corner from Wisconsin into Q Street. While he's taking me in behind those *Men in Black* shades, I mosey down my skinny street. The going is slow because what was once a glorious sunny morning has become a grizzly snowy twilight. We've got three inches of powder on top of sleet—and on my rental car, I've got no snow tires.

What's more, I've obviously got no electricity, either, because my garage door opener is not operating. I park the rented Taurus behind my neighbor's BMW—and wonder if he's gazing out his window at me and pitying me for my bad taste.

My bodyguard seems to ignore me in favor of doing his duty and casing the dead-silent street. I grab my briefcase and get out.

While I climb my steps, I note he has a pointed jaw worthy of Dudley Do-Right and a composure that reeks of former Marine or FBI. His presence here is like a red flag, screaming, *Here, here, look at the elected official who's in a mess.*

"Oh, suck a nut," I grumble, but silently once more give thanks that my daughter is not here to be exposed to this. *To be frightened by this.*

But I am, I admit in the inner voice I know belongs to none other than Carly the Eight-Year-Old Wuss, cringing at the sounds of Mama and Daddy roaring at each other down in the kitchen while she burrows into her covers and holds her kitty-cat tight.

Well, I don't burrow well at my advanced age. No, indeedy. I know how to go up like a flare and scare the buzzards away.

"Nice night, isn't it?" I greet Dudley as I mount the last step to my porch.

"Yes, ma'am." No smile, no nod, no personality, thank you, ma'am. I unlock my front door, step inside, fall back against it, and remove my snow-filled shoes. In my stocking feet, I pad past my living room and head for the kitchen. My housekeeper Ming was here this morning and I can smell the pine cleaner she uses on everything she can get her hands on. Hell, she'd wash Abe with it if she could.

I fling open the kitchen door and there he sits in the evening shadows. In his cage, he has his arms folded, unhappy to be confined. But tonight, unlike last, he has not scooted his crate across the tile. No one, I could conclude, has been snooping in my home today. The presence of Ming here earlier has mitigated against that. Or they got what they came for yesterday. Geez, who knows? One thing, for sure, Dudley on the door is a visible deterrent to intruders.

I loosen the latch. "Hey, Abe, what's happening?"

He chitters at me.

"No prowlers today?"

He smacks his lips, which I take to mean, *No, none.*

I toss my head back and forth. He imitates me. I chuckle. He does the same. Is there something wrong with a woman whose main companion is a chimpanzee? Ouuu, should I answer that?

Probably not.

Abe climbs up on a barstool and nods to the bowl of bananas. Abe is the kind of man many women want: no arguments, no hormones, no resentments, no agendas.

Except two.

Companionship, followed closely by food.

I toss him a banana.

He grabs it midair and spins on the stool in glee, pleased to be eating and out of his cage. Ming always says he should be free because he is named in honor of the Great Emancipator.

True, my Abe has similarities to the gentle giant.

He's kind, he's courteous, he's scrawny, he is definitely ugly, poor thing, but we gotta call a spade a spade, don't we? Besides, he's not offended, he knows his looks are his signature brand. He really does look like his namesake, especially when I am still sitting reading in my armchair in my living room after ten or so and the timer makes the table lamps go dim. If he's sitting in his chair, book spread in his lap pretending to read, too, but dozing (picture that chair pee-wee-sized and red-lacquered), he definitely resembles that brooding man who sits in that huge chair, head bowed, at the end of the Mall. Now, you might think that's unpatriotic, to compare a chimpanzee to our sixteenth President, but we never had any intention of insulting old Abe when we named him. Nope. He came to us, if I am real honest about it, from God. He showed up one day about six years ago on our back porch. Sitting there on the edge of the patio, he had a little coat on, bright blue with red buttons. He also wore a little white shirt, red string tie, and navy pants. Trousers, to be precise. Someone, we never did find out who, let him out to the wild world of Washington, D.C. But Jordan saw him first, named him "ape," which of course was not quite polite or accurate. So, after we got over the shock of a monkey on our doorstep and took him to a local vet and had him checked out, we registered him with the local authorities for rare and exotic species, then decided to bring him home to live with us. Smart monkey that he is, Abe knows us well and what we need.

Like now.

He finishes the last of his treat, then waves his hands about, repeatedly going toward the front door.

"Right," I tell him. "This guy is our new buddy."

Kiss-kiss sounds come from Abe's puckered lips.

"No. No kisses for this guy." I start to unbutton my suit coat jacket, debating if I should mix myself a gin and tonic now or go learn who our Cerberus calls boss.

Abe makes a sound that I interpret as, *Really?* (Picture eyebrows of loving chimp rising here.)

"He's here to be our friend, but not our best friend." I put my fist to my chest, Jordan's and Abe's gesture that means love and devotion.

Abe does a raspberry.

I laugh.

That brings me perspective, so I get my legs under me and going toward the door, for surely, how hard can it be to ask a man where he came from?

I retrace my steps, swing open the door and get a blast of frigid snow in my face. "Hi, there," I greet the nonplussed gentleman before me. Upon close examination, his jaw is definitely pointed and his eyes are beady behind those dark glasses. Not such a looker after all. "Come in, please." I stand aside.

"No, ma'am." He shakes his head once. Snowflakes dance on his nose and eyelashes. "I can't do that."

"On duty." I might've known he'd give me air.

"Yes, ma'am."

"Very well." I cross my arms and I notice that my protector does not blink an eye as he stares down in awe at a chimpanzee that is crossing his arms in imitation of his owner. "We'll talk where you stand. Who sent you?"

"Ma'am?"

Not a complicated question. "Are you Capitol Police, private contractor, what?"

"Capitol. Plainclothes detail."

No foolin'. "How long have you been here?"

"Since three."

Abe snorts as if to say we don't need or want him.

The guy's not so dumb, because he interprets it correctly, looks Abe in the eye, then me, and says, "Yes, ma'am. We are here to protect you."

That unfavorite word again. "Protect me. From what?"

"Anything, ma'am. Neighbors, nuts, reporters."

And burglars. "Okay, okay. Are there more of you?" I nod my head toward the inside.

"Yes, ma'am, all over."

"How many?"

He smiles and it definitely ups his handsome quotient from homely to passable. "Three. Front, back, roof." He nods across the street. "Over there."

"For how long?"

"Long as it takes."

"Are you here for the night?"

"I'm the three to eleven shift. That's all I'm authorized to say, ma'am."

"Great, well, thanks." I begin to step inside. Recalling my experience with police patrols before, I know enough not to try to pry info out of him with offers of breakfast, lunch, or a before-dinner drink. "Too bad about the snow." I shut the door on him and lock it behind me. "Nice enough guy, huh, Abe?"

Abe tosses his head to and fro. Middling acceptance from a wise creature.

"Yeah, well, we have a few things we gotta do, kid. Get some candles lit so we can see—and then, if the electricity comes back on, try to get Len and Jordan on the phone in Tokyo."

At the sound of Jordan's name, the dearest friend in all the world to Abe, he grins, all teeth, all white, all the time.

"Yeah, well, it's not going to be a happy call."

The smile dissolves.

"Jordan's friend's daddy is going to be buried in a few days after the police finish an autopsy, and tonight—if the phones work minus electricity—Len and I are going to fight about Jordan coming home to attend the funeral."

The gaunt little face droops.

"I know, it's not happy stuff," I croon, and put my hand out for Abe to grasp, "but I've got to tell them all this."

Abe catches my attention when he ambles over to the front window and pulls back the drapes to see our guard. He is worried about this stranger remaining outside our door. "I don't blame you for being concerned, Abe. But he's there to watch over us."

Abe nods, but is clearly more troubled than before.

"Tell you what, let's get undressed and comfy. Then we'll hope that whatever Ming made for dinner, we don't have to heat up."

Abe claps his hands. Interpretation: *If it includes food, it sounds like a plan.*

We're doing well, me in my jammies with a second gin in production and Abe snoozing on the sofa. It's after eight, the house dark as sin, save for the two candles I've lit on the end table. Dinner was tuna from a can and limp lettuce. But I'm enjoying the peace of snow silently falling outside my French doors. Sitting in an oversized chair with an afghan over me in a quickly chilling house, I'm contemplating how realistic it might be that Iverson and Scott know that the Capitol Police have guards on duty for me—and if they consider that is adequate for their new keynote convention speaker.

Scott, after all, had known I had visited the good detective this morning. One of the original Special Forces assigned to our Saigon embassy back in the fifties, Scott knew how to pry intel out of a kitty-cat. I could lay odds he had learned Brown's other plans for me included ol' Dudley at the door.

I surely cannot call anyone, even Lou, to talk it over. In this storm, not only is the Potomac Electric Power Company down and out, but so are satellites for cell phone use. I know for certain because I have tried repeatedly to call Jordan—and have given up, realizing that the time zone difference would have her in bed long ago.

I'm quiet, I'm lonely, and fretting about not being able to talk to her. Mostly, though, I'm grieving for Alistair, whose life was ended so sadly. He had problems, women and money and professional ones, to boot. But he didn't deserve that kind of ending. I'm fighting a tear or two, staring out through the French doors, when a shadow seems to ooze down over the snow-white wall like a huge black crab.

Now, I don't do horror movies. Not since one of those *Alien* flicks got to me with those drooling beasts trying to take a slurp of ol' long, tall whatshername. But, swear to god, this shadow looks like a cross between one of those creatures from Hollywood and the Satan that every Bible-thumping preacher pictures for his congregation.

Lucky for me that I know what to do about Satans and Aliens. I get my gun.

I stay in the shadows, gliding backward toward my kitchen island. I slide open the drawer, quiet as a little mouse, and there it is, right up tight next to the recipes for my daddy's beef barbecue and my mama's first housekeeper's margaritas. Rightful place for a gun, in a drawer with two other things that can kill you.

I slither the drawer wider. My fingers dig in, wrapping around cool comfort. The SIG I always liked, fitting right into the palm of my hand. Makes me feel like a woman, I tell ya, to know I can bring down a man with this, if nothing else. Gives a girl balls. What every woman needs, now and then.

I recede farther into the shadows, back flattened to the wall, agile in my pj's. But I've got my bedroom slippers on and, unsure of my footing for the task of felling a critter, I kick them off. I inch along the wall that at its other end stops and gives me a better view of the garden in the far corner where my visitor has sequestered himself.

I wonder where my back-door protector might be. For surely this varmint is not of the same ilk as the dude at the front door. He's faster, slinkier—and for sure, he is not sent by the same *jefe*. No matter, this is my home to protect. Mine. And Abe and I are not going to die at the hand of a black-clad slug.

So I lick my lips, congratulate myself that I always have a full magazine—and chamber a round. With both hands on my weapon, I whirl toward the other wall and, flat against it, skim the garden. Cloaked in white, my back yard looks like it's been smothered in melted marshmallow. I scan the muted silhouettes of my rosebushes and my forsythia, my cherry tree and tiny yearning impatiens. Amid every petal, every flower, every branch, he is not there . . . and not there . . . and not there. Where, where, where?

I glimpse a shadow growing against the window and gauge if I can get the door open and swirl up, aiming to fire at the top of the trellis which he seems to be—but how *can* he be?—crawling across. So if he's up there, he can't see me. And if I reach out, pull down the doorknob, furl the door open, and fling myself outside, I will have to roll, gun in hand, point upward searching for my mark—and I figure I can't be any more agile than a guy who can scale a wall like he did. So my gut says I have got to open the door and throw something out, see if he tails it, and shoot. *Go, Carly* . . . and I rush the doors. I am outside when I am rolled down to the snow like a feather. I turn over and over, my gun falls away, and I kick upward, but a weight hits my chest like a ton of bricks, crushing the air out of me.

I'm flat on my back, arms and legs spread like a two-bit hooker at a bachelor party gone bad, and the creature I'm looking up at has eyes that flash like electric sparks and a balaclava that covers the entirety of his face, but lets him croon to me through the material, "Ah, the congresswoman of the hour, I presume. Damn, you are better-looking in person than those news clips. They did not tell me that, and they definitely should have."

Clearly, the guy thinks that flattery will get him somewhere. But breaking and entering is not the way to this girl's heart.

Using the only advantage I have, I knee him in the nuts.

He doubles over. I slide out and away while he suddenly finds himself wrestling with forty-two pounds of mad monkey on his back.

I'm panting like a boxer as I stretch across the patio snow to reach my SIG with greedy fingers. I grasp it tight, years of practice with it bringing reassurance to the grip. This huge dark creature in my garden is one I'd enjoy ripping into with this, his proximity ensuring I could blow him to smithereens with just a few bullets. I get my back to the wall and train the SIG on him.

"Enough! Leave Abe alone. Now . . . slowly, get up," I order him. "Okay, Abe, you can back off, babe. I've got him."

Abe objects.

"Honest, Abe, I'm cool." I wave the muzzle at our guest. "Take off your mask."

"Not fair, having a savage hop on me like that."

"Life's little surprises, huh?" I sound nonchalant. Fancy that. "Take it off, let's see the cut of you."

He whips off his skin-tight head gear and in the soft grays of a snowy night, I'm looking at one of those spare and sculpted faces you see on the Sci Fi Channel. All muscle, his face is so symmetrically proportioned I'm questioning if he was born this way or if plastic surgeons have nipped and tucked him to this rare perfection. His eyes look absolutely radioactive. A flash of gray, blue, silver. I squint, almost unable to look at them, they seem so bright. And his face reminds me of the angular symmetry of some of the figures in Jordan's digital GameBoys. He is every American man, literally, rolled into one triple *A*—Anglo, Asian, and African-American. A flesh-and-blood example of twenty-first century American melting pot. With every breath he takes, every move he makes, he is much more than that: He is definitely military. Strack. Buzz cut to the point of nearly bald, but handsome with a capital *H*.

"Sorry about the entry," he apologizes, but doesn't look contrite at all. "I was told you knew I was coming."

"Whoever gave you that info got more than one thing wrong."

"Check." He tilts his head toward my family room. "Let's go inside for this talk."

Sure, the winds have whipped up and it's cold enough to freeze the stink off manure, but damn if I'm gonna let my guard down. "What makes you think we're talking?"

"Your lips. They're blue. And your toes are going to fall off from frostbite soon. Here." He sounds like a lounge singer now, dulcet as Bayou jazz. "Take my weapon." He hands over a small black gun that resembles a peashooter. Light as one, too.

No ordinary man ever gives up his advantage. But this is no ordinary man. For one thing, he must be a polar bear because he's not shivering like I am. And for another, his gun is nothing I've ever seen before. Too tiny. Too sleek.

"Come on." He's got his hands spread wide as he inches backward into my house. "I'm here to pro—"

"Shut up and get inside." If he was here to kill me, he would have done it before now. And since my logic says he is sent by Iverson and Scott, I need to know what they plan and who he is.

"I was going to say that I'm here—"

"Yeah, yeah. I've heard this all day. Now move."

I slam the doors shut behind me, step into my warm slippers, and tell him to get over against the far wall in the corner. If he decides to rush me, I have time to plug him full of holes. With my gun *and* his.

John Wayne–style, I stand braced with both weapons trained on his guts. "Who sent you?"

"You really do not need those." He must be deciding otherwise, because he's raising his hands like I might just make him dance to my bullets.

"That's my call."

He steps forward.

"No, back there is good. So. Who is it? Iverson?"

He shakes his head no.

"Scott?"

No, again.

Let's work on the opposition party, then. "Woodruff?"

"Really? Do you think they have any reason to come to your aid? Woodruff has a strong resentment because you wouldn't compromise on your budget vote last year. He's also not crazy about your demands for more increases in the Border Patrol, either."

This guy knows a lot about my politics. "Well, who, then?"

In the flickering dance of candlelight, he mashes those pretty lips together in a *sorry to say this* look. "My employers are never revealed to me."

"Why not?"

"No need."

I am not buying. "Don't you want to know who you're fighting for?"

"Once I get the description of the mission, I know what I'm fighting for. That's enough."

"And here your mission is what?"

"Protect and assist you. Learn who really killed Dunhill."

"What if I'm guilty?"

"You? No."

I might be gratified, but what's it worth coming from a cipher? "How are you so sure?"

"Probabilities of success. I work them all up before I take a case. This means lots of homework. In this case, about you."

"How time-consuming."

"Necessary pre-op planning," he corrects me.

"For a soldier of fortune like you, doesn't that make for boring work?"

He smirks. "Predictable. I like to collect my entire fee for a mission. So if I am well prepared, then I deliver the goods, and I get paid. Simple."

"What if your research is wrong?"

"Not usually."

I cluck. "What's written is not always accurate."

His eyes flare with satisfaction. "What's between the lines is."

"And you are . . ."—my gaze has strayed to admire the nonfat content of his biceps in the sleek black cat suit—"a thorough researcher?"

"And a noble student of the Second Mind."

"Cults." I knew about them from Texas. A few of them in my district were so nutty, they'd scare the hide off a bison.

"No, it's a discipline of the Shao-lin monks. Says trust your knowledge. Trust your instincts." He's tapping his skullcap against his thigh, surveying my family room, getting ready to get comfy.

In a pig's eye. "Instincts," I snort. "And yours about me say what?"

"That you would argue with me about my services," he reveals with confidence.

"Did it also predict I have a short fuse?" I was getting antsy here, jawing about Second Minds and wanting only to kick him out, and sit or sleep, perchance to dream.

" 'Know thy subject' is my first rule—and you"—he fixes me with those X-ray eyes—"might be hyper occasionally, but you are also squeaky clean. You did not kill Alistair Dunhill."

I indicate both guns. "I could kill you."

"But won't."

I am envious of his certainty, ticked at his smugness. "Headline here. Without a substantiated alibi, I am a prime suspect."

"You did not do this."

"No?" Does he know who did? Was he sent by someone who did? Ouuu, that gives me the creeps.

He steps forward. "You don't approve of violence."

I brace myself for an attack. "And you would know this be-cause of what?"

"Your stance on gun control."

"Yeah," I argue, "but I also approve of the death penalty."

"And beefed-up police forces."

Hmmf. He certainly has done a yeoman's job of Carly 101. I am impressed.

He tilts his head a bit. "Shall I tell you more?"

Let's see what else he knows. "You're on."

He comes another step and I catch a waft of eucalyptus and saddlewood. "You like your life. Living alone, one child you adore. You can be stubborn, but you will compromise. Makes you a good congresswoman. A great negotiator. If you were ever a hothead at home with your husbands, that was yesterday. Plus now there are no husbands. No distractions. Your passion is not making men bleed physically—or cutting off any part of their anatomy. Your passion is winning. Your way. You are not a mur-derer."

The lights flicker. I blink. My guest steps nearer, but he's behaving like a gentleman.

The lights blink again.

He licks his lips. And as the electricity holds for a long minute, I can see they are full and firm, but they are also silent. He's thinking.

So am I. But the lights dim and I back up to the counter, gaining protection from the rear. "You did your research quickly, to learn all this in such short time."

"Not hard to learn. The *Post* likes you. They run too much copy about you, if you ask me." As if on cue, the lights go on again when he moseys up to stand inches in front of me. Isn't it odd for a burglar to smell so good? And what about it being criminal for one man to be so dangerously good-looking in black spandex? I mean, no love handles, no lumps, ladies—well, except . . .

My eyes zoom to his, and I return to the topic of the moment. "I'm not crazy about how they delve into my life, either. But if they play it fair, I won't complain."

Too long an explanation. He takes the advantage and does a fancy around-the-world kick that sends my SIG and his whatever-it-is flying out of my hands and crashing into the kitchen wall. And I am quite suddenly flat on my back. Again.

"There, now . . ." He croons, pinning my hands to the floor as he settles over me, squatting, his legs trapping my thighs while I inhale his exotic scent. "Let's get down to being friends."

Friendly is not what I feel so much as the heat coming off him in a big red tide. "Looks like you are currently in charge." Though from the corner of my eye, I see Abe saunter forward.

"I apologize." Good god, he sounds sincere. "But tell Abe to back off." He thrusts a palm up to ward off my chimp.

"Okay, okay. Abe, be a good boy and sit down."

"Great. I don't want to hurt either of you."

"Gee, thanks, but I'm not very comfy here."

"Sorry, but I like the advantage."

I wiggle on the hard floor, my body beginning to sweat in all the places that touch his, and knowing that heat like this is not all attraction, I suspect something intriguing about his attire. "Who's your tailor?"

Both of his brows shoot up. "You like my duds?"

Oh, yeah, the fit, the form. "The fabric is?"

He smiles, appreciative of my observation. "M5."

"The military's newest ballistic fiber." Developed in a chemical lab, this stuff could be stretched, burned, frozen, shot at, bombed, and still survive. In the congressional budget, the line item for this paper-thin fabric that fit this guy like his second skin was costing Uncle Sam an arm and a leg to save the hide of our GIs in combat. Which meant, since this guy had it, he had to

earn big bucks to afford it—and he had to have the right con-
nections to get one made. "You are very lucky. I've seen swatches
of M5, but never in the flesh—or correction, on it."

"Great product."

"So great, it's no wonder you weren't concerned I'd shoot
you."

He grins even wider. "Right."

"I couldn't."

"Right."

I fold my arms and frown at him. "Since we agree I am harmless, can I get up now?"

"If you promise to be nice."

"And do what?"

"Accept my help."

I shake my head. "Hard to do when I don't know what your
services will cost me."

"Not a dime."

"Dimes don't concern me. Votes do. And if you don't know
who hired you and I can't be certain of it, either, then that leaves
me with an obligation to a godfather whose name I do not
know—and whose payback I don't know, either." He thinks that
one over and I squirm under his pressure. "Besides, it's tough for
a woman to trust a man who keeps her pinned down."

"Okay, but no getting the chimp to jump me, or we're down
here again."

"Truce."

My defender rises to his feet and offers me his hand to help
me up.

I don't take it. Call me independent, call me miffed. "This is
not a cotillion—and even if it was"—I stand up, brush myself
off, and straighten my jammies—"I couldn't dance with you, since
we haven't been formally introduced, Mr. . . . . ?"

"Jones."

What a hoot. "Jones. What kind of a name is that?"

"Mine. For now. With you. Here."

I examine him a long minute, brooding on the implications of his ordinary name. My imagination, my work with the Defense Appropriations Subcommittee—and a knowledge that our commandos usually "retire" into white ops private sector work—combine to give me the heebie-jeebies and a rationale that spills out of my mouth. "Meaning what? It changes?"

"According to need."

I throw up my hands and go to the end table to retrieve my gin and tonic. "I should have guessed." What I have here is a private bodyguard, expensive, secretive, adaptable, and blind to his employer. I sip my drink and examine him. "Which begs the question, if you're so noble, how come you don't just knock on the front door, like my other guard dog, and present your credentials?"

"Now, ma'am, you know why." He ambles farther into my den and gestures at the sofa, asking to sit.

I wave my hand in permission. "Let's say I don't."

He settles down, looking like a hunky black panther on my couch, one leg crossed over at the ankle. "Two reasons. One, we are not from the same company."

I note he doesn't say "force" but "company." That's terminology from a government operative. FBI or CIA. Current or past? Matters not; my Second Mind, as he would call it, says so. "Lucky me. What's the second?"

"I'm here but not."

"Totally untraceable."

"You could say."

"And so what did you do to him and his buddies, that you were able to get inside?"

"They have a little cocktail, harmless, odorless."

"Delivered by . . . ?" I raise my brows.

He smiles. "Dart."

"Cute." I drop into my chair. "Are you alone?"

"Tonight solo, yes. Occasionally I recruit others."

"I don't suppose you carry an ID. Your driver's license. Or a credit card."

"Sorry." He pats nonexistent pants pockets. "Traveling without them tonight."

"How did I guess." After all, where precisely would he put them? With intriguing thoughts of where to conceal weapons against that well-honed body, I ask for clarification. "How'd you carry your little peashooter, there?" I incline my head toward his stapler-sized handgun lying on my floor.

His electric eyes twinkle with humor. "Easy to tuck it inside my suit. M5 is flexible, but doesn't stretch out like some anamids."

The guy can talk the lingo of high-tech protective gear. Call me very impressed—and a tad more afraid of him than I was before. But I hear a scrape and I look over to see Abe picking up the gun. I'm out of my chair. "No, Abe, give me that."

My hand is out, my heart in my throat. How's it going to look in the *Post* and *Express-News* tomorrow when they learn that my monkey shot me and himself with a bullet that can't be any bigger than a gumdrop?

My guest is right in front of me with his hand out to Abe. "Hey, there, my man, nice little toy, eh?" He puts his hand on Abe's. We're both bending down and I'm reaching around to comfort Abe.

"Please give me this, Abe." I'm pleading. "It's okay, buddy, honest. This might hurt you."

"Give it to me, Abe," says Jones. "I promise to give it back."

Is he bonkers? "Don't lie to him. He knows—"

Jones turns to me, his face as close to mine as kissing cousins can get, and he is telling me the truth.

I narrow my gaze at him. "How can that be?"

"Let me show you." He gets Abe to hand it over and then he cups my elbow so I can rise. When we're standing, he takes my hand, palm out, and slaps his toy gun into it. "Shoot me."

Oh, would I love to.

"Go ahead."

"You're nuts."

"Aim at me. Shoot me."

"I'm a sharpshooter," I warn him.

"I know. Do it."

I put my finger on the trigger—and pray whatever this gun does I don't die for it. I pull back and . . . the trigger pulls, an action occurs, but ladies and gentlemen, we have no bullets ejected from the chamber. "How can that be?"

"It's not your gun."

"No foolin'." Just for chuckles, I pull the trigger again. And . . . nothing is what I get. Except relief. And curiosity.

"Abe could not have fired it on himself, either." Jones takes his toy from my hand and performs a twist on the barrel that evidently locks it, because he then tucks it inside his M5 suit. "The gun fires only for me because the trigger is tripped only by my fingerprint."

And by the look on his face, he is not feeding me a line of bull. I stare at him.

He resumes his place on my sofa. "I am having one made just for you."

You have my fingerprint? "I need one?"

"Hopefully, you will never have to fire it. But, yes, you are in a bit of a pickle, and you just might need the services of a gun that you can shoot but no one else can."

Since I have already seen the value of such a piece demonstrated, I ask no more questions, but resume my own seat and say, "When might I receive this?"

"Tomorrow. I will deliver it. Personally."

"Great. Good. So. Then." I reach for my drink and take a swallow. "Your mission is to bring me toys, Santa?"

"Work with you to learn who killed Alistair."

"So that you can share this with an employer whom you don't even claim to know? Pardon me. I don't think so."

"Come on, now." He skewers me with skeptic's eyes. "You need help. Who've you got at the moment? Abe?"

I scowl at Jones. "Watch it. He's perceptive."

We both look at Abe, who is scowling at Jones.

"Okay." Jones crosses the other ankle over the other leg. "I'll prove my worth."

"You can try." Doesn't mean you will.

"Why did you ask for a meeting with Scott today? You needed intel about Alistair."

All of Washington probably knew by noon that Scott and I had had a tête-à-tête. "I don't have to go to Scott for that."

"Sure you do. You need info from anyone you can talk to. Senator Rawlings, Minority Leader Scott. Your own receptionist. There are a host of people you need to interview."

The lights come on and this time, they stay that way.

He rises from the sofa, giving us distance and me perspective. He is graceful as a dancer, and I get the full length of him. In the M5 spandex-type cat suit, he is an elegant animal. Not too tall, maybe five-eleven, not too broad, with arms made from years of hard lifting and thighs made from miles of tough marches, his bod matches his face. What little fat he's got on this frame is not showing, except in one place. His round, firm, and fully packed buns.

He closes the drapes across my French doors. Suddenly the room is cozy and, with him in it—electric eyes, tight buttocks, and bulging family jewels—it is suddenly like a furnace in here.

"Hungry?" He must detect my wayward mind because he asks this innocent as a kid at a Sunday social.

"Pardon me?"

"Looks like the lights are going to stay on, and so I say let's eat, while you tell me what you know. I know you made a big pot of marinara sauce the other day."

I go to stone. He was the one who'd been snooping in my shed and trash and read my journal? "You know about my marinara?"

"Yeah, you really are a good cook, ma'am. Your sauce could use more basil, though."

I push the hair from my eyes. "Gee, does this mean your real name is Julia Child?"

"Don't get smart, now," he chastises me with an East Coast nasal I want to say is Jersey or Philly. "I know you're confused, afraid, but you don't need to be. I'm cool." He strolls over to my silverware drawer, asks if he should set the table, and I'm thinking, what if he's really Mafia? How would they be interested in little ol' me?

"So, then, because you give me advice on my spaghetti sauce, I should trust you to take good care of me."

"That's about it, yeah."

His *yeah* is Baltimore, maybe? "Who made you qualified?"

"My mama."

"Excuse me?"

"I make some kick-ass bruschetta, too. Got any tomatoes and basil? I could make us a batch, and then if the electricity goes bust again, we've got game."

Someone I know talks like this, but who? "I don't recall you were invited to dinner."

"You should ask me, though."

"Cuz you're staying whether I ask or no."

"That's about right, yeah." *Yeah*, again. He's definitely from Baldamer. "We have info to share."

I'm fed up with this chitchat. "I am sharing nothing with you. I have no idea who the hell you are and I don't want you in my house. So now is the time for all good boys to leave." I stand up. Screw him.

I walk to my fridge, pull out my marinara, and plunk it on the stove. I open a cabinet and extract a plate.

"Guess I'm not included, huh?"

I grunt.

"All right. Here it is: You cannot do this on your own."

"That's why we have the police."

He snorts. "Right. And we both know how much you trust them to do a thorough job."

I feel a nasty revelation coming on.

From the corner of my eye, I see him, leaning against the

counter, arms folded. "Your daddy's disappearance never did get resolved. Is that because the sheriff had an eye for your mama and forgot to look at all the evidence in her closet—or could it be that you wonder if the DPS sent you their number one idiot to investigate his best friend's untimely departure?"

The Department of Public Safety sent us the Texas Ranger who was my father's buddy and who, as I remember, could not tie his shoelaces without assistance, let alone follow a trail to find my father.

How on god's green earth did this man know all this? I have never told anyone what I questioned about my daddy's walk into the sunset.

"You're quiet," Mr. Jones offers.

"You're pretty gutsy," I reply lamely.

"Right on, too, huh?"

I go to my pantry and pull out a package of capellini.

"Want me to tell you about your fears about Alistair's murder?"

"No. I want you to leave." I take my pot to the sink to fill it with water.

"You didn't touch him the morning you found him, but you did the night before."

I whirl. "How the hell do you know that?" How did he know *anything* about the crime scene and how I found the body? This was a murder investigation in one of the most secure areas of the whole wide U. S. of A., and the likelihood that Detective Brown was sharing facts with a break-and-enter kinda guy didn't wash with me.

His eyes drill holes into my brain. "Sources."

"That you are not going to share with me." My god, I was so frightened to say this to Brown, I couldn't wrap my lips around the words this morning. Did I actually leave some trace of me on Alistair when I touched his cheek and he kissed my hand?

"I doubt you'd believe me."

"Well, too bad, buster." I turn back to stirring my pot of marinara, scraping the bottom of the pot for some courage to face this bit of evidence that this man, of all people, knows. "Cuz unless you play nice and share, we're not playing at all."

He's not answering, and I am damned if I'll look around to see some kind of smirk on his face. At the age of forty-two, a woman with half a brain and all her hormones working can smell the testosterone burning in a man's brain.

I'm bending over to smell my sauce. And it does not need any more basil. I face him and note he was taking the virtual reality tour of my legs that most men do with a whole lot of pleasure. Except tonight my curves are covered in shapeless flamingo flannel. His eyes say, *Nice.* Mine say, *Fuggettaboutit.* "Fact is, Mr. Whereveryoucomefrom, you've worn out your welcome. Adios, buddy. You can leave the same way you came in."

"Tough cookie, aren't you?"

"You might say that." I turn on my water and my marinara. Wish I could put a fire under his ass, too. "I did not get here solely by flashing my tits."

"Your tits aren't your weapons of choice for politics. You use logic and one-liners. Better than sex in this day and age."

I glower at him. "Your stamp of approval does not thrill me."

He frowns and the eyes go hard as steel. "Suppose I told you that whole groups of people want to save your curvaceous ass."

"Sorry, pal, that is not late-breaking news."

Frustrated, I pick up the phone and there still is no dial tone. If this guy is leaving, it is not with the help of any 911 call from me. "Get out. I do not want you."

I sit down, tired and cranky. Abe, wary of our visitor, comes to sit by me.

"I had hoped we might be friends," he begins.

Me, I've got my hand up. "Wow. I must commend the Pentagon for teaching you how to be persistent to the point of obnoxious."

"You helped make it so."

Let us note that he has just admitted to having been in our

military. One point to the lady in pink. "Did I? Memo to me, read the fine print on all appropriations for secret operations."

"You're getting grumpy now. Doesn't become you."

"You're getting preachy and remaining vague. Neither buys you into my life."

He sighs. Shifts in his chair like he's staying awhile. "How's this, then? Today, Scott told you there were a cluster of women and men in Alistair's life that you had to investigate."

I can't help it, my mouth falls open. Shades of my discussion with Scott. I don't like the memory or the conclusion I come to. "How do you know this?"

"It's intel I received when I was briefed."

"By Scott?"

"In writing. My orders are always in writing."

"Orders?"

"Instructions."

"I need a specific name."

"And I don't have one. What I do have is the ability to investigate those facts you can't. And Alistair's sexual escapades fit that category. So you see, I am going to help you whether you want me or not."

"Don't want you and don't need you. Because just in case you have not followed this conversation closely, Mr. Jones, you have told me what I've done today. Which proves you are good at one thing." I fold my arms. "Collecting data."

He smiles, pleased as punch with himself.

"But it's data I already know. So unless and until you can come up with some fact I do not know, of what value, sir, are you to me?"

He looks contrite. As he should. But only for a second, and then he steps forward, undaunted once more. "Fair enough."

"Good. Now get the hell out of my house and for god's sakes, I hope you'll revive Detective Brown's men before you leave the premises. I would like some"—oh, boy, my favorite word here—"protection."

Ol' Jones pushes back a sleeve to reveal a band of fabric that must be a watch. His eyes flick up to mine. "They will resume full consciousness in twenty minutes five seconds."

"Super. You can wait outside for your coach, Cinderella."

He rises. "A few words of advice."

"Lock my doors?"

"Ha, ha. Go to the shooting range. You haven't been in months. Improve your marksmanship. Let up on the gin and tonics. Keep up the treadmill."

Get ready for trouble was the scary message here. "Do you also have advice on how I find time to do all that?"

"Yeah, go to bed earlier, get up earlier. You're not sleeping with anyone, so you'll get your beauty rest."

Fuming that this perfect stranger knows how I sleep at night, I make a mental note to check my lingerie drawer for signs of rummaging. "How often should I brush?"

"Twice a day." He grins, points to his teeth, and makes a circle with his thumb and forefinger.

"Take a hike."

He makes his way toward the French doors and, with hand on the doorknob, pauses. "I'll be back."

As Schwarzenegger, he just does not thrill me. "Toodles." I roll my fingers at him and Abe imitates me.

The doors click shut and the two of us watch him leap up our garden wall as if he had wings. "Wow, Abe. We got it wrong. The man's not a crab, he's a goddamn raptor."

six

$\mathcal{M}y$ first visit the next morning in my temporary digs is with a group of Girl Scouts from San Antonio, twenty-three strong, strapping girls who look like they need to go on a diet. Texas, big in so much else, is the third fattest state in the USA. No record I'm thrilled to point to. These poor things are going to have a hard time getting a job, let alone a man. So being a Girl Scout for them is probably a condition of eternal virginity.

We flow from that meeting right on into the next—and this one holds more joys and more terrors for me.

In Texas, we have an old saying that you gotta dance with the one who brung you. Bubba Gardener heads up the Southwest Texas Cattle Ranchers Association, a group of hard-riding, smooth-talking landowners who have escorted me to dance in Washington from Day One.

He comes to visit me once a year in D.C. A little jaunt, a deduction to take off the organization's tax forms, never hurt a man. He's sitting in a rickety chair Aaron commandeered for me, pawing the brim of his black gambler's Stetson. Bubba has a face brown as a nut and wrinkled as a prune, a body that's a long, stringy piece of rawhide in his starched jeans and shirt and hand-tooled leather jacket.

"Ya'll know how I love this town," he opens, poking his way through the preliminaries of our meeting, careful as a chicken with an egg cracked inside. We talk a spell about my support of the agriculture bill that will increase tax relief to landowners who raise animals. But sure as hell's hot, he has got to have Alistair's murder on his mind, too.

I sashay right past that, saving it for last or not-at-all. "Have you been over to Arlington yet?" I ask because he always visits his grandfather's and great-grandfather's graves on the hillside cemetery.

"No, ma'am, not yet. Tomorrow, I reckon, bright and early. Me and the missus'll go."

"Hopefully, the rain will stop so you can lay your wreaths." The sleet and snow of yesterday have now become an occasional rain to add to the mess.

"This here sprinklin'? Shoot, them's angels' tears. You been here too long, you know that?"

My ears perk. I try not to straighten my spine. But I am alert to his hint that my presence at home has been scarce of late. "True, I haven't been over to see y'all in a couple of months. But I'm slated again for the annual Barn Raising in Fort Davis in June."

"Good, cuz we miss you." He leans forward, confiding in me.

That translates into: *We have a need to talk turkey.* I'm smiling. "Okay. Why don't we plan a little private get-together with the board of directors while I'm there?"

"We'd like that." He sits back. "We'll lay in some tequila and limes."

Texas body shots, meant to straighten you up or lay you out flat for the mortician, put glue in my feet faster than I can blink. I've killed more plants than a twister at these watering events by surreptitiously pouring liquor in the flower pots. But I gaze wide-eyed at him like I'm eager. "I'll do my rundown of current bills." He nods. "And I'll have Esme come over from our Uvalde headquarters." Esme has been one of my two congressional office managers in West Texas since I first won office. Cheerleader material, everyone calls her.

A grin splits his lined face into old crepe. "Esme." He is nigh unto crooning. "We'd like that a whole lot."

Esme, my secret weapon in her five-county territory, is a real born-to-it champagne blonde with a figure shapelier than an hourglass, brains faster than a speeding bullet, and gumption bolder than a blind burglar. My Esme has the savvy to keep the men of my district salivating while she pours on enough revival talk to please a preacher's wife.

"I'll have her make reservations for me for the night at the Hotel Limpia and have them hold the back parlor for all of us to meet. How's that sound?"

"Fine, real fine. We have got to talk about your next election, you know."

Donations from this group have always been free-flowing. Their members would send out their families for me for door-to-door electioneering, not a small project when many folks owned ranches topping hundreds of acres. Even their kids would pass out leaflets and collect pennies from their classmates for me. If I don't keep them happy, I don't know where I'll find the votes to replace them.

"What's worrying you, Bubba?" Money? Taxes? Murder?

"Coyotes."

"What kind?"

"Them that's in sheeps' clothing." He leans toward me, his skinny face hard with intent. "We got tree-huggers movin' in to Uvalde at the old Leber ranch and another set of them Harry Krishna's putting up a mosque or whatever they call their churches outside Eagle Pass. I tell you, the Indians over in Eagle are even screaming about them takin' over and desecratin' their ancestors' graves."

"Bubba, I understand your concern. Tate Mullens and his foreman were in last week—you remember Tate, don't you?" Tate was once head of the oil drillers' lobby in Marfa and still called the shots, though his son was now head honcho.

Bubba is bobbing his head. "Sure. Who doesn't know ol' Tate?"

"Well, I have to tell you what I told them—the Hare Krishna sect that bought that land did so legally and paid for it in cash. The title search on the land showed no claims other than the Hawthornes' going back to 1910 or more. Same for the Evergreen Society buying up the Lebers' spread."

"Them Evergreen boys I s'pose we can live with. They got respect for water and such. But them bald-headed bell-ringers. Look like Tinkerbells on Halloween, I tell you, marching through the Mercantile, asking for seeds and nuts and dry bone powder. Hell, why not have a T-bone? Those boys are so thin, they could lay down under a clothesline and not get a sunburn."

We're both chuckling, but I'm winding down as I see Aaron heading toward me.

"Excuse me, ma'am. Mr. Gardener."

"It's all right, Aaron. What is it?" Unhappy at the interruption, I listen to him tell me I have an urgent phone call from Detective Brown.

"If I can call him back in a few minutes . . . ?"

"No, ma'am, I already asked that. Sorry." He shakes his head at me and Bubba.

I sigh. "Pardon me, Bubba, this will take just a minute." I hope. I motion at the phone to get Aaron to transfer the call here.

"If you want me to walk into the hall, I can give you some privacy," Bubba suggests.

"Stay where you are," I reassure him, hoping he takes back to his buddies the fact that I felt free to talk of the murder in front of him. The red light on the phone board lights up. "Hello, Detective. What can I do for you?"

"I need you to come take a look at something."

No hint what that might be. "I have appointments this morning until ten-thirty and then a special Friday session opens at eleven." I'm also doing lunch with an old friend at the same restaurant Alistair dined at the night he died, all in the interest of learning who he ate with—and if I can, maybe even a bit more than that.

"When can you come?" By the time I could get the car up out of the garage and drive from Southeast to Northeast, we could be talking twenty-five or thirty minutes, depending on traffic, the slush—and if any paparazzi are able to find and follow me. "I'll walk over later this afternoon. It'll be faster than me trying to drive. Plus, I hate the Taurus I'm renting." Why not dig him a bit for the inconvenience he's causing me?

"Sounds good," he says, and without even a thank-you, hangs up. The man needs to cultivate his manners.

"How's that goin'?" Bubba eyes the phone.

"Slowly."

"We're pulling for you, you know."

I mash my lips together. "Thanks."

"Bad luck, to have him killed here."

I hear where Bubba's going with this, fishing with such a long pole. "He was a skillful congressman and tried to be a good father."

"Good friend o' yours?"

"Not really. I worked with him. Worked well, usually. He was the party whip."

"I know. No man gets a leg up without an assist, but that means he's got a lot of enemies, as well. Any of them your enemies, too?"

"I've been thinking about that." Boy, have I.

"Making a list?"

"Checking it twice," I try to look nonchalant. I have so many lists—in the kitchen, in my briefcase, in the bath—I could paper a few rooms with them.

"Who's naughty on there?"

I shake my head. "Depends how you slice the word."

"Well, you know the drill, ma'am. First thing, you round up the mavericks."

Mavericks. Cattle who slip the confines of the fence and roam free. Yes, I understand that. For Alistair and me, that means two in particular who have always dealt with us as if we had no brains and less importance. George Freiburger, the congressman from Minneapolis, and Holly Ireland, a former congresswoman and now a lobbyist for a senior citizens group, stand high on my list and Alistair's, too. Both have been pressing for later retirement ages for Social Security so that the Baby Boomers could rest easy they'd get their just desserts.

"I have a few ideas who that might include. But there are others I need to look at." In my own delegation, Jimmy Jeff Holden, my buddy down the hall, and Alistair had been having a Mexican standoff on immigration regs. Jimmy Jeff wanted to free the reins, let anyone in for a period of two years. Alistair adamantly opposed his plan.

"You look real hard, cuz you got to cover your assets." He's looking congenial.

I'm feeling queasy. "I hear you, Bubba."

"I expect you can't talk too much about how he was when you found him."

I shake my head. This morning's *Post* had told once again what little detail Detective Brown was permitting of the tale— plus my formal statement of grief. Knowing Bubba, he'd read the paper cover to cover before walking over from his hotel. Demure, I try to be ladylike. "Terrible, to see a man like that. Not like going to a wake when the body is all dressed up and peaceful-looking."

"Death ain't pretty. Ever. Whether or not you killed the buzzard—ugh, sorry, didn't mean that he was one."

I try never to speak ill of the dead, the result of good manners Sadie taught me. "Bubba, I understand your point of view. Congressman Dunhill knew that he was not always the most popular man." As whip, his job was not to be popular but to garner votes in accordance with the party line.

"I realize you gotta work with folks like this. Yankees, I mean. But hell, ma'am, he wanted to raise our taxes. We already got too many weighing us down."

"And I am fighting to make sure we keep them low, Bubba."

"I know you are—and we 'preciate it, we do. But you got to understand that we are not grieving Dunhill is gone. It's folks like him in the party that hurt you and your chances, ma'am. I don't know whether to be tickled Dunhill's gone or scared out of my drawers that he went in your chair."

"Either way, you are telling me how you see it—and I am grateful for your honesty." He must have had conversations with a few of his buddies yesterday before he flew up here. If I knew who, I might discern who among them questioned if I killed Dunhill—and who was pleased I might have. "I have only the truth to serve me, Bubba, and truth is, I didn't hurt one hair on that man's head." Part of me thought, hell, why do I have to declare my innocence, but part asked, why not say it and just put it out there? Kind of like asking for someone's vote. As in, she who does not ask, does not get. That's me, obvious to a fault.

"You couldn't kill a flea, ma'am." Geez, he sounds like Jones. I frown, listening to him as he drones on about bein' a mite concerned about some of the younger ranchers who haven't had a chance to talk with me lately. "A couple of those boys need to see the whites of your eyes—and more often than the annual Barn Raisin'."

"Good advice." Reaching across the desk for my PDA, I tap the screen to life and wait till my calendar pops up. I'll combine this trip with the one home, making my mama happy as well. "What do you think of weekend after next?"

"The twenty-first?" The fact that he knew the date meant he'd walked in the door with this meeting as his goal.

"You'll call them together just for this?" I'll play up to him.

"For you, anytime."

"I'll fly into San Antonio Thursday night, go down and visit my mother for a day, then drive over to you all Saturday morning. I'll get Esme on my way and we'll see you about dinnertime."

"Sounds good to me. You think you'll be finished with this here murder by then?"

"I don't see why not." Watch the little lady lie through her teeth. "That's the responsibility of the police. I discovered the body, that's all." I'm skeptical about what I'm saying, but I'll be darned if I'll tell him that.

He rises, gives me a bone-crushing hug and a handshake, taps his hat on his head, and moseys out the door.

I'm watching him wave so-long to Aaron as he enters from the hall.

"How'd that go?" he asks.

I fold my hands in my lap. "Seems I have another skunk by the tail."

"And another one on the phone."

"Who now?"

"Your ex."

A big stinky skunk. "Great. Put him through."

"Jordan called that boy," Len says to me without so much as hello. I don't correct him.

"She has a right to, Len."

"Behind my back? No."

She does what she has to do, a real daughter of mine. "There is no harm done. In fact, a lot of good. Zack needs a friend."

"Listen, Carly. She's crying most of the time and wild, like I have never seen her, yelling at me about coming home to be with him."

"Len, I will not convince her otherwise." Get used to it.

"Carly!"

"Len, listen to me. You have nothing to lose on this. You're still talking with Mitsui about tilt-rotor helicopters, or whatever you're hyping these days—and she's left alone. Stop the talks and go around with her for a day or two. Give her the vacation you promised. Alistair's funeral won't be for a few days."

"Who told you?" His voice is petulant.

"The only specifics I know are from what I read in the *Post*." Chucklehead. "Alistair's sister is his only next of kin and she has not decided between a funeral or a memorial service. The police have not yet released the body. This means we're looking at a few more days before any kind of service occurs. If Jordan wants to come home before that, I have no rationale to stop her. Do you?"

That puts a burr in his britches. "To satisfy her, I booked reservations at a Buddhist temple in Nikko for the rites of spring. If she insists on coming home, we'll never get in again in this lifetime. Rooms are more than four hundred smackers a night!"

Ah, yes, our candidate for Father of the Year. Reservations and money are more important than the natural inclination of his daughter to stand by her best friend. "Len, if she wants to come and you don't put her on a plane, what will the four hundred be worth to you in your lonely old age?"

He goes quiet for a spell. "I'll have her call you tomorrow morning, tonight your time."

"You do that. I have got to go. 'Bye."

Listening to all this, Aaron's got a hangdog look to him. "What can I do to make any of this easier for you?"

I run a hand through my hair. "Get me a ticket to Tahiti?"

He shakes his head. "I felt like a failure getting squat from Alistair's chief of staff about dinner Monday night. But he was so damn tight lipped, a crowbar could not have opened him up."

"Detective Brown has probably been pounding him—and warned him, too, about talking to any of us. We'll see what I can learn when I go to lunch over at La Colline."

Aaron scowls. "Are you sure you don't want me to go with you?"

"No, thanks. I need the privacy."

"Oh?" Aaron usually knows when my shoes need polishing, including the intricacies of my schedule. I certainly am not going to tell him about the party's offer of protection—and last night's intruder—black M5, balaclava, hard buns, and all. But he knows I am longtime friends with my luncheon date, Dez Harlan, and so I tell him I'm meeting him. "Dez knew Alistair socially."

"Allll right. Sounds good to me." His eyes light up. "You walking over?"

"Yep. Keeps a girl in shape." I glance outside. The rain has stopped, at least. "I seem to be able to dodge raindrops as well as reporters by going out the front door instead of escaping from the garage in my car. That alone should put serenity flowing through my veins."

I grin at him, thinking, *Fat chance.*

I'm thinking about my luncheon date—and my less delightful one to follow with Detective Brown—as I walk onto the floor for a vote on the Medicaid bill that Alistair wanted me to support. The bill has grown to twice its size with amendments that are irrelevant and benefit providers' pockets, including drug companies. Against Alistair's direction of last week—and Monday night, too—I'm going to vote against this bill. Anything that denies Americans of their right to adequate health care has my no vote.

I'm looking for Jimmy Jeff, thinking I need to pay a visit to him and talk about illegal immigration and drug-gang wars flaring up on our Rio Grande border. Suddenly Mirinda Pace steps out into the aisle to talk to me. She's a party diehard on all recommended votes, and this one is no exception. She's been vocal about it, and like a lemming to the sea, she's gonna throw herself off the nearest political cliff to side with the party on this one. Her constituents think she's lovely to look at, delightful to hold, and a pleasure to listen to. I think she's a weak sister, shoring up her voting record and her spine, taking the easy way out so she doesn't have to think for herself. Amazing to me, the media love her. I could be catty and say it is mostly for her sultry good looks.

"Hi, Carly," she whispers, "I wanted to talk to you about this bill."

I smile and nod, not in the mood to be hustled. "I'm in a rush, Mirinda."

"I'm certain you are, what with the investigation and your temporary move over to Cannon."

For a woman who holds the party line as if she were Davy

Crockett bleeding all over the walls of the Alamo, she sure can sound like an idiot when she tries to garner your vote. My tolerance today for her lack of politesse is very thin. "Yes, and . . . ?"

"I really want you to reconsider this. We cannot afford going into debt any more than we are. This bill would save the government millions of dollars that we do not have and simply cannot afford. Won't you—"

"I'd rather cut money for research into extraterrestrial life or one of our spy missions, Mirinda. I told you this last week."

Her eyes go beady and mark me for death, for sure.

Okay, not a good move to anger Mirinda Pace. I have seen her temper flare before . . . and seen it fire up with Alistair last week when I walked into her office next door to mine and they were seething at each other about this same issue. Evidently, from her current support of this bill, Alistair won, didn't he? "Look, I am sorry, Mirinda, but I am preoccupied, as you might well imagine. And I am not sleeping well. I am going to vote against this bill, no matter the debt incurred. Maybe you and I can have a drink sometime soon and discuss what we can cooperate on. How's that?"

Her agreement is as thin as her lips. "Sure. Next week, maybe?"

After the funeral, I'm thinking.

"After the investigation is over," she prods with a smile that is fake as a three-dollar bill. "You'll hopefully have more time."

Ah-hunh. We have an old saying in Texas that goes, avoid doing business with folks who deal in fried lard. I roll my shoulders, cuz I've got that greasy feeling. "Pardon me," I tell her, and walk around her down the aisle toward my seat.

On purpose, I arrive half an hour early for my luncheon date. It's twelve-thirty and the crowd looks like the usual mix of well-heeled staffers, judicial types from the Supreme Court offices, plus a few business leaders and lobbyists. I recognize faces, but recall no names—and the opposite is true of the diners, clearly, from the way quite a few look up and stare at me as I chat with the maître d'.

"I am expecting a gentleman to join me, Renard."

His complexion is parchment. His body, very tall and fluid but so blasé he could be mistaken for Charles de Gaulle's twin. "Would you like to have a table now, madam, or will you wait?"

"I'll wait here a few minutes, thank you." What I want to do is talk a bit with this man who hardly ever leaves his post—and subsequently knows who dined with whom, when, and sometimes even why.

"Very well. Please, make yourself comfortable." He gestures to a few chairs out here expressly for this purpose.

"I'll stand, thank you."

Renard tends to the party behind me, and when he returns, we are alone near his podium.

I smile politely at him, look out the glass front, examine my boots, not wanting him to suspect I am here to pick his brain— or to fear he'll get in trouble with the police if he talks to me.

He comes over to me and puts the menu in my hands. "While you are waiting, you might like to review this."

I glance down and he is so right, I would. Atop the menu, he has given me a slip of paper. Folded once. I open it and read, "Table for 3. 7:15. reserv. Cong. Dnhll."

I clear my throat, all choked up that this gift has simply fallen into my lap. I gaze up at Renard, poised, Gallic in that beak-nosed disdain so indicative of his countrymen's attitude toward Americans. To what I owed this honor, I didn't know. I could not recall any kindness I had ever shown him. Except perhaps politeness. I lick my lips. "This is good to know. I cannot thank you enough."

Another group, rowdy for this early hour, enters the glass doors and he turns away to seat them quickly and sequester them.

I pocket his note.

When he returns, he tells me in a hushed tone, "Only two arrived that night."

I sidle closer. "Yes, that's what I understand."

The tension drains from his long face and he says, "A lady joined our friend at eight or so."

"I see." I move closer, eager now to know more before someone else enters and disrupts our solitude. "Did you perhaps know . . . ?"

"No. She was tall, brunette, with an elegant visage. They fought. She left in tears." Renard does a little frisson in revulsion while my first thought is, wow, this woman might be Krystal. My second thought is, gee, Alistair was fighting with a boatload of people lately.

Then I question myself. Who was Alistair to dine with, that he would invite me to join them as well? I stand there, clueless.

A foursome makes its way toward the front door, breaking up our tete a tete.

"I am grateful for your assistance with this, Renard," I say as I hand him back the menu.

"Anytime, madam. I am at your service." He gives me a nervous smile. "It seems your party is very late. Shall I seat you, do you think?"

"Yes, that would be a good idea."

He leads me into the dining room, where patrons now seem to be more interested in their food than me, thank goodness. Nonetheless, Renard seats me in the back in a corner where the height of the banquette seats obscure so much from so many. As he places a napkin in my lap, he offers me another tidbit. "This was the table for our friend's last dinner." He pauses to look into my eyes. "I did not overhear words, only loud voices."

"I see. Thank you, Renard." I smooth my napkin. "Could you have my waiter bring me a spring water while I wait?"

"Of course. With lime?"

"Yes, please. Oh, and Renard?"

"Yes, madam."

"My luncheon partner's name is Harlan. Desmond Harlan."

"Very well. I will bring him to you immediately when he arrives." He steps backward. "Enjoy your lunch."

I will. I think.

I am rummaging through my brain, madly searching for a way to interview Krystal for myself and see if she came to meet Alistair here Monday night. I'm coming up with a big zero when Dez Harlan leans over to peck me on the cheek.

"Hey, there. Long time no see, Carly." He slides into his chair opposite me, while the waiter gives him a menu and drapes his napkin for him. "I was delighted you called this morning. I've been concerned about you."

"Thanks, Dez. You and me both."

"You look wonderful. As ever."

"Ha! You are still a silver-tongued devil, kind sir." Dez, who graduated from high school with me, flies a desk over at the State Department. While his title is long and dignified, his job is to coordinate spooks across State, Defense, CIA, and NSA lines. Of course, the only way I know this is because his mama gives out the story back home. In this town, however, he is probably the only one who truly knows his job description. To top it off, he not only looks like an angel—blond, buff, and broad-shouldered—but he speaks like one. "That's why they keep you on over there in Foggy Bottom."

"Make no mistake"—he twinkles sea-blue eyes at me—"that's why they pay me the big bucks." At forty-two, Dez looks a decade younger.

"You obviously enjoy it. How is Anna?"

"Wife, great. Son, good, too. And Jordan?"

"Good."

The waiter arrives and we both wave him off for a few more minutes.

"Seriously," Dez asks, "how the heck are you dealing with this?"

"One more madcap item to add to my frenetic schedule, that's how. I feel like crap. Sleeping is a nonexistent activity. Len is being a royal pain about letting Jordan come home to console her friend who is Alistair's son—and I have got to fly home more often to keep the folks on the range happy. Other than that, I'm cool."

"Right. So how much do you want to talk about this? You are probably bound by police injunction not to."

"I am—but I can walk around it and get where I'm going." Getting info from Renard had not been difficult, so I was feeling lucky that I could strike oil again with Dez. The challenge was, what could I reasonably expect to learn from a man who was also bound to secrecy?

"Well, let me say I don't think you killed him."

"Let me say thank you."

"A lot of people know that, Carly."

"Join the chorus and sing it to the detective in charge, will you? Until they find the real dude, I am officially The One."

The waiter floats nearby and Dez nods, bringing him over to take our order.

Afterward, Dez moves his chair closer. "Alistair had problems."

Our eyes meet. I don't ask how he knows this, but I do share what I know. "Two kinds. Sexual and financial."

Dez nods gravely. "One connects to the other."

Oh, god. This just gets worse, everywhere I go, everyone I speak to. "How many suspect that?"

"Suspect? Quite a few. Know? I'd say three people. You, now, makes four, five is tops."

I bite my lower lip, thinking I'm one, Scott is two, probably Iverson is three, Dez is four. Who is number five? Careful about going where I may not be welcome, I test the waters of Dez's knowledge. "For these others, should I be looking in my own house?"

He levels those sea-blue eyes at me, aware of my double entendre. "All roads lead home."

I inhale and take a drink of spring water.

Dez draws patterns in the condensation on his glass with a finger. "Let me change the subject."

"Please." A diversion would be good until I can get up my gumption to head back where I should not go.

"Come to dinner tomorrow night. Anna is doing Chinese and it's been too long since you two had a good laugh."

Anna was one of my best friends in high school and we can still act like giggling girls when we get together. "I would love to. You won't mind having such a notorious woman at your dinner table?"

He grunts. "You need to come. For fun, for Anna, for the company."

"Who's my dinner partner?"

"Iverson."

"Interesting." I cannot help but smile. "Know him well, do you?"

"We play golf occasionally. Nice guy."

"Is that so."

"You are not convinced, eh?" Dez is amused by my reluctance.

"Maybe tomorrow night will turn the tide for me."

"Has he been in contact with you about Alistair?"

"I can't be sure. No one is being official, but someone or -ones have the idea that I need help, protection, or a bodyguard of some sort. Maybe those someones include Iverson, maybe Scott, maybe the Tooth Fairy—who knows?"

"Do you need one?" The blue eyes are warm but sharp as a razor's edge.

"Not certain on that point, either. What I do know is that I don't want to accept such services and then owe my soul to the company store."

"Sometimes we give a little to get a little. Aside from the payment schedule, I ask you again, do you need protection?"

I shift in my chair.

Our waiter appears with our salads, and Dez and I dig in as he departs.

"So, do you, Carly?"

"Yes." I'm thinking of who snooped in my house—and feeling vulnerable because Jordan will be home soon.

"Well, then, my advice is accept the things you cannot change."

"How do I know when I have what I need? I mean . . . do I just accept the present on my doorstep?"

"From what I hear, the present on your doorstep is courtesy of the Capitol Police."

I cannot tell if Dez is being coy—or truly does not know that I have some other entity assigned to my safety. I chew my salad a bit, swallow, then go for broke. "Do you hear of any other presents that appeared in my garden?"

"No." Dez examines my eyes for a long minute, evidently reading there the explanation he needs for my statement. Issue clarified, he decides to reach for more bread, frowning into his greens. "I could check, though."

"Do, please."

"You don't seem to be frightened by this appearance."

"Well, at first I was, yes. But there is something about him that says he is from The Farm . . . or Fort Bragg . . . or Langley."

Dez smiles in spite of himself. "To know one is to know them all."

"This one has a unique character to him."

"How so?"

"A jigger of James Bond with a chaser of Michael Corleone."

Dez gets a belly laugh out of that. "Well, think about this. Would you send a scruffy-looking guy to *your* front door? Correction, back door?"

"Surely not."

"No." Dez waves a fork. "I'd send someone with style and humor and—"

"Looks."

"Is that right?" He's amused.

I nod, unamused.

"You haven't looked at a man in more than five years. This one must be eye candy. Do me a favor, don't tell Anna. She'll be pea-green with envy."

Now I am chuckling. I can't tell Anna because she'll think I'm nutty. "You are dreaming, my boy. When Anna married you, she knew she would not have to look at another man for the next millennium."

"Come to dinner tomorrow night and let's see who can tell you more about your shadow, me or Iverson."

"I'll be there." Early.

Feeling slightly better about my future after lunch, I make my way toward the door and see three people I know well at scattered tables. Show is nigh unto everything in politics, so I rise to the occasion and exit like I'm doing the runway at a beauty queen pageant again, nodding and saying hello and good-bye, dripping good will and vague pleasantries all the way out to the sidewalk. I curse the slippery slush and go as fast as I can to get a burn, fire in my stomach that Dez has a point about my lingering disinterest in men.

I'm not interested in Jones. Okay, a little. More than that, I'm irritated. Frustrated that he might be a present from my party leaders. Amused that he is so very engaging—and all-fired attractive. A man you'd love to have hang around, but never want the neighbors to learn about. Or in my case, my daughter.

I'm walking briskly, thinking, and when I hit the Taft Carillon just as the bells are chiming the quarter hour, I realize I am walking west on the Mall instead of east toward police headquarters. I pause beneath the pristine limestone monument and gaze at the likeness of the once-powerful senator from Ohio. He had lost his bid for the presidential nomination against D-Day Invasion General Dwight Eisenhower. Shows you what a military man can do, on and off the battlefield, abroad and at home. Shows you what power anyone can wield when name recognition and circumstances are on their side. Ike had both. Robert Taft of Ohio had only good buddies and family tradition. What do I have?

Guts. Dedication. Legs. Tits.

My party hierarchy wants to use them, too. Hadn't Ike used his? Well, all right, not his tits, but his balls. Careful about who he showed 'em to, Ike had bided his time, surviving decades in dusty little western Army posts with no prospect of promotion or glory anywhere in sight. He'd been an organization man. A schmoozer. That's what won the day for him. From sticking in when times were lean in the Army of the thirties, to toughing out a choppy Channel crossing and Nazi bunkers on the shores of France, to defeating this man before me—Ike and I were alike. We stuck to our guns, our talents. We were well liked, easygoing, plodders, planners.

"Think he might have made a good President?"

I jump at the intrusion. But I recognize the Baltimore accent and I register the conversational attitude. "Do *you*?" I ask my intruder as I take a good hard look at him in the light of day. And, be still my heart, the man is a visual roll in the hay. Taller than me by only an inch or two, sculpted like a statue of David, with big hands. Well. We know the myth about a man with big hands, don't we, Carly girl?

"Ah-ah." He sidles up next to me, jamming one of those big hands into a chocolate leather jacket that enhances the gold in his complexion, and with the other pushing aviators up his nose to hide his electric eyes. "I asked you first."

"Taft would have been unique." I decide to parlay, learn more if I can about Mr. Jones here. "Not what any of his party would have wanted. Not what he would have predicted for himself, I am certain. He thought he was an isolationist. Thought he wanted nothing to do with overseas alliances. But he would have soon seen that he couldn't stay home alone."

"The Russians would have overrun Europe without NATO."

Ah, not just a pretty face, the man knows foreign policy history.

"He would have gone in and blasted the hell out of Castro,"

I add, "before he got a foothold in Cuba. Plus, he would never have allowed the Russian premier to come here and bang his shoe on the table at the UN."

"Sweet." Jones smiles up at Taft.

But I'm admiring the living man before me. My first thought is that his profile is sharp, and as I suspected last night, Mediterranean. Italian, I bet. With a bit of Mexican thrown in—and from what I remembered, but couldn't see behind the sunglasses now, double-lidded Hawaiian eyes. So, "sweet" was definitely a term I could use to describe the man himself.

"You think Taft was a man for our times, eh?" He draws me out of my examination of him.

"Hmm. In Texas, we would have called him a hold 'em and hit 'em kind of guy."

"Bringing justice to the world."

"Like you?"

"Like me." He gives me a smile that shows me big white teeth and huge compassion—and I find myself wishing I could see whatever complimentary emotion lies in those zinger eyes. Like he reads my mind, he slips his shades into his inside coat pocket. Oh, god. The eyes are jolts of fire and ice. Hard. Intense. "Did you figure out yet who cased your house day before yesterday?"

"Aside from you, you mean?"

"I was smoother than they were because you never knew I was there. I got inside just before you got home. Saw the way they botched the thing. Bad show. Amateurs."

"No, I haven't discovered who it was," I tell him, and want to kick myself for the instinctive response to trust him.

"Neither have I." He reaches inside his jacket for a cigarette, lights it with a flame so tall it could singe his long and much-too-thick eyelashes. Then he hands it to me. "Take it. You need it. Come on," he urges as my mouth drops open and I snap it shut. "You like a bit now and then. Yeah, I know that, too."

"Homework," I mutter, take it from him, and yet, glance around.

"No one's watching. I made sure."

"*You* told me to get fit."

"Yeah, well, tomorrow is another day. Here." He hands it over, butt first.

I'm inhaling, hating my vice, loving the rush.

"I've got other presents for you."

"Be still my heart." I take a drag and scan the lawn to see if anyone appears overly interested in us. The FBI has added cameras to the Mall, but they're not telling where and I wonder who's watching us, aside from J. Edgar from heaven. "What could you possibly—"

He draws his little toy gun from his pocket. "I promised you one. Made just for you."

I exhale through my nostrils. "Cute. Even if I wanted it"—*or do I?*—"I can't take it now. I've got an appointment with Detective Brown in a few minutes and then I'm going back to my office. I'll never get through the metal detectors with it."

"True. I'll leave it in your bedroom."

I choke on smoke. "Pardon me?"

"I won't break the lock."

"That is far from my objection."

He gazes off into the distance, then zeroes in on me. "Ma'am. Let's not stand on ceremony here. You know I can get in, did get in, without a trace."

"Yeah, right past my official guards."

"Down deep, you also have to know that I am not there to destroy anything . . . or to see what your panties look like. Although I gotta admit"—he scratches his cheek—"I like the emerald-green bikinis."

Enough! "I have a million things to do without smoking in the snow with a dude who likes my underwear."

"I come bearing more gifts," he says, soft and low so I stop fuming and consider his mouth.

"Like what?"

"Alistair's receptionist."

"What about her?"

"Krystal is a beauty, I'm told. Anyone who sees her remembers her."

My cigarette is burning low, and so am I, to know what he's learned. "Who specifically?"

"A Capitol policeman on motorcycle duty Monday night. He saw her walk over to La Colline about eight."

"Good for him. The maître d' just told me that, too." *Good grief, Carly, shut up. Why share your hard-earned info with this man?*

"But did he tell you that when she left—crying, I might add—she went to get her car, parked off Louisiana Avenue, and then she drove west on Independence?"

"No, the maître d' did not know anything about how she left the restaurant."

Jones grins.

I try to remain logical. "And did your policeman follow her?"

"Oh, yes, ma'am, he did."

Jones is going to draw this out, I see, so that his credibility is forever stamped in my brain. "And? What?"

"He followed her home and spent the night with her."

"He *what?*"

Jones revels in his triumph. "He dates her. They are an item. Have been for months. He claims he is going to marry her."

"Is that right."

"Gospel." He holds up one hand in pledge.

"And I should believe you because . . . ?"

"Check it out. You'll find it's sound intel."

Great. "In my copious free time."

"Right. Verify this, then you'll accept what I give you as god's truth and you are good to move on to intel only you can gather. Makes sense, no?"

"No. How do I know you are not hired to mislead me? Why should I consider that I am worthy of your interest? Aren't I rather small potatoes for a man of your training and experience?" Last night, after he departed, I figured his speed, his agility all pointed to a man who had been trained in Delta Force or the SEALS. Maybe something deeper, darker. All of which gave me the shivers then—and now.

"Someone likes your potatoes. Wants 'em saved."

"Groovy. Tell 'em thanks, but no thanks." I take another drag, ready to stomp out my cigarette and leave him in the snow.

"I hear your challenge. Yeah, if I were you, I'd be skeptical, too."

"I don't want to afford your protection. Saving my integrity is my most important job."

"Saving your hide is your first one."

"To be effective, you'd need my cooperation. One phone call and you are gone."

He smacks his lips. "But you need me. There are only so many bases you can cover to find out who eliminated Dunhill. Get used to it."

I take another drag, throw it down, and grind my heel on it. I turn east, the wind in my face, him at my heels, temptation to accept help from this stranger the stupidest idea this good gal ever had. "Go away. Tell your owners I said so."

"Aw shucks, ma'am. No need to get huffy."

I keep walking, pick up my speed.

"Besides," he says in that *who's your daddy* bass of his, "you can't reject me."

"Watch me."

The wind whips up and I clutch the neck of my coat closer. This guy needs to go away when he's told—and I suddenly see a way to rid myself of him. A D.C. police patrolman in his cruiser is camped on the corner and I sense my guard dog has spotted him, too. He doesn't want to attract any attention to himself, nor risk that he might appear to be stalking me.

But I contribute to the illusion and cast a fervid glance over my shoulder. As I swivel my head back, I glimpse the cop stiffening. I pick up my pace as the policeman steps out and slams his door.

"Good afternoon, ma'am." He looks me in the eye, one hand on his baton. Since 9/11, D.C. police are very aware that an ounce of prevention is worth a world of cure. And kidnapping someone who works in and around Capitol Hill could be a swell ploy to net a million bucks or cause a major panic.

"Good afternoon, Officer." I straighten my mouth with tension and cast my eyes to the side.

He saunters in my direction, slowing Jones down.

I hurry on. Knowing I am running later than expected, I call Aaron, but he's out, so I tell Rayanne to push my appointments back today—and add to my schedule in-office work tomorrow, plus dinner tomorrow night at the Harlans'.

Despite the trophies I gained at lunch and the knowledge from Jones, I enter the side door of the police station, pulse vibrating in anticipation of this next interview with Detective Brown.

So when we are into our conversation, I'm sitting in his bile-green chair, gazing at his bile-green walls, and thinking slimy thoughts to match, and he tells me that he has the results of the glass shards in my shoes, I try to be thrilled.

He plunks what looks like a petri dish from high school biology in front of me, but then rubs his face like he's considering what words to pick.

But when he says the fragments show a trace of red dye and he wants to know what lipstick I wear, I get angry. I grab my purse from the floor and empty it on his desk. Plink, plank, plunk, everything clangs out to the metal. "Lipstick, eh? One color only, lately. Peach M·A·C cosmetics. You can get a sample from any department store that sells the line. Here." I snatch up the two tubes of lip gloss and drop them in his hand. "Have a ball."

"You're not being friendly."

"Makes two of us, huh?"

He scowls. "We also have a partial fingerprint."

"I assume you have mine on file from the House, so let me know if you find points of similarity. You could, you know.

Assuming that the glass fragments are from my set of glasses in my office."

"Why wouldn't they be?"

I shrug. "I have no idea. You are the detective, you tell me. I am only saying that lots of glasses are alike. Especially cheap ones. Mine were cheap. And let's ask my chief AA where they came from." I note how he agrees with that, reluctantly so. "When can I get back in my office?" I am riled now.

"Next week."

"Specifically?"

"Can't say. I want to make certain the carpet has been totally processed."

"Me, too. How about my car?"

"Not finished with that yet. Maybe middle of next week."

"Where is the CSI team when you need them?" I grumble.

"We're not running an hour-long TV show here. We're eager to get this over with, too, ma'am. But I can only go as fast as technology allows."

So I ask one of the questions that has been churning up my stomach contents lately. "And the FBI isn't helping?"

"Because of the death of an elected federal official, we are consulting with the FBI."

I bet you are.

"But the chain-of-evidence rules demand that the organization that began the investigation continues it. Barring any undue change in the tenor of the case."

"Meaning what?"

"As long as we have cooperation from you, we will continue to process this like any other murder investigation."

Goody, goody for me. "And your team of guards, are they still in place?"

"Yes, ma'am. No more break-ins, right?"

His men never suspected they'd been violated. Jones was that good. Maybe I ought to keep him around just because no one else could match him. Or catch him.

I'm getting a headache from double-double-think. Worse, this whole process is so enervating that I feel like a rag doll. I struggle up from my chair. "Can I go now, Detective?"

"Yes, ma'am. Thank you."

"You are welcome, Detective." I can barely hear my own voice.

I must look washed out, because he offers, "Can I get you a cab?"

For the first time, I would rather ride than walk. "Thank you, yes, you can. I need to go back to Cannon—and do a bit of work." And thinking.

Who was Alistair drinking with in my office?

seven

It wasn't Krystal. Nope. She'd disappeared through Door Number One into the arms of her honey, a motorcycle policeman employed by the Capitol Police. That info valid only if I cared to put my trust in Jones—and supposedly in the Capitol policeman who gave him the story.

Oh, brother. I rub one temple, my headache growing thorns and horns.

Detective Brown steps out onto the street and raises his arm for the first taxi he sees. "Get some sleep. You look like you need it."

"Thanks, Doc. That little prescription is tough to take when everyone thinks you've killed your superior." A big yellow cab screeches to a halt, making me wince.

Brown opens the back door for me. "Maybe if you stop looking for clues, things will come to you that might be useful for the investigation."

I gaze at him like he has gone woo-woo. "Right. Thanks." I climb in, lean over, and tell the cabbie, "Cannon Building—" and before I can say please, we are off like a shot.

If I had a headache, now I've got whiplash. I squint at the dashboard at his license. Wherever he learned how to drive, it was in a town where yelling was the way to clear your competition from your path, and beating the steering wheel with your fists in artful ways substituted for conversation with your fellow passengers. We arrive, none too soon, and I leap out and pay him, thrilled to still be among the living.

I look at the front door, lick my lips. Where the hell was I in my deductions?

Women and men. Money and sex. Lipstick on my collar. Or my glass. Or maybe not my glass. But it must be, right? Only it could not be Krystal's lipstick. So whose?

I am about to walk into Cannon and come full stop. What time is it? I check my watch: 2:40.

If I have any luck today—and survival of my taxi ride tells me I have a guardian angel watching over me—I can catch Harry Woznowski before he goes home from his shift.

I turn toward Rayburn and in minutes, I enter the front door. Despite the fact that the lobby is flooded with traffic, everybody going through security, I spot Harry and wend my way over to him.

"Afternoon, ma'am." He touches his cap.

"Hello, Harry. How are you?" I let my eyes ask him how he has fared with the detective.

He raises his brows. "Good, ma'am, and you?" He reaches for my purse. "May I?"

You bet. "I wondered if . . . ah . . . you might have any thoughts on the logs for Monday evening."

He's going through my bag like he's panning for gold, so I figure he is honoring my line of questioning, if indeed he didn't expect it. "Yes, ma'am. A few." His eyes are circling the foyer. "You might want to visit with Jim—"

"Hello, Carly!" Holly Ireland steps into my line of vision. When she was a congresswoman, we never bonded. She being a pushy broad—and me not appreciating anything less than finesse. "How are you doing? You look tired."

No foolin'. "How are you, Holly?" *You look like a truck ran over you.* She'd always favored the no-makeup hippie momma look, long skirts, shapeless shirts, odd colors of prune and saffron. Today featured the hues of a pumpkin patch. She had kept her seat lo, those sixteen years, clearly, by her work, not by her fashionista tendencies.

"Wonderful. You know, after all this is over with for you, you and I need to do lunch. We haven't in a while and I want to discuss our thoughts on the new Medicaid bill."

Oh, joy to dine with Holly, who favors seeds and nuts and flowers in her salads, vegan that she is. But I need to hear her latest thoughts because she represents the largest lobby of senior citizens in the country and nearly half a million of them live in my district, so I nod and say, "Let's. Maybe in two weeks or so."

"Will the investigation be done by then?"

I shake my head. "No idea, but I certainly hope so. We all need resolution on this."

"You do, for sure." She puts her hand on my forearm and squeezes. One of those women who has a handshake that crushes your fingers, Holly makes me smile in pain. "I'll call Aaron and get on your calendar."

I'll tell him to make it breakfast, so that I can have her meet me at the HealthNut on Mass Avenue, where they serve every food pure as the driven snow, vegan or otherwise.

Harry and I watch her walk—well, waddle, really—out the doors.

I gaze into Harry's eyes and he rewards me with, "Quite a few were late Monday night. Jimmy Jeff. Pace. Ireland was here, too, to visit Sonderberg—and Scott."

Scott. He never so much as sneezed in my direction that he had been here late Monday night.

"And that's not all. There's—"

Harry's supervisor looms at the periphery of my vision, so I put my hand out for my bag. "Thank you, Harry." I raise my voice. "You gentlemen keep us safe and sound."

"Hello, ma'am." His supervisor tips his hat. "Everything okay here?"

"Absolutely," I tell him, sling my purse over my shoulder, and make a beeline for the stairs.

I climb them, realizing that my old pal Detective Brown has the log with the complete record of those who were still in the building between nine and ten Monday night. Me, I've got to work with what I've got. Jimmy Jeff, Mirinda Pace, and Holly Ireland. Pace wears lipstick and works next door. Holly Ireland hasn't seen a tube of lipstick in so long, she'd confuse it with a tampax. Sally Sonderberg from Minnesota has her office around the corner from mine—and she puts her lipstick on her pale and delicate face with a trowel. Do any of them wear M·A·C in peach tones? Darned if I can recall. Then there are Jimmy Jeff and Scott. Neither one wore lipstick, to my knowledge. But I need to ask Scott, Sally and Holly about their meeting late Monday, just for the record and my peace of mind.

I enter my office and about four of my staff look up at me in unison like they've seen a ghost. Aaron scurries over. "Hello, ma'am. Do you need something?"

"Yes, come with me."

I note with a *humpf* that the yellow tape of the police line is still strung across my door, and I make for Aaron's small office, which features four glass walls, though they are as soundproof as cardboard. I lower my voice. "I want you to go have another discussion with Dunhill's chief of staff. Coffee, lunch, whatever."

"Sure, boss, but I doubt he'll be able to talk with me. They are in a mess over there."

"I'm certain they are. Detective Brown and his merry band are going slowly—well, as fast as technology allows, they tell me. But I need to know more about Krystal Vaughn. Evidently, she—"

Aaron is shaking his head.

"What's the problem?"

"She quit."

"What? When?"

"This morning. Rayanne and she are good buddies and she

told me this morning that Krystal was going to quit today, no two-week grace period."

"Why?"

Aaron is now whispering but turns so that both our eyes track Rayanne through the glass partition.

I tell him, "Invite her in here."

Aaron takes a step and opens his door. "Rayanne, could you come inside and talk with us for a minute, please?"

Rayanne enters, kneading her hands and looking like I was going to chew her up for mincemeat. "Yes, ma'am, what can I do for you?"

Lots of things, because first of all, I'm examining her lips. "What color is your lipstick?"

She blinks. "Pardon me?"

I try to smile, but I don't feel really friendly at the moment, especially because her mouth is decorated in a gloss so similar to mine. "What color do you wear?"

She puts a hand to her lips. "I—I'm not sure. I mean, I'd have to check it. I have it with me, if you'd like to borrow it."

I try not to flinch. "Could you please get it and tell me?"

She thinks I am ready for the funny farm, but she zooms out and returns with a plastic tube that I know even before she holds it up for my perusal is a M·A·C product. What's more, it is a bright peach. Swell. She reads it to me and I close my eyes. The same color as I wear. Wonderful. "I bought it," she adds in apology, "because I saw your shade and loved it and thought, gosh, I need to have that."

Imitation is the sincerest form of flattery. I am so thrilled that it has happened to me. I wince at her. "Thank you, Rayanne. One more thing before you go. If you would, please tell me about your friendship with Congressman Dunhill's receptionist, Krystal Vaughn." So what if I am treading on police territory and asking someone to talk about facts in a murder investigation? What can they do? Accuse me of being aggressive and protecting myself? If I'm going to my own necktie party, I'd rather die knowing I at least tried to figure out who killed Alistair. Besides, Rayanne is my staff. Ultimately, she reports to me, then god, and only after that, Detective Brown.

Rayanne squirms, narrows her eyes, and furrows her brows. "Why?"

"Because I wonder what her relationship was with Congressman Dunhill. Do you know anything about that?"

"Yes," she says firmly, "I do. And I will tell you what I told the detective. Her relationship with her boss is so over with."

"What was the nature of that relationship, Rayanne?"

"They were . . . friendly. Very friendly. But that's done with. She told him so."

"When did she do that?"

Rayanne examines Aaron's features and then my own. "Monday night. She went over to talk with Alistair at La Colline. I mean Congressman Dunhill. She—she knew he was going there for dinner and she had to talk with him sort of privately. She told him she wanted to quit. She couldn't work for him anymore."

I purse my lips. "Do you know why?"

Rayanne crosses her arms. "Yes. Yes, I do. She . . ." She stares at me, like a prizefighter ready for the match. "She wants to change her life. Make a clean start. With a new man."

"Do you have any idea who this man is?"

"She loves him." She is justifying her friend's steps and not answering my question. "She deserves to have a decent life."

Right. Got that. But is he possibly the man that Jones says he is? "Who is he, Rayanne?"

"His name is Jimmy Marchetti."

More than I had hoped for—a name. "Have you met Mr. Marchetti?"

"Oh, yes, ma'am, I have." She is beaming at me. "He is such a nice guy."

"And what does Mr. Marchetti do to earn your approval as a nice guy, Rayanne?"

"He's kind and sweet. A real gentleman. Plus, he's . . ."

I wait.

"A cop."

My heart does the two-step around the floor. "For which force?"

"Capitol Police," she announces, and I'm thinking, bingo, so Brown must know this little fact, too. Rayanne's rushing on, "That's how she met him. He was on duty and one night her car stalled and he helped her by putting cable jumpers on and getting her home."

I go for a fact Jones fed me, testing his veracity—or Marchetti's. "So these two are going to get married, I guess?"

She nods. "Krystal is really excited."

"And what will she do for a reference for a new job now that she's quit without giving notice—and at such a time as this?" I pursue the subject to its ultimate conclusion.

"She doesn't care about a reference."

That stuns me—and I guess it shows, because Aaron puts a hand on his hip and asks her, "Doesn't she know that no one will hire her without a reference, once they learn she worked on the Hill?"

"She doesn't care, I'm telling you." Rayanne is adamant about this. "She is so done with this scene." She quiets down, now contrite. "I told you that, Aaron, this morning when you asked about her." She seems to be pleading with Aaron to confirm her honesty. And I wonder why she needs his stamp of approval.

I pinch the bridge of my nose, forehead tight with confusion and alarm at her tone of voice. So alarmed that I deduce that Krystal probably was indeed having an affair with Alistair, found true love with Mr. Marchetti, then wanted to live the clean life. If she hadn't gone home Monday night after talking with Alistair, it sounds like she might have had a good motive to stab him. Maybe even emasculate him. As it was, her boyfriend claimed she had gone home. So, now, did her best friend.

Unless both of them are lying to protect her. And unless the entry log shows she reentered the building, Krystal could not have killed Alistair. This means the odds were that Jones had delivered the honest goods to me.

I flick my eyes to Aaron, who says, "Thank you, Rayanne, you may go back to your desk now." She does. Then, to me, Aaron mutters, "She's scared."

She's not the only one.

And I have to return to work. Only my job is to learn who else had motive and opportunity to kill Alistair in such a hideous manner—and I have to find out on my own, don't I? Or else I have to be happy with the service a certain Mr. Jones can provide. And therefore, also happy with the remuneration due from me after his services are concluded.

"Mom!" Jordan has called the main line in my Rayburn office just as I'm headed for my tiny, solitary office over in Cannon.

"Yes, honey, what—?" The line crackles with static from Japan.

"I've been trying to get you. I just got a call from Zack and they're going to have his dad's funeral Tuesday." So Detective Brown had completed his work on the body—and he hadn't given me any hint. "I told Dad I wanna come home—and he said yes."

"Good. Put him on." What a relief, I don't have to fight this battle on top of conducting my own little murder investigation. I run a hand through my hair and reach for a pen.

After a bit of rustling, Len growls into the phone, "Hello, Carly. Well, I have decided to put Jordan on a Continental flight from Narita Airport tomorrow. It gets into BWI at seven-fifty your time Sunday night."

"I'll be there. Are you coming, too?"

"No. I have work to do here—and I can't afford the time to leave and then have to come back again. The airline assures me Jordan will be just fine. The flight stops in Houston, but she stays on the same plane. So no mix-ups are possible."

"Okay. Wonderful. What's the flight number?"

He tells me and I jot it down. "Len, thank you for this. I know Jordan appreciates this more than anything."

"Yeah, well, I'm not very pleased about it all, but there's nothing I can do except make her happy, right, princess?" Len sounds accepting and fatherly. I can picture him hugging our little girl and giving her the comfort she needs. I even hear her from afar chirping with excitement, "It'll be great. I get to travel alone like a real person."

Len says to both of us, "I wish I could fly back with her, but I need to have a few more meetings with Mitsui."

In consolation, I hasten to add, "I understand, Len, and I'm sure Jordan does, too."

"Yeah, well . . ."

"Don't fret, Len. I will be there at the gate to get her."

"Go ahead, Jordan," I hear him tell her. "Get ready for breakfast. I need to talk with your mother a minute."

"What's up?" I ask him, ready to lay odds we are about to discuss Alistair's funeral.

I'm right. He wants to know what I know about this, to which I tell him, "Nothing. It's news to me that the body has been released. You even know the funeral is to be Tuesday."

"And then they are taking him back to Montana for a private service. Don't they have a service for members of Congress in the Capitol?"

I cannot remember any deceased member of Congress lying in state in the Capitol. "Not sure, but I think all who lie in honor there must be approved by a joint resolution of House and Senate."

"Or maybe," Len ponders, "the powers that be decided the victim of an unresolved crime should not receive such a public honor."

"Could be."

"Look, Carly, I want you to promise me that you'll keep Jordan out of the press for this funeral."

Exasperated that he mentions what to me is a given, I roll my head back to stare at the ceiling. "I will do my best, Len."

"I've got a paper in front of me here with a photo of you walking up the steps of your house. Can't you get a restraining order on these reporters?"

"Not unless they step onto my property and cause a disturbance, Len, no, I can't." And part of me does not want to draw any attention to myself, other than what I've already garnered. "You have my word, I will do whatever I can to make sure Jordan is not harassed." I turn my face to the nearest wall in an attempt to keep my conversation private. My staff is wonderful, but only human—and human interest like children's privacy is really a very sacred subject with me. "She is not the public commodity, here, and I can hope for their good sense and decency."

"And when did that ever become a priority of the press?" Len offers with snide derision.

"One consolation will be that I will be with her—and they really want pictures of me, Len."

"I hope you're right, Carly, because Jordan is very upset over this murder and I don't want it made worse."

Like I can control the media. "Neither do I, Len. So rest assured, I'll do anything in my power to make it easier for her—and for Zack."

"One more thing." He lowers his voice and I can hardly hear him. "I think Alistair's sister is talking about moving Zack back to Arizona with her. Jordan's really broken up about it."

I can understand that. "He's her best friend, so I'm certain that would be a bummer."

"What's going on with the investigation?" Len switches horses too smoothly for me and I count my blessings once more that I had the intelligence to divorce him. Oily, my mama always called him.

Briefing him on the status quo, I decide to press him if I can on Krystal. "You know the woman you talked about the other day who knew him?"

"Hunh? Who knew who? Alistair?"

"Yes, and the other person whom he'd been good friends with?"

"Good friends. . . . Oh, you mean Krystal? Sure, what about her?"

"She quit today. No grace period. Don't you think that's odd?"

He gives a gruff laugh. "Not really. From what I heard, with what she was into, she better quit. Now that ol' Alistair's dead and gone—and someone offed him—she has to cover her pretty tail and get outta town."

What she was into, he said. What *was* that? "Could you explain this in more detail to me?"

"Ahh, well, not really, because I don't know that much."

"But you just said—"

He grunts. "Big Brother probably has this phone tapped, don't you think, Carly, girl?"

Indignant at the mere idea, I blurt, "They'd need a court order to do that."

"Carly," he scoffs, "sometimes you are so naïve."

Maybe so. But naïve people do best to stay on the right side of the law. And stay smart. So I say, "Yeah, but when you get home—"

"I know nothing, Carly."

You most certainly do, Leonard Underwood. And I need to learn it. To save my own hide—and our daughter's happiness.

We hang up, him nasty, and me fuming. What else was new? That was the way we ended our marriage. It was a relationship that had to die.

He had never thought of me as his equal, but as his *woman.* Living back in the last century, Len would always think of females as commodities, appendages. Men who did that had a patronizing attitude that glorified a girl for what she could do for them, not what she could do for herself.

Len's problem was that he had married me thinking I was his

arm candy, and learning I was my own tigress in charge of my own lair. He should have known that a woman who can stand for Congress serves as her own eye candy and runs her own lair. Anything less than that, her weakness is an invitation to the lions of the game.

And she can be eaten alive.

How many women here are like that?

Time I looked at a few, up close and personal. Especially the ones who had stayed late Monday night.

Sally Sonderberg has an accent almost as funny as mine. From upstate Minnesota, she sings her sentences like a Swedish yodeler. I bet if the two of us were ever on TV together, someone would whip out a guitar but never get to bar one for laughing.

"I'm glad you could see me, Sally. Especially on the spur of the moment." I've taken a seat opposite her in her inner office, the door to her legislative aides' offices left wide open—and by her hand.

"Happy to, Carly. There are so few of us that we have to stick together." She has settled into her chair, a swivel that she is using like a rocker.

"That was my thinking, too. I wonder if you could help me with something." *Not with the shade of your lipstick, clearly.* It is red. And as I look at her, pristine porcelain skin, baby-blue eyes, and platinum hair, I recall that I have always seen her in reds, never pinks or peaches.

"Anything at all."

I hesitate. Sally has a good reputation for someone so new. She's serving her second term, a Grace Kelly ice goddess who is the opposite of salsa-hot Mirinda Pace, and not a party hardliner, either. In fact, she tends toward being an independent, as only the woods of Minnesota and New England states tend to grow 'em.

She stops rocking. "What, Carly?"

I lick my lips because I am about to stretch the truth—and I hate that. "I recall seeing you still here working late Monday night."

"Yes, I was here." She gives me this with a stony face and tone.

"Did you know I was?"

"No. The police asked me that, too, but no, I had no idea who else was working late."

"Would you tell me please if there were others here in your office with you?"

Her spine straightens—and I fear she's gonna throw me out. "The police have cautioned us not to discuss the case with anyone."

I nod. "I understand. But I was hoping you might help me out and tell me more. I am in a bind and naturally, they are not telling me anything."

She gives me a consoling look. "None of my staff were here. I was alone."

"No one dropped in?" I press her, trying not to get angry at her prevarication. Harry had no reason to lie to me and tell me she had seen Scott and Ireland, if indeed she hadn't.

"I wish you would stop this." She's nigh unto pleading with me.

"Okay, okay." I put up a hand. "One more small thing. When you went home that night, you saw no one in the hall?"

"No. Nor on the elevator down, either."

I inhale, wishing she were more loose with her tongue. But I hesitate to badger her for fear she'll run to tell Brown—and I'll be charged with interfering in the investigation of a capital crime.

"What did you think of Alistair?" I'm wondering if he ever tried to put his hands up her skirt.

Her eyes go round while she hesitates a tad too long with a response. "Well, I thought he was extremely good at his job."

"Congressman or whip?"

She gives a wan smile and says, "Both."

"Why?"

"What?"

"Why do you think he was good at both? Did he persuade you to vote on some bill lately in a way you didn't really want to?"

Her features shatter. "Yes." She examines her wedding ring, fidgets with it, shakes her head a bit, then pushes back her chair and walks over to her door to close it. When she is back in her chair, she's clutching her armrests in what I would say is a death grip. "It happened over a month ago. The energy bill."

"Ah," I say, hoping for more, now that we have privacy.

"I . . ." She fades away, out of words, pondering again for overly long. "I had to give him that."

"Sometimes we do. You are still new at this and—"

"I was not happy about it. I'm still not. I am, in fact, very mad. More at myself than him or the system. Just, well, I never thought I would have to compromise so much, so often. It is maddening. Unnerving. I have to go home at night and write down what I gave away, so I can remember it all."

"I think I did a lot of that my first few years." I never wrote down what I gave away, because I never did budge on issues that were important to me. What I did write down were rules to live by—issues I would die for, programs I would fight for, battles I would never march off to.

"And so how do you deal with it now?" she asks, eager to find a solution to what is a gnawing frustration. She shows it, too. Her knuckles now are white. "I mean the good old boy network, the hours of work, the effect on your family?"

This woman has more troubles than a rancher with no cattle. I cross my legs, feigning nonchalance, afraid she is losing her cool. "These good ol' boys seem just like ones back home to me. Give 'em a portion of what they need and they're happy for a while. The hours of work, well, I stay healthy." Except for my love of gin—and an occasional cigarette. "I do tai chi and my tread-mill." Sally looks as piqued as if she counts sheep regularly. "And as for my family, I have one child who is a dream to take care of. But you have how many children?"

"Two. Ages five and six."

"They are very young still," I acknowledge.

"And my husband . . ." She slowly swivels to look out her window. "Oh god, Jerry hates it here." All I can recall is that her spouse is a lawyer. "He left his practice when I was elected. He was better off alone than with . . ."

I stare at her, not wishing to be forward and ask, letting her volunteer the name of her husband's employer.

She reels around to face me. "Reed, Green, and Barton."

Ah, yes. The Seventeenth Street law firm that is counsel to anyone with a name, an ego, and bucks big enough to hire them. "Perhaps he would feel better going into practice on his own here, too," I suggest.

She mashes her lips together. "Not possible. Takes money to do that. Buckets of it. We don't have it. In fact, when we moved here, we were so blown away by the cost of everything that we had to borrow from my father to help buy our house. The damn thing was built in 1923 and every time I sneeze, I think I'm going to blow it down." She laughs in spite of herself.

And I laugh with her. "Where is it?"

"Chevy Chase. Easy for both of us to get to work, but the housekeeper charges one arm, and the nanny, two legs."

We're both chuckling now. "I hear you."

"How have you been able to do this? I mean . . . if you don't mind my asking."

"I was lucky. My first husband left me a bundle as life insurance. I get child support from Jordan's father, my second husband. Plus, I invested a lot of the money I'd won as a barrel-racing queen and Miss Texas when I was a kid. The way the stock market grew in the nineties, I have a cushion if I ever need it, but my congressional salary suits me just fine."

She sighs. "Wish I could say the same."

"Sally, you have to pick what you want here. Choose what's right for your heart and your head and your pocketbook. Then you gotta stick to your guns."

"That's easier said than done. And there are too many extra ways to make money."

Yikes. "Most of them are not ways you want on your record," I advise her.

"You got that right." She fidgets with her rings again. I note how very large her hands are—and how she rubs them together almost . . . compulsively and she cocks her head to one side as she reveals, "I was here Monday night talking with Holly Ireland." Her statement comes to me, I see by the expression on her face, in gratitude for the girl-to-girl support. "She left about nine-thirty."

And was Scott here with you both? I want to ask, but can't because I am not supposed to know he was here, too. But it is too much to hope for that I might learn that easily.

She's giving me what she can. "I went home later, but I can't remember when. They must have it in the log."

Right. And only if I can corral Harry again unobtrusively can I learn what time that was—and how it relates to others. So I get up, offer up my heartfelt thanks and encouragement to meet her challenges, then head back to my office.

Working here, being elected to this august body, has brought Sally Sonderberg more pain than pleasure. If I knit her painful circumstances together, then by god, she had been here in the building, giving her opportunity—and she had a few resentments against Alistair, giving her motive. But were they sufficient for her to have killed him?

I halt in the middle of the hall, a hand covering my eyes, my fingers kneading my temples and the headache that seems as big as all outdoors. I inhale, look up, thankful no one has seen me, and continue back to my staff.

Working here, being elected to the House of Representatives, brought anyone a thousand challenges and a million pitfalls they never looked for, never expected came with the title and the staff and the power and what little glory or thanks they got for helping drive the largest democracy in the world.

Nice work. If you could get it.

In my case, great work. If I could keep it.

eight

"Peking Duck takes forever to prepare. Kind of like steering a bill through Congress, I'd say." I grin up at Anna Harlan, pausing in my chopping of ginger and scallions to watch her dunk one carcass in boiling liquid. She sets it down, then throws heavy twine over her pan rack to hang up the duck by its legs. "You look like you're preparing a noose."

"For hanging a duck—a dead one of any kind—let us recognize that patience"—she smiles widely with her Julia Roberts mouth—"is the main ingredient."

I raise the knife I had been using to chop the vegetables for her broth. "You want me to cut any more scallions?"

"Not right now."

I reach for my glass of Coke. Not ready yet to discuss Alistair and the way he died, I say, "Tell me the principle of what you're doing here."

"You have to submerge the duck a few times to ensure that the liquid sears him inside and out. Then you have to hang him, preferably ventilated so that the air circulates well around it and dries his skin. Meanwhile, the fat is dripping from the cavity and the skin is separating from the flesh. This means that when it cooks, the skin crisps and browns while the fat renders nicely from the bird."

I am bemused. "Sounds like the opposite of politics, where

rendering the fat from a bird hardly ever is part of the process."

Anna chuckles. "No one yells fowl"—she lowers the carcass again, well into our metaphor—"unless they have a bigger pet project for the taxpayers' money."

"And the only hot oven it gets into," I lament, "is in committee, where the poor thing is sliced and diced so that later it can be larded up with fat."

"Speaking of hot ovens"—she zeroes in on my eyes—"tell me what's going on with you and this investigation."

Grateful that she hasn't used the *M*-word, I give her the rundown, minus any names of suspects, to protect the innocent.

"And you have no idea who might have done this to Alistair?"

"A few. But you know how flimsy any conjecture might be." I recall what Dez told me at lunch the other day, confirming what Scott had said about Alistair having financial and zipper problems. Sounded almost like Sally Sonderberg, but in different ways. And I wonder if I dare ask Dez to tell me more about a subject that might just be classified info, courtesy of some spook organization in town.

"Yeah," Anna affirms, "you never know who is telling half a story or a total myth."

And she ought to know, married to a guy who learns and churns myths with reality on a daily basis. I try to look nonchalant. "In this town, we are so used to being politic, it is bred out of us to be blunt about anything, including where we get our dry cleaning done."

She grimaces. "Tell me about it." She's working on suspending the second duck from her makeshift lasso, concentrating on looping the string around the ankles sufficiently to get it to hold. "Living in a glass house grates on the nerves. God knows I've been there, done that, when we were in Hanoi. I worried more about the effects on Charlie." Charlie was Anna's and Dez's only child, now eight. "But I worried for nothing. He talks about it all the time, memories of the embassy, and especially the fireworks during Tet. Children accept more of what they see, largely because they have little to use as the norm." She slides her gaze to mine. "How do you think Jordan will take the media glare?"

"Well. She rolls with the punches of her mother's odd life." I don't want to get into the details of the controversy between Len and me over this. Here with the Harlans to have a good time for a few hours, I want to keep as many negative subjects at bay as possible. I sip my Coke. "I hope Jordan will bear with the inconvenience. I'll do my best to shield her, but she and Alistair's son are the best of friends. I know she'll want to see him, visit him." I envision what the press will make of that—and pray they will respect two children's affections for each other. "I'll try to emphasize to her that it is only for a few days until they figure out what really happened there."

"When does she come home?"

"Tomorrow."

"Good." She smiles. "The press will notice that." She looks at the huge pile of scallions I've been chopping. "Scrape those into this dish, will you?"

"Right." I do as I'm told, then pick up all the utensils on the counter and walk to the sink to plop them in the water. "How could they not notice she's home?"

"How many reporters are there?"

I'm washing the cutting board and knives. Ugly things, knives. "A lot but fewer today than yesterday. Mickey Gonzales is there, though, night and day."

"The reporter from the *Express-News*?"

"My pal," I add with sarcasm.

"What do you call him? Your python?"

I get a good laugh on that one. "Hey, that would do, too! But, no, I call him my scorpion. Sweetest of guys."

"Well, as long as he and the rest of them remain respectful and don't knock on your door or get weird."

"Does following me in my lovely rental car go into the category of weird?"

Anna shudders theatrically. "Tell me they didn't track you here."

"I didn't see anyone," I tell her, and that is the truth. Even the one man I expected to see hadn't followed me to the Virginia countryside this afternoon. "But they're resourceful and I wouldn't put it past them to find me." She's cringing, so I suggest on a smile, "We could walk outside the gates and check it out."

"No," she says emphatically. "Anybody who'd do that deserves to be reamed—and by a man."

"Why, my sweet lady, have you become a chauvinist?"

"You bet. Years of living in two communist countries make me appreciate the power of a big strong male. The bigger, the better. I'll have Dez go check outside and shoo any of them off when he finishes getting Charlie and his friend set up with video games."

"Yeah, well, I didn't see anyone," and part of me wonders if Jones's employer paid only for a few days' protection. The idea of being dropped fills me with glee and anxiety. Damn, I hate to be conflicted about anything, and here I am, asking myself, do I want a bodyguard—or not? I'm washing the knives and wondering when was the last time I was ambivalent about a man's attention. Darn, must be years and years. I snap out of my reverie and say, "But hey, it's the weekend. Maybe they're taking turns on duty to get some rest. I wish to god they'd just get a new congresswoman to hound."

"You're not getting morose about Alistair's death, are you?" Anna asks, an edge in her voice because she remembers how grief-stricken I was when my daddy went missing when I was sixteen.

"No, course not," I reply quickly, but just as fast concede, "Maybe." I try to chase my memories of my father by concentrating on washing a knife. But I wind up speculating how much strength it takes to plunge one into a man' chest—and how much anger it takes to sever his penis from his body. A lot, I bet.

And suddenly I'm recalling how big Sally Sonderberg's hands are, and how she was in the building late and how she and her husband are having marital problems. And career problems. And money problems. And she was having problems with Alistair. But Detective Brown had never mentioned her name. Not to me. Not that he should.

"Earth to Carly," Anna insists.

"What? What, I'm sorry. Daydreaming here. What did you ask me?"

"What indication do you get that the police have suspects?"

I purse my lips, considering that she is one of my oldest friends and she has not said *other* suspects. I take a big breath, satisfied for such support from my truly diplomatic friends. "None. The detective on the case is very closemouthed. But I think that is par for the course." I remember our county sheriff and the Texas Ranger who investigated my father's disappearance were never overly communicative. At least, not with my mother and brother and me.

I put the knives in the drainboard, glad to get them out of my reach, if not my thoughts. But I'm still staring at them, rubbing my hands down my apron, when Anna thrusts a towel in front of me.

"Carly," she whispers. "It's okay. Wipe your hands on this."

I do and sit at the kitchen counter. "Anything else I can do to—"

"No," she cuts me off. "Just sit down there and drink your Coke." And I do for a few minutes while she works on in silence.

"Ahh, sorry, girls." Dez sails in to the kitchen from the upstairs. "Getting the boys settled in for the evening takes a bit more time than I envisioned."

Anna grins at me. "Consecutive translation: Dez likes to play video games."

"They're educational!" he affirms, and she rolls her eyes at him. "America's Army. Charlie loves 'em and I am just along for the ride."

I raise my glass to toast him. "I'd say you are using up all that testosterone you don't get to use at work!" He and I sparred often about what State would and could not do to rectify crisis situations.

"Ha, ha! I'll let one go by me." He rubs his hands together—and peers at our glasses. "All right. So, what are we drinking? Holy cow. Coke and water? Damn, are you both not feeling well?"

"Hey," Anna retorts, "we're playing Emeril here. Sweating over a hot stove and a chopping block."

"Calls for a good white wine, if you ask me." He wiggles his brows. "What do we have for nibbles to go with that?" He pulls open the refrigerator door and sticks his head in. "Gorgonzola? Salami?" He pulls out a wedge of blue-veined cheese, a giant deli wrapper—and a wine bottle.

"Dez!" his wife objects. "We're having Chinese!"

"Not for openers, we're not. We've got—what?" He glances at the clock. "Two hours before the others get here, and I am not waiting to have a drink till then. Nor will I drink without something in my stomach. What'll it be, Carly? Another Coke or my superb Prosecco?"

"Your superb Prosecco. With lots of cheese to soak it up, please."

"That's a girl. Anna?"

"Sure." She's laughing.

We're eating and chatting and doing a thorough job on the bubbly stuff when I notice Dez blink at Anna with wide eyes. It's a momentary flick, undetectable if I hadn't been aware of them at just that instant. Smooth as glass, Anna excuses herself to go check on Charlie and his friend, then change her clothes before the guests arrive.

I croon, "Ahh, alone at last."

"Not too subtle, huh?"

I close one eye to stare at him. "For a man of your profession, sir, you and your wife must develop a more covert high sign."

"Tomorrow's task."

"Tonight's"—I grin—"is to tell me what you have learned about my bodyguard."

He savors his wine a moment before launching in. "We know of sixteen companies here in town who do the kind of work you are talking about. Thirteen of them are new since 9/11. Three of them are as old as the Cold War and very well known. Two have gone worldwide in the past decade, and done very well. They are legendary for taking high-profile subjects and offering protection or investigation. Both charge enormous fees, but clients gladly pay because they have never lost a case."

"Lost a case?" I ask for clarification, a huge lump of trepidation in my throat.

"A client."

"That's what I thought you meant." I swallow hard. "And what about the third firm?"

"Well, the third is intriguing. More Prosecco?" He reaches to fill my glass. "Word is that they are as renowned, as successful, maybe more so. Their intelligence is consistently without peer in manpower and technology. And the shroud of secrecy under which they operate is thicker than the others."

"How can they be so hush-hush and still get clients?"

"Few of these companies ever advertise," Dez points out. "This one relies solely on word of mouth."

"So I imagine they have a lot of friends." My statement is really a question.

Dez mashes his lips together. "On both sides of the law."

We're both staring at each other, our glasses going in slow motion to our mouths. I'm thinking, *You know this because you've dealt with these guys.*

Dez is saying, "No one will give me any indication that that's true."

"But you bring them up because—why?"

"They have a reputation for hiring the best and not always revealing who the client is, if—as in your case—the need to know might impede the project."

I gulp down a piece of cheese. "So, let me get this straight. In this third security company, it is possible to have someone come in—"

"Or call."

"On a secure line, I bet."

"What else?" Dez shrugs.

"Then they plunk down a chunk of change—"

"Maybe six or seven figures," he elaborates, cool as the Foggy Bottom cucumber he is.

Hold on, I wanna shout, *you are not blowin' smoke here.* "Okay, and for this tidy sum, they order up a bodyguard or—"

"Or a private detective."

"Or both," I add.

"Could happen to be combined in one neat package." He's nodding.

"And maybe the client injects into the contract a clause that says no one has to know who's paying the retainer." I utter these words, feeling about half as smart as a wooden Indian, playing cloak and dagger in my feeble mind.

"Which could be the case here."

"Terrific." Confirmed once again: To the lady on the kitchen barstool, the prize. One bodyguard. Origin unknown. Cost to the lady, to be determined. "I have got to get rid of him."

"Maybe. Maybe not."

I glare at Dez. "If this company is so shady, if the client is so anonymous, if the retainer is so large, and the payback so . . . so . . . undefined"—I'm waving a hand like a crazy lady—"if this ever gets to Mickey Gonzalez of the *Express-News*—or any of my opponents in South Texas—my ass is grass, Dez."

He licks his lips, tilts his head, and contemplates his glass for far too long.

"What?" I pressure him. "Talk to me here."

Dez gazes into my eyes with a sadness that shocks me—and makes me very afraid of what he's about to say. "If someone hired a guard for you from VentureX, there was a good reason.

A need. Face it. You are still the only suspect they have so far in this murder—and yet you did not kill Alistair."

I close my eyes. Fighting back terror at being tried and convicted for something I did not do, I bite my lower lip. "I believe in justice. In technology. In facts. I. Did. Not. Kill. Him."

"And if that detective really thought he had an airtight case, he would have had you arrested before now. But let's be real here, Carly. The longer he goes without any other solution, the more he will look at you. Sad to say, but plenty of folks have been sent up the river for crimes they did not commit. Circumstances played against them."

"All right, I hear you."

"With the kind of money this man's being paid, he is yours. Whether you like it or not. You have no choice."

I frown. Jones's words of yesterday. Suddenly I am not happy with Dez. With what he has told me about where Jones might have come from. A company as real as a mirage. With a name and owners I probably can't trace. With the potential to make my reputation disappear, if anyone ever found out about this tidy arrangement. I sag in my chair.

"Excuse me, Dez." I'm weary from fighting all the forces I cannot seem to change. Sliding off my stool, I stick my thumb in the direction of the spare bedroom where my dinner clothes hang. "I'm going to change."

I'm halfway down the hall when he calls to me and I turn to look at him. "Don't search too hard for his origins, either, Carly."

I wait, feeling the chill of a warning coming down on me.

"It's not healthy to look too hard into these companies."

"Thanks for the advice, Dez. But I'm going to live my life doing what I can to keep my integrity." Or die trying.

Dinner does nothing to get me out of my funk, either. The duck is crisp, the fried rice fragrant, the stir-fried veggies crunchy. But my taste buds are deader than a fly in molasses. Oh, I'm polite, hey, even funny. But sitting next to Tommy Iverson, chatting about the weather and the Orioles, I feel like I'm the bird that's been plucked and cooked. With eight people at the table, how can I ask him if he hired a bodyguard for me out of national party funds?

"What do you think, Carly?"

Dez stares at me.

"Sorry, I was appreciating the wine too much. Ask me again."

"Don't you think it's time you went on a junket to Beijing? You've been talking about the rising commerce going through your district."

I nod. "True. I've been thinking about that for a couple of years. I want to go, but it is tough to fit it in my schedule. Careful about the school year and Jordan, you know, I want to be fair to my constituents, too."

"I didn't know you were interested in going," Iverson says.

"Sure I am. I've got containers coming through my district by train through Del Rio from the Mexican coast at a rate of thirty-three percent growth per year. I worry about possible imports of weapons of mass destruction inside those containers."

Tommy Iverson sits back in his chair and scratches his gray beard. "I understand that China's biggest imports in those containers are not the nickel-and-dime stuff going to the big retailers, but the illegal drugs and herbs coming through those ports of entry."

Anna looks at her husband. "No, I thought the Chinese outlawed all that and put more officers on their customs inspections."

"Bah!" Dez shakes his head. "Old-fashioned squeeze, just like they used to have in the old treaty ports through the cohongs, still operates. This time, it's back with a communist vengeance."

Another guest, one of Dez's co-workers at State, leans forward. "Now they have a new import. Pills. Banned by our FDA as lethal. Pearls of Love."

Glenna Iverson, Tommy's lovely wife with coal-black hair and eyes, hoots, "Is that the stuff that they talked about on *60 Minutes* a few weeks ago?"

"Yes, indeedy," Dez confirms.

Tommy Iverson snorts. "Makes you horny as a triple-X porn star in a gang bang."

"Wow," I say with innocence. "I wouldn't have any concept what that is."

Iverson lowers his bushy brows at me and feigns severity. "Nor should you. You are a virginal congresswoman from a god-fearing district."

"That is so right," I acknowledge. "We Texas women know nothing about sex at all."

Anna harrumphs. "Our mamas told us to tie a ribbon around our legs until we got a ring around our fingers."

Iverson chuckles. "Don't get near any of these, then. I understand one engorges the labia like that!" He snaps his fingers. "Makes you hop on anything from gearshifts to pogo sticks to get off. Works within fifteen minutes. But afterward is bad. Heart palpitations. High blood pressure. Wears off in spurts of craziness and horned toad activity to give you the worst hangover of your life."

In total shock for his bluntness, the rest of us sit there dumb as stones for a long minute.

Intrepid, I walk into the void. "Well, count me out. I wouldn't know what to do with one man, let alone gearshifts and pogos. Plus, who has the time?"

Iverson, unaware or just into his topic like a pig in mud, marches right on. "Like Ecstasy, I hear this stuff spaces you out so badly, you won't worry about time."

His wife, whose eyes bugged out during his monologue, clears her throat and glares at him. "Or place, evidently."

"Oh." He surveys the dinner table, silent as it is. "Sorry."

The conversation devolves into the stuff of too much wine and not enough substance. Dessert done, without the courtesy of chatting in the living room for a decent interval after dining, Glenna announces she's bushed.

I'd been so keen on talking with Iverson to bring up the issue of Jones and VentureX or one of its clones that I had been certain the moment would arrive when I could get him into a corner to broach the subject. But no. The entire evening is now a wash. We're leaving. Getting our coats. My overnight case. Making our ways to our cars on the circular drive.

So I sidle up to Iverson and lower my voice. "I need to talk to you for a minute, Tommy."

"Sure, what's on your mind? Go ahead, Glenna, get in. I'll only be a minute." He faces me.

I inhale. "Your present," I begin. "The bodyguard. I'm grateful, but—"

He zeroes in on me with the intensity known to kill at ten paces. "What the hell are you talking about? I have not sent you any bodyguard."

I stare at him, looking for truth, not finding anything but a stone wall. "Lou told me, Tommy, the other day—"

"*What* did she tell you?" he demands, angry now.

Exasperated with having to repeat this stuff all the time, I throw diplomacy over my shoulder. "Lou called me the other day and told me she had been talking with you."

"True."

To hell with cooing in his ear, I put a hand on my hip. "Did you or did you not tell her you would send me some help?"

"I did say that and I considered it. Verbal. Image and damage control. Press release strategies."

"That's all?"

He looks around the driveway, and I'm guessing, by the expression on his face, he doesn't find any answers there that thrill him. "Carly. I have not sent you any man. Honestly. What I did do was discuss the possibility of different scenarios. One was to hire you a bodyguard. But as far as it got was discussion. You know what Scott told you about us supporting you, our faith in you that you did not hurt Alistair."

"That's it?"

He's digging his car keys from his pocket, avoiding my gaze. "Yes."

"Why?" *I need to hear your reasoning. And I need to see your eyes when you tell me.* I step closer to him, invading his space.

And I win when he gives me a glare. "I didn't think you needed more than that."

The more he talks, the more I know. So I keep working it.

"I'm hoping that's a compliment."

"A vote of confidence," he corrects me, plastering a pained smile on his face and softening his tone. "Why not ask him who sent him?"

"Oh, believe me, I have. Repeatedly."

"And what did he say?"

"That is what he will not reveal." Will not. Cannot. Does not know. Pick one. Hey, pick all.

Tommy hitches a corner of his mouth up and it makes his goatee look lopsided. He's thinking and buying time to see if I cool my jets.

I try for the softer approach, called Carly as Girl in Trouble. From the old school of gentlemanly behavior, Tommy has been known to crumble to female vulnerabilities. I run a hand through my hair, frustrated femme fatale version. "This whole thing is making me crazy, Tommy. The murder. Finding Alistair like that. The police and the media, then this guy."

"I can see how it all would, Carly. Just sit tight and let the investigation proceed. As for this bodyguard, who knows where he comes from? Call the police, hear me? Don't let him in your house."

"A little late for that," I bite back, the damsel in distress now gone, gone, gone. "He's been in my house."

Tommy fixes me with a vacant look that does not make me confident of his outrage at this invasion of my abode—and

I decide to test his veracity. Mix up the facts. Rattle his cage and see if he bites. "And my shed."

"Your shed?" He is honestly shocked.

I can't figure out if he's innocent or guilty. Ever valiant, I test again, just for insurance, you know. "Yes, my garden shed, and my trash, and my daily journal."

"Bad joss." He is commiserating so blithely he sounds like he's consoling me for having lost the two-dollar lottery instead of a breaking-and-entering.

I blow a gust of air out of my mouth. "Right." *Thanks for nothing.*

"You've got a real problem, there." He sounds like sweet reliable Mister Rogers now. "Call the police. Get him carted away."

Ah. If he were that clumsy to be caught. Alas, Jones has not a clumsy bone in his beautiful bod. "Check. Thanks, Tommy."

"Do that—and call me to let me know he's gone." He moves toward his car. "Look, I hate to run, but when Glenna declares the night is over, then I need to get home."

Though the Sir Galahad in him has emerged, I can't care. "One more question."

He raises a finger to his wife. "Just a minute, Glenna. Sure. What?"

"In your opinion, who would have the resources and reason to protect me?"

He winces. "Your mother?"

My mother. Never thought of her. "Not probable."

"Why's that?"

"She thinks I can take care of myself." I cross my arms and tilt my head in innocence.

"Oh?" He chuckles. "Can't say that I've ever thought that!"

What did he know? Tommy had met Sadie all of twice. "I shoot better than she can. Always could. Anything from near or far, I'm a bull's-eye."

"I see. I won't get in your gun sights, then." He's chortling— but it's forced cuz he knows I'm not real happy with him.

I mutter, "Good thinking." But I have another point I need to cover. "Do you think Scott would hire someone for me?"

"Without telling *me,* you mean? No. He wouldn't dare. Plus, he can't tap money to do that kind of thing. Only I have funds sufficient for that kind of hire. If I could find the right fund to tap." He ends this trip to nowhere with a sardonic smile that shows his diabolic logic.

What a *cover your ass* statement that was! But who am I to disagree, since I have no proof, and never would have the means to find any, that such hidden funds exist for heads of political parties. "Oh, sure," I say for the record. "That was my thought, too." I nibble on my lips and gaze at the starless sky. "Anyone else you'd list who might do this?"

"Lou? She likes you, thinks you can go far."

Very true. "But where would she get money in the six or seven figures?"

"She's well set but not flush," he tells me, and he knows, because he keeps track of who has major means and who does not, especially in a day when everything an elected official spends is subject to scrutiny by a horde of commissions or oversight committees. But his logic leaves me cold and I am still staring at him—and he is catching the arctic glare of my regard.

He sees he's rung no sale with me and kind of rolls his shoulders. "Look, I wish I could help you."

"So do I, Tommy. So do I."

"Gotta go. Good night." He scuttles away, climbs in his side, and revs the motor, a bit hasty if you ask me, and pulls out just as fast.

I've already hugged Dez and Anna, so I trudge over to my ugly rental, throw my satchel in the back seat, and slam the door. Bitter, I curse the results I've gotten here.

It's been a bad night all around. And even the crisp April night air does nada to improve my sour mood.

I wave one more time to my host and hostess, then haul ass out of the drive, headed for home along the Virginia two-laner dumping down into GW Parkway.

Cuz if there is one thing we do real well as Texans, it's drive.

We drive to survive. Herding cattle nowadays with four-by-fours instead of horses, we are bold as brass. We drive for serious events, with bigger-than-Dallas cattle guards welded to the grilles of our Suburbans, also known as Texas Cadillacs.

We drive for serious enjoyment. Going "up the road a piece" to visit family to us usually means more than a hundred measly miles touring at a cool eighty, eighty-five, like Comanches still want our scalps for belt decoration.

We drive for fun. Drinking hard stuff or a frothy "roadie," we work the distance joyfully. Until a few years ago when the legislature got a lick of sense and passed a law against having a beer and cruisin', we could even do that legally.

We drive to work off anger. And this is the most dangerous. Cuz we drive, putting new meaning to the phrase *hell on wheels,* riding over dirt and cactus and heartache like every rock we encounter is meant to be crushed smooth beneath our true and noble souls.

Right now I drive to work off my anger. Anger that I've been dealt a hand of cards I'm supposed to play with half of them covered.

In fact, it is downright infuriating to me when I punch on the radio and can't find a jazz station where I can croon to some torch song to relieve my frustration.

And it is damn disconcerting when I look in my rearview mirror and the brights that are blinding me crawl right up my Taurus's trunk and begin to push me across the road toward the cliff that drops straight down into the Potomac River.

nine

I hit the gas.

Pulling away from him, I sit straighter, drive more consciously. The night is starless and, courtesy of cloud cover, deep black. The George Washington Parkway is a winding road that borders the Potomac River the same way roads skim the Rio Grande. The Potomac, once the river of the Paw-to-Mac Indians, can run shallow and peaceful as a baby at sleep. But in the springtime, it runs wild and high from spring rains that dump into the Ohio River and careen down to the Potomac and the Chesapeake Bay, then out to the Atlantic. The snow of the other day, melted now, plus recent torrential rains in the Midwest, mean the river is nearing flood levels. In South Texas, flash floods often kill more people in twenty-four hours than traffic accidents in a whole year. In 1998, one washed away my aunt and uncle and two cousins, never to be found again. I hate water, except the stuff that comes in plumbing pipes or bottles.

In my tinny little ol' Taurus, I can hear this river, whooshing and rushing and scraping the rocky banks.

I slip off my stiletto heels and hit the gas pedal with a lead foot. The damn car gives me another five miles per hour easily, but the steering wheel is doing the shimmy.

The road climbs higher, then dips and rises steeply. I'm heading southeast, back to Georgetown along the Virginia side of the embankment. Two cars, moving northwest toward me, hug the side of the road that abuts the river. The headlights of the car in back of me recede as I put more distance between us at a cool seventy. That's much too fast for this terrain and this car, but hey, I'm eager to put miles between me and the crazy man there.

Except for him, no one else is traveling my way at this hour of the night. Not even Mr. Jones.

I wonder where he is, if he is not on the job tailing me. Has he quit? Did his employer run out of dough? Or desire to see me live a long and happy life?

I'm frowning over that.

And suddenly I hear the roar of an engine. And the same idiot as before zooms right up to me, high beams snapping on and his bumper connecting to my trunk in a snug clunk, nudging me so that the Taurus's wheels seem to plane.

What the hell?

I pull the steering wheel right to drive the shoulder. The car shudders and I'm cursing rental cars and detectives who make them necessary.

The guy behind me gets in the shoulder, too. Is he drunk? Some punk kid with joyride ambitions?

I try to look back, but his beams are up and I can't see jack. I flick the rearview to nighttime reflectors, but I get no better glimpse of who's inside. He must have blacked-out windows.

I lick my lips, and now I have sense enough to get scared.

He wants to play rough?

He has no clue who he's dealing with. Chances are, he has never played chicken with a Texan. Correction, a Texan woman.

And I may never have competed in any NASCAR race, but I sure as heck won medals and money driving a horse around barrels.

True, I have never until now transferred the concept from horse to car. But you do what you must when the time is right, yes?

"Come on, brother," I seethe, "get your gumption out of your ass and let's see what you got under that hood."

I'm not betting on what I have under my hood, but countin' instead on what I have in my head. "Please, God," I'm praying, "let me be good here."

I hit the pedal again and before he can cuddle up close to me, I am in the left lane, and faster than a jackrabbit in heat, I'm in the right again.

I'm sending up another request to heaven that no one is ahead of me, cuz if they are, we're all road kill, barrel-racing agility or not.

I have no idea how much weight he has on me. But he is definitely bigger than I am. So I decide I'll play with him. I know this road fairly well. I've traveled it at least once a month for the past two years, going to Girl Scout events with Jordan and taking her to visit her friends up in Leesburg.

I know there's a long stretch up ahead where I can speed up and pray for a policeman with a need to fill his ticket quota this month. And so I hit the gas. My shadow is right behind me.

He's far faster, too. Too agile. I swerve and he follows. I zag and he falls back a bit, not wishing to send himself across the median into the river instead of me.

But I don't anticipate the red horses in the road that signal construction up ahead. I curse. Ease off the gas. He's gaining on me and he swerves over to push me left closer to the median. My back teeth grind.

Who is this?

And who's in the next car barreling up in back of him? One of his compadres?

If this car, too, wants to see me swim with the fishes, then I'm across the other two lanes—and gone to God in only a few more minutes.

But I don't think he realizes he's got a tail behind him because he nudges me over to the left more. Now I've got my left wheel on the grass and the right on the paved shoulder. My ride is jarring, the ground is mushy, and I'm stunned the Taurus has any traction.

I have few choices. Slow down, dig in my brakes—and face off with him, *mano a mano*. Not a way I want to go, but I've brought my SIG. Tucked between the console and the passenger seat. But damn if I can reach over and grab it, cuz I've got all I can do to grip the steering wheel while I chug over mud and loose stone.

I've got to surprise him. Shake him up. Shake him loose.

I jerk my wheel left so that suddenly I'm running totally in the median and the tires are grinding in. But I am going too fast still and I wonder if I am going to flip, the propelling force stronger than these puny brakes.

But I've got no time to ponder, because the huge black vehicle that forced me over whizzes past me. The car following him has rocketed up behind him and the two of them speed past, the second closing hard on the first. In the dark, in my fright, I concentrate on the Taurus, whose wheels are churning and grinding mud and digging in so that I come to a bone-jarring stop that has me gasping for breath—and wondering if I am going to die from the shock of it.

Amazed that I am sitting in one piece on this lonely road, I begin to shake and tears spring up like geysers and roll down my cheeks. I'm crying, silent as a dead woman, when I see another car heading toward me and grind to a halt. It appears to be a Volvo sedan—and I know no one who owns one. I lean over and push down the lock on my door. Something says this is the car that chased off the big black one. But I'm not in the mood to take chances that Volvo owners are more friendly or less nutty than others they chase.

I reach down against the console, dig out the SIG, chamber a round, and point my gun along with my gumption at his approaching figure. If this person so much as looks cross-eyed at me, he will soon look like swiss cheese. He's not a trooper, but in plain clothes. Black pants. Black tee. Running toward me.

I raise the barrel, lower the window enough to poke the barrel through, and double-hand the gun to give me a steady bead on his heart.

"Carly!"

Oh, Jesus! He knows my name?

"Who the hell are—"

"It's Jones!" He's leaning over and there's just enough light from my dash that I distinguish his features in relief.

I dissolve like sugar in water. When I open my eyes, this man looks better to me than any I've ever known.

"It's okay now, Carly. Put the gun down. Carly . . ."

I'm delighted, I'm grateful, I'm mouthing funny stuff to myself that I'm fine, really fine, and alive.

"Open up, Carly. Let me see you. Are you hurt?"

I flick the lock.

He flings wide the door. His fingers are all over me. Face, head, nose, neck, shoulders, arms.

"Okay, okay!" I assure him, coming back enough to reclaim some dignity. "I'm good. Nothing's broken."

"Yeah, right," he retorts, now working on feeling up my thighs and my knees, my feet. My bare feet.

"Hey, that tickles."

"Thank god it does! What were you thinking, back there?" He uses a colorful array of curse words while he takes my pulse.

My head is flung back on the headrest. "What are you doing here?" I'm talking slowly and tonelessly like I'm using one of those voice distorters. "Why did you come back?"

"My first job is to protect you."

I chuckle, and for a long second I recall the only other man who ever told me that—and then kept his word. "Oh, well, then. You sure did a great job of that. Tell me, do they dock your pay for failure to keep your pigeon alive?"

"Ha, ha. Very funny." He's crouched beside me, surveying my face and form. Putting a hand to my eyes and widening one lid to look at my pupils, then the other.

I slap his hand away. "Stop that. Did you get his license number?"

"No. None."

"None?"

"Did you hit your head when you stopped?"

"No."

"Feel fuzzy?" He runs his fingertips over my scalp.

"No! Tell me how he could have no license plates," I insist.

He grunts. "You have a one-track mind. That's good. Means no head injury."

I grind my teeth and my jaw suddenly hurts, so I chide him, "License plates, focus here, Jones."

He mashes his lips together, unhappy with me and himself. "He must've removed them."

"Removed them?" Damn. I shake him off. "What make of car?"

"Ford. Excursion. Black or navy blue. Did he hit you?"

I concentrate, narrow my eyes, and relive the moments of terror. "Crunched me."

"Think he scraped your paint?"

"Could be."

"Don't move. Just rest. I'll check it out."

"You do that little thing," I murmur as he pushes up. Chills begin to trickle through my bones. The aftermath of an adrenaline high is never pretty.

One, two minutes tick by. I breathe more evenly.

He returns, bends down beside me again. "Let's get out of here, what do you say, before the Virginia State Patrol cruises through?"

"Sure. It's not much farther home."

He's looking at my companion seat. "You brought your SIG-Sauer." His eyes, electric with anger, snap to mine. "Didn't want to honor me by using the pistol I left for you, eh?"

I close my eyes, rub my forehead. "Yours looks like it came from the toy section of the Mercantile. Me? I'm packin' dum-dums."

He whistles long and low. "Taking no chances, are you? Well, good. Fact is, I really don't care what you carry, as long as you do."

I shudder, not sure if it's fear or the frigid night air that's causing it. I turn over the ignition and turn on the heater. "Let's get the hell out of here." *Oh, boy, did I just invite this guy home with me? How could you, Carly?* I ask myself, and follow it with, "You don't think he'll come back, do you?"

"No. He saw me coming and decided to peel off at that last exit. Lucky for him, I needed to come back and check on you."

"I wish you *had* followed him." I sulk over the lost opportunity to track the bastard.

"Not to worry. I think we can get a paint sample from your trunk where he bumped you. We'll find him."

"Yeah? And how long will *that* take?" Frustration and fear begin to blend, turning me into an A-Number One Shrew. "And in the end, will you tell me who it is or do I have to deduce that myself, too?"

He shakes his head. "Yes, of course I'll tell you. You're working too hard, trying to investigate this murder—"

"And you."

"And me." He gives me another once-over with his X-ray eyes. "As soon as possible, I promise, I'll know what year and color this car is. I'll make it a priority of our lab. Let's get you home."

Feeling feisty now, I'm rankled that he didn't prevent this attack. I mean, isn't that what he's supposed to have done? "No, bad idea, Sherlock. I am going home alone. Close the door."

His jaw twitches. "We need to talk."

"Well, you know what? I don't know that you earned that, buddy. When all this was happening, where *precisely were you?*" I hate to say it with such venom, but I'm weary, and worse, I sound needy.

"I was at the Harlans', too," he fires back, "doing surveillance across the street from their gate in the woods. It just so happens, ma'am, that it took me a while to get outta there because Iverson came back to talk to Dez."

That raises my hackles and lowers my depression.

"What do you suppose that's about?" he presses me, adding to my bad mood.

"Wish I knew."

He lifts his brows, in a look that's a cross between haughty and buoyant. "Good to know you missed me, though."

His affirmation that I value his presence fries my oil. I open my mouth to fire back and the pain stops me flat.

He's leaning closer, reaching for me. "Did you hit your chin on the steering wheel?"

I pull away from his grasp and move my chin. "Ow. Maybe."

"Lemme see." He's touching me again. "Does that hurt?"

"Yes, it hurts!" I try to talk without moving my lips and figure I look like a bad ventriloquist. "What do you think?"

He's unperturbed, lightly fingering me again. "You don't have a broken bone. Great." He slaps his knees. "Let's get you home and look you over in the light. Think you are good enough to drive?"

"Sure." I give in to the offered help and show how really big and strong I am by revving my ridiculous Taurus engine. "If I can get out of this median without churning up and digging in, I am good to go."

"Try it." He circles his fingers.

The wheels grip and grind, then spring out of the muck. "Okayyyy!" I call back. "Let me close the door."

He jogs forward to me and bends over. "Listen up. Go no more than forty, you hear me, just in case you've damaged the alignment or your tires. I'm right behind you. Pull over if you have problems; we'll leave it on a shoulder and you can ride with me." He starts to walk away and turns back, circling his hand to roll down my window. "Because of the reporters outside your house, follow me to let me park down on O or P Street and get in with you. I'll sink down in the front seat so your Capitol Police detail won't spot me when you pull into your garage."

Great. My big Saturday night out. Topped by smuggling into my home a man of dubious origin—but slightly proven devotion.

Even if he's got sketchy abilities to protect me from the coyotes of this world.

I'm gazing in my bathroom mirror at my jaw when Jones comes in to stand behind me and lean in to gaze at my reflection, too.

"Ouch." He winces in sympathy and draws closer, his front to my back, and his heat warming my cold, cold heart. "That looks like you'll need lots of concealer for a few days. Leave it. I've made us a pot of coffee and put out crackers and cheese."

"Made yourself right at home again," I grumble, but take this golden opportunity to study Jones, up close and very personal. His eyes never fail to arrest me, the silver and blue shocking to behold. But the rest of him is sure easy on the eyes. The square jaw with the late-night swath of heavy beard. The high cheek-bones. The nose, straight, roman, perhaps, but once broken and artfully repaired.

I pivot to reach into my linen closet and grab my heating pad. "I'll put some heat on it."

"No. Ice. It's gonna swell otherwise and you'll look like Rocky after a run-in with a truck."

"Thanks," I tell him deadpan. "But I don't have an ice bag."

He lifts the heating pad from my fingers. "Come with me." He leads me by the wrist into my kitchen and directs me to my easy chair. "Sit there and be quiet." Throwing my afghan around my legs, he marches off and pours us both some coffee. "How do you like yours?"

"Half and half. No sugar." I'm thinking, *Hey, it's perfectly all right, Carly, to take what comfort's available after some fool just tried to kill you.* "Thanks."

"Welcome." He hands me my tallest mug and returns to the kitchen. I'm sipping as I watch him, reaching in one drawer to pull out a hand towel, then opening the freezer to grab handfuls of ice, wrapping them in the towel, and bringing it to me. "Lean back and drape this around you."

Shoot, it was cold. And the blanket wasn't helping to warm up the rest of me. I close my eyes.

"How was your visit with Anna Harlan?" he asks after a few minutes of total peace that I am grateful for.

"Fun."

"And with Dez?"

I open one eye and turn my face toward him. "Not fun."

"I guess that means he gave you the rundown on security firms, public, legal, or otherwise."

I point a finger at him. "Got that right."

"And your little tête-à-tête with Tommy Iverson there at the end was not very forthcoming about employing the likes of me, either, I gather?"

I open the other eye. "Should he have been?"

"Beats the hell out of me."

"Thanks." I roll my head down on the back of the chair again and close my eyes. "No one wants to take credit for you."

"Figures."

I sigh. "Agreed." I'd come that far in my investigation of Jones and his ilk, that I was now able to understand how no one would wish to take credit for a paramilitary detective bodyguard type who had access to nifty weapons and clothes and had a remarkable ability either to read minds or had one whale of an investigative organization behind him. Including a lab to analyze evidence like paint chips.

"Did you get anything worthwhile off the Taurus?"

"Yeah." He sips his coffee. "Good amount. It'll work, not to worry."

"But I do." My eyes are still closed and I hear him step into the kitchen, filling his cup again. "Whoever that was, I don't want them coming back. Not here." I don't give him my specific reason. *Let's see if he knows that Jordan's coming home.*

"Right. I doubt they would, though. Not with that car—which now they have to ditch somewhere. And they won't come here, not with this detail here, night and day." He returns to his chair, opposite mine. I hear the cushions squish, accepting his weight. "No idea of anyone who owns an Excursion?"

"Nope. I don't catalogue stuff like that in my brain. Too much else to remember." I rub my forehead again. For a woman who hardly ever gets a headache, the last few had been strong enough to stop a bull at ten yards. "How reliable do you think these boys on the front and back door really are, given the fact that their track record with you is rather checkered?"

"Oh, they're good." I feel the radiation in his smile from five feet away. "But I'm better."

"Affirmative on that one, brother."

A moment ticks by, when he opens with, "I heard Dunhill's funeral is Tuesday. Private viewing in Bethesda tomorrow night and Monday. Memorial service at the Washington Cathedral."

"Yep." I don't move a muscle. "I'll go."

"I figured."

I wait for what else he knows.

"And when does Jordan come home?"

Ah, the crux of my concern about home security and folks in black Excursions. "Tomorrow night. BWI. Continental at seven fifty-eight."

"I'll follow you."

I sit up, and my head pounds like a jackhammer. "What's your opinion of whether I tell Detective Brown about the Excursion?" His eyes and mine lock.

"You can, but if he puts a detail on you wherever you go, then it limits what I can do for you."

"So I have a choice to make, you or these boys." I pick up my coffee mug and drink. "Perhaps if he were to learn someone tried to run me off GW Parkway, he'd get the idea, too, that I am not his murderer."

"No guarantees there. Plenty of criminals make up things to throw police off the trail."

"I could show him my trunk."

"You could. But you could have gotten that scrape anywhere—and you have no eyewitnesses except me."

"Whom I can't call on to corroborate."

He nods. "It's a matter of who you're gonna trust."

I swallow trepidation on that note. "Tell you what. Let's make a deal."

He considers his coffee and purses those *kill me with kisses* lips. "If I can."

"Bring me the paint analysis. The name of the owner of that car. Tomorrow." I glance at the clock. "Twenty-four hours. One A.M. Then I'll have some evidence you're on my side."

"You've got that already," he objects with a metallic glint in those eyes.

"Let's say I need more."

"Or you'll do what?"

"Tell Detective Brown about you?"

"No, no, no." He's shaking his head. "Won't work. I'm not part of Brown's ken. Hell, operatives like me are not part of any-one's ken . . . until they need me. Until they have to accept my help."

"Twenty-four hours." I'm bargaining like a busted gambler, but I've got to force his hand.

He inhales. "I'll do my damnedest. On one condition."

I give a wan smile. "What?"

"Who've you been talking to about Alistair and the murder?" He puts his hand up when I open my mouth. "Please. No politically correct answers here, ma'am. Someone doesn't like you or what you're doing. That means you're prying into matters—digging where you're not welcome. So." He curls his fingers and gives me the *come on* waggle. "Fess up. Who?"

I hate being backed into corners, but I loathe being used as a target so much more. "Scott. Dez. Iverson. Sally Sonderberg."

After a silent moment, he asks, "That's it?"

"So far."

He snorts. "You are incorrigible."

"Not the worst thing I have ever been called." I sniff theatrically.

"All right." He lifts his chin in the direction of my coffee cup. "More before I go?"

I hold it out. "Please."

He takes it and fills it up, hands it back to me, then orders me to tuck my afghan higher up around me if I'm going to sleep here, which I may.

Doing what I term the *man of the house* thing, he gives the first floor the once-over, checking the windows and doors. Back in the kitchen and family room with me, he twirls the lights down to dim, then inspects me, hands on his hips. "Sleep tight. Where's the gun I gave you?"

"Top drawer over there."

He digs it out from beneath my recipes and places it on the side table within reach. "Use it. The SIG is fine, but this has the extra added ability to keep others from grabbing it."

"You doubt my abilities with a gun."

"Being a sharpshooter merits you zippo if you can't keep possession."

I bristle. "You don't know that I can't."

He throws me a tolerant look. "From the other night when I had you down on this floor, I know you've never taken a martial arts course in your life. Therefore, you're vulnerable to anyone who has—or who's bigger than you are—or faster. The first rule of warfare is take the other's guy's weapon, and the second is never lose your own. So, do us both a favor, carry this weapon. Just in case somebody wants to use yours on you."

I nod.

"All right," he croons, happy at my agreement. "Time for all good boys to exit."

I want to show my gratitude, but don't want to go over the top and give him any ideas he might now be welcome here. "Thanks."

"Sure," he tells me, proud of himself, but prouder he saved my skin. Our eyes lock. "Not a problem."

Blinking, I break the mutual stare. "How will you get out without our buddies seeing you?" I try to ask with a nonchalance that has a purpose, just in case I ever need the info myself. "I assume you have no darts at the ready tonight."

"Nope, none. But I can leave without detection. From where they usually stand post, there's a blind spot covered with bushes leading to the fence of your next-door neighbor. I'm going to turn the lights off here completely so there's no light shining in the garden."

He's got his hand on the French door, ready to go, when one more itty-bitty thing occurs to me. "What if . . ." Ah, hell, I go for the big enchilada and ask, "What if . . . I ever needed you? How would I get in touch with you?"

His eyes sparkle like he just won the biggest buckle at the rodeo. "Gosh, ma'am, and here I thought you'd never ask."

ten

My Sunday mornings in D.C. consist of two obligations—one to my soul, the other to my mind. Both are not being saved today. Hours ago, I decided to skip Mass and threw over my lame tai-chi attempt at Daughter-over-the-Mountain, too. Skimming the *New York Times*'s and the *Washington Post*'s coverage of Alistair's death gives me nothing more than a bad case of approach avoidance that makes me grind my teeth.

I click on the tube, going for the drama of Sunday morning political shows. Down in rural Texas, we don't receive the wealth of cable channels available to the metro areas, meaning we can't tune in with ease to just any ol' show. So when I stay in D.C. on weekends, I love to surf for what I call the Sunday Funnies. Only this morning, I'm not laughing too hard.

I'm in the same chair Jones left me in. I've plunked his newest gizmo for me, a sleek two-ounce-tops cell phone (that masquerades as a silver business card holder, mind you), within reach of my fingertips on my side table. In one hand, I hold a fresh cup of coffee—and in the other, my remote control. Abe, who was such a good boy last night, never making a peep in his cage when Jones was here, is now sitting on the floor, pointing and chittering at the face and form of William Preston Scott. My House party leader, oozing his southern gentleman gravitas in a navy suit and red bow tie, has just covered all the high points of this week's floor events in words that would make watching paint dry more exciting. Now he's been asked the question I have certainly been waiting for, lo, these past twenty minutes.

"Congressman Scott, what do you really think," demands the moderator, an old coot who resembles *Tyrannosaurus rex*, "really happened in Congresswoman Wagner's office Monday night— and how do you think she or anyone else in your party can survive the scandal?"

"I can't know what happened to Congressman Dunhill, Ned. None of us should speculate on that. But I do know one thing: Congresswoman Wagner has been cooperating with the Capitol Police on this investigation."

Thanks, buddy.

"Wait, wait," the moderator, who's been yelling at people on this show for more than twenty years, interrupts him. "Just a minute, Congressman. We don't want to hear the party line on this. We want to know the truth."

Cretin. How does he expect that Scott knows the truth? Or could tell it if he did? Tarnation, I discovered the body, and I don't know the truth!

"Do. You. Believe. Congresswoman Wagner. Murdered. Him. Or. Not?"

No, he doesn't.

"No, I don't. Listen, Ned, she and Congressman Dunhill got along famously. We all did."

Gee, did I detect Scott's nose growing longer with that statement? *You had an argument with him the day he died, for god's sakes.*

"Dunhill was an effective whip," Ned the Yeller offers as consolation prize. "But he had his foibles."

You can say that again. But, man, you better not list 'em on national TV.

Scott, a credit to his years in the hot seat of his party's leadership, smiles congenially. "Ned, Congressman Dunhill had a few challenges personally."

Eeeek. We're really not gonna go there, are we?

Ned nods. "We all know how tough it is to make policies, keep constituents' needs uppermost, run offices here, district offices, staff, the obligatory flights back home each weekend. . . ."

Or not.

Scott agrees. "But I prefer this morning to focus on those aspects of Congressman Dunhill's long career in the service of his country. First as an infantry lieutenant in Vietnam, then as mayor of his hometown, and serving continuously in the House for his district for more than a quarter of a century."

Ned gets in the praise game. "A great American with a distinguished record. We'll miss him."

Liar, liar, pants on fire. Ned misses no one and no thing. Except when a scheduled guest does not show, then he screws you by not letting you on again till you offer him a juicy controversy to launch here.

"You bet, Ned. Alistair Dunhill was an integral part of our team, working to gain votes for the bills our party is devoted to, like education and veterans' benefits and—"

Oh, boy, this is the blah-blah-blah factor, up with the party, down with the opposition, rah rah rah.

But Ned steers Scott back to the story that obsesses us all. "By next week, do you think we will have an arrest in this murder, Congressman?"

"Oh, I have every confidence in the Capitol Police that they will pursue this case as thoroughly and as quickly as possible."

Ned scowls and points at Scott. "Doesn't this tarnish the image of the Congress? A murder in our midst?"

Scott, bless his heart, doesn't squirm, but looks Ned in the eye. "No. This is the work of one madman. A crime. One of passion. We work together in this town, on both sides of the aisle, to make democracy move along. One person's abhorrence of the law does not diminish the good work we do every day here in Washington together. Whoever did this, we will find him."

"Or her," Ned interjects, and I shiver.

"Or her," Scott affirms. "Absolutely. And we will deal with this person. Then we will all go back to doing the work of the country. Our nation has survived so many foibles—"

"Scandals, Congressman Scott. Wilbur Mills, who was stopped by local police, found to be intoxicated while his companion jumped into the Tidal Basin—."

"Ned." Scott blushes such a bright pink I think the TV tube is going to burn clean through. "That was more than thirty years ago."

Yeah, and why is Ned bringing up an incident that sounds like sexual misconduct? Does he know about Alistair's penchant for lots of women . . . or is he reacting to the lurid details of his emasculation reported in the papers?

"Ned, I hasten to remind you and our audience that this republic has survived so much else. Assassinations of our Presidents, impeachments—"

"Financial misconduct on the part of presidential advisers and House members," Ned points out.

Oh, baby. Does Ned know about Alistair's sexual *and* financial problems? *Detective Brown, are you listening to this?*

"Yes, true. We are a microcosm of the greater society in many ways," Scott adds. "But we are also leaders who overcome adversities. We have, as a democratic republic, done so for more than two hundred and thirty years, and we will continue to do so because—"

I flick him off. I already know his god-bless-America speech.

And my needs today are greater than a refresher course in patriotism. It's only eleven A.M. and I need to get ready for Jordan's arrival home tonight. I scoop up the scattered *Post* and skip reading the rest of the *Times,* dumping the armful into the recycle bin in my pantry. They all say the same thing anyway: The Capitol Police need to work free of all political involvement to examine the facts and the suspects to charge one with the murder of Alistair Dunhill. Just because Carly Wagner seems the most obvious suspect does not mean she committed the crime.

I wonder what they'd all report if they knew I'd been attacked last night, pushed toward the Potomac. They'd find a few sympathetic bones in their bodies. If they believed me.

And what about other suspects? Brown was not going to list any for me, was he?

By now he had to have not only a list of who stayed late in Rayburn that night, but also who had motivation and who had the strength to plunge a letter opener into a man's chest. And who had the violent fury to cut off a man's penis.

I pause.

With a letter opener?

My opener was sharp—at the point. And it could puncture skin. But did it possess the shearing ability of a knife? I imagine myself holding it and . . . sawing off an organ.

I clamp a hand over my mouth, forcing back a gag.

Now, I have seen death a hundred times. You don't grow up on a ranch, work with animals, domestic and wild, in the heat, in the wind, in dust storms and floods, and not see how death comes in all guises. It comes as dehydration in a climate that can roast your brain if you're caught too far from water for too long. It comes as an attack from predators like coyotes and bobcats and wild boars, whose instinct is to kill to survive. It can come as an attack from another human, who might have too much access to his rifle when he's more than a mite riled. Oh, yes, I'd seen dead creatures, dried, fried, mauled, and bullet-riddled. I'd seen them killed accidentally and on purpose. I'd even seen them slaughtered purposely and butchered.

But I had never seen one purposely badly butchered.

And if my letter opener had a sharp edge—if that truly was the murder weapon—then Alistair was slain in a way no human deserved from another.

And I have to take myself outside for fresh air. Breathing deeply, I stroll through my garden. My spring flowers are straining their necks toward heaven in the sixty-degree sunshine and I, too, close my eyes straining for some brilliance, some clarity. My, my, what zany weather we've got in Washington, that my forsythia, which the other day had spread crystal arms of ice from the snowstorm, now waves yellow fronds in the gentle breeze. I pad across my patio and along the flagstones through my rosebushes, past the flat of petunias that Rayanne bought and I've not yet found time to plant. The aromas of caffeine and sweet florals soothe my senses—and I orient myself to welcoming home my daughter, who now must deal with the first death of someone important in her young life. The death of her friend's father. I think of Zack, too. His loss. A blow to any child, but to one who had lost his mother when he was four, this of his other parent is doubly cruel.

How much does Zack know of his father's personal troubles? Chances are, he sensed them, if indeed he did not know the specifics. Children feel the chaos of dysfunction. Just as I felt the discord between my parents when I was small. As adults, we lose that ability to intuit . . . or bury it with the veneer of maturity or diplomacy.

I stand frozen for a moment. Reliving scenes I'd witnessed of Alistair with others. With Mirinda Pace. With Jimmy Jeff Holden. With Sally Sonderberg. With Scott. Yes, I had dismissed those encounters, in a sense, because they were none of my business. But perhaps now that someone had stabbed him in my office, those scenes, those arguments, have come to be my business.

How can I learn more about each of them?

I need to talk with someone who will level with me. But who could that be? Surely there is not just one person who will know the answers to my dilemma. All of Washington is filled with authorities, but each knows pieces of pieces.

Discouraged, I survey the blue sky and my neighbor's rooftop when I spy one of the Capitol patrolmen on duty to protect me from the wolves outside my door. Too late, boys. The wolves have already besmirched my name and reputation by killing one of their own in my territory. In my inner office. Not satisfied with character assassination, last night someone also decided to do me bodily harm.

I sink down to my garden bench and consider my flowers. Ever valiant. Budding. Trying.

Hey, kids. That's me.

At least I've got one person working for me. I'm laughing. "Right, Carly. One you can trust just as much as any other so-called friends."

But who has saved me from assassination by automobile? Jones. Who has given me clues about Krystal and a few about Alistair? Jones, again.

And if he could learn who had been driving that Excursion, old Jones might gain a place on my list of good guys. Until I could dump him.

As if I didn't have enough problems, I have Jones to disturb me.

But so does that attempt on my life last night.

Who wouldn't that disturb?

Someone had followed me to the Harlans'. Or knew I was going there. Knew, when I left, that I was alone on that road home. That the road was treacherous and that they could shove me off it. That they had a big car and I had a puny one—and they might be successful. And they planned it, too, because they had removed their license plates before hitting me.

It could have been anyone.

Even someone aligned with Jones to let him save me and prove him to be a good guy. Someone I could trust.

I spring up from the bench like a crazy lady.

I was doing the triple-think again. The nutty *who can you trust* game that might drive you to drink or drugs or resignation from frustration. Well, I am not going there. I have never quit one damn thing I tried. Except my marriage to Len—and that was his fault. Or mostly.

So.

Who would Jones not disturb in this town?

An entry like a cat burglar, a mission without a boss, a nothing name like Jones. Knowledge or intuition of facts he should not know about me. I snort. *Who wouldn't he disturb?* Lethally delicious-looking, tantalizing in his skin-hugging bulletproof zoot suit, self-assured to the point of downright cocky, chock full of information he shouldn't know, Mr. Jones is a bucketful of trouble. A feast for a woman with an eye for . . .

Men.

Ohmigod. As my daughter would say.

I do a full circle in my garden.

But like a child who has just seen a wish come true, I am skeptical of what I have just recalled. I check my memory. Oh, there is no doubt of my conclusion: There does indeed exist one woman whom Mr. Jones would definitely not disturb. One woman whom last night's attack would not disturb. And she is my party crony. A fellow member of the same garden club.

Patricia Tipton had once needed a bodyguard extraordinaire to protect her. It was perhaps a decade or more ago, when Patricia was in her late fifties, blond, buxom, but otherwise willowy as a teenager. The daughter of a former President, a three-time wife, an umpty-ump-time mistress of CEOs and sheikhs, one French pastry chef, and even one hotheaded matador from Madrid, Patricia knew men like a book. Never had one lived she could not charm, would not seduce for the enjoyment of having him lavish his libido and his wealth on her.

Evidently, though, there was one whom she decided she did not want, and he, given his walking papers, decided he did not want her living. So he began to lay traps to kill her. He persuaded one of Patricia's housemaids to put berries, to which Patricia was highly allergic, into her health shake one morning. When she failed to drink it, he drained her brake fluid at her villa overlooking Naples and caused her to run her Maserati into a convenient rock that stopped her rapid descent down a jagged ravine. Then he placed a bomb in her bedroom in Vail, but detonated the damn thing when she was sleeping in her other one in her house in the Hamptons. Patricia, call it her Irish luck, got tired of anticipating this loony's next move and so she asked her third husband, a former senator from North Carolina, to hire her a super-duper security man. According to Washington legend, the man appeared and made like Hercules. And Adonis. He not only swept her house for bugs and thugs, but swept her off her feet. He was young. Maybe twenty years younger than she. He was tough. A lot tougher than her seventy-five-year-old hubbie. Cuter, too. And talented. In bed. Not so bad out of it, either, because she kept him around for more than three years, long after her stalker was forcibly retired to jail for his crimes of passion.

Long about the time the then-President, an old pal of hers for whom she had personally raised beaucoup election bucks, talked of naming her ambassador to Italy, she gave up Sweet Cheeks. No one knew what had happened to him, as he receded into the mist from whence he came.

But she might know where he'd come from.

And if Patricia knows where men like hers came from, I stand a fighting chance of learning where Jones came from—and who paid his fees.

Patricia and I are faithful members of the Georgetown Rose and Shamrock. The female version of an Englishmen's club, R and S—as it is called by the initiated—evolved during the nineties from a wives' society chitchat group into a professional women's networking mechanism. Patricia, older but just as spry and wise at the game of politics as she has ever been, attends every luncheon. A serene widow in her sixties now, her years of playing pogo with every guy she savored are done. These days she pours her heart out onto her flowers while she nurturs her status as doyenne to the party and a few relationships with females, most of whom are elected officials in the House or Senate. This keeps her at the top of her game in the hearts and minds of politicos everywhere, to whom she is a classic Washington society hostess—and, by all accounts, a mover and shaker. Still.

I should be so lucky at her age to be as involved. As revered.

Sure as the sun's gonna rise tomorrow, that'll only happen if I am absolved of this murder in my office.

I shiver, wrap my jean jacket around me, and lift the brass knocker once more to tap Patricia Tipton's large green Federal front door. After a protracted set of two more, a horse-faced girl in a maid's uniform of white doily over shapeless black opens the door. She is polite but cool—and worse, she has one of those French accents that sounds like she wears a clothespin on her nose. Now, I have never learned French, so you could fool me if she's putting me on or the real McCoy. But she eyes me up and down and clearly disapproves of my western attire for one o'clock on Sunday afternoon. Too bad, cuz I'd dressed for a horseback ride to clear my tension long before I got up the gumption to call Patricia and ask if she'd receive me today on the spur of the moment. So I plunge onward and inform Frenchie that Madam Ambassador is expecting me. *Ah, may we*, she intones, *I will of course present you.*

You do that little thing, I want to reply, but hold my sharp tongue.

Like low-flying aircraft, she hovers around me, divesting me of my coat and purse, then glides away like a wraith.

I wonder what Patricia likes about her. The nasality, the homeliness, the total lack of personality? Patricia was known for her peculiarities in staff as well as her penchant to hire and fire them by the carload. If anyone was late, inept, unkempt, loose-lipped, unethical, any little trait at all that Patricia did not care for, she would sack them so swiftly they had no idea if they were coming in the door or out. Kind of like Sadie O'Neill. Neither one tolerated slackers.

So I settle into a cushy Chippendale chair to await my hostess, congratulating myself that I understand Patricia Mayfield Curtis Tipton, née Reilly.

Minutes later, pulling open her drawing room doors with a rush, she sweeps in like an actress of the silent screen. In a plum silk dressing gown that hugs her still-gorgeous figure like a glove, she trails a tea-length skirt with train. She welcomes me with open arms and air kisses on both cheeks. She's flashing her collection of rings, carats dripping from her fingers like boulders, but sedate pearls in her ears. No diamonds above the wrist before seven, she keeps the old rules of dress. Even to the matters of how shoes and hat should match. And makeup, she once told me, "even for breakfast and always before male servants."

I know because she and I had enjoyed a few drinks one afternoon about a year ago after one of our garden club meetings. I had invited her to cocktails because I needed a perspective on the new leftist Italian premier and his government—and she knew him well from her tenure in our embassy in Rome. She graciously accepted my invitation and she'd been more than informative. She had been downright enlightening—and as a result, I had felt better about our declining military presence in the European Union.

If I had been worried about how I was going to hop, skip, and jump to my subject of choice, I was suddenly without a drop of it. With women like Patricia, one never can worry about anything in her company. She envelopes you, consumes you, absorbs you into her skin. She focuses on you, all ears, all eyes, all smiles. Your health, your family, your policies, your views, your favorites as she places a gin and tonic in your hand and fires your imagination with her perception and her intuition about your day. Before you know it, you are sipping a refill and chatting about subjects you have hardly raised from your subconscious, let alone articulated to anyone, much less a woman you have spoken with fewer times than the number of fingers on one hand.

"Do you do yoga, my dear?" she asks me as she returns to her credenza and pours herself a second martini, dirty, two olives. "I find it stimulating. All that stretching. Good for the posture, the digestion, the soul." She turns, hoists her glass, and winks. "But so is this."

I tell her I walk a lot, especially lately, and do tai chi. She rejoins me, sitting like a queen on a throne, spreading her skirts out so as not to wrinkle them over the Chippendale chair that matches mine. I wonder as I glance at her if I could ever possess as much elegance.

Her turquoise eyes drop down my body. "You were once Miss Texas, I recall."

My lord, she's done some research. "When I was eighteen. Scared to death."

"You sang for your talent?"

I consider my gin and grin. "I still do a mean imitation of Ella, but only in private."

"You placed in the competition, am I right?"

"First runner-up."

She assesses my body again, cool as a talent scout. "You are forty-two and still have firm breasts, trim ankles. You should wear more skirts."

I usually don't get flummoxed. With Patricia, I blush.

She captures my gaze and holds me in thrall. "That's why they want you, and you must let them use you for TV."

I blink at her. She knows that Scott has offered me the keynote at the convention?

She inclines her head. "I knew about the keynote, yes. I suggested you, my dear. But so did quite a few others. All men, I might add."

"I didn't think they considered me podium material." I have frequently questioned if my Texas drawl was too thick, if my stance on the death penalty was too far right, and my support of universal children's health care too far left for anyone to seriously consider me a contender for center stage. Or a higher profile.

She loses the smile, all guise of the hostess replaced by the face of the power broker. "You want to be, don't you?"

A thrill goes up my spine. I initiated this visit. I brought my agenda. But she has transformed it into hers. I am not happy with her usurping my plan, but I am not unhappy that the subject is my ascent within the party. "Of course. Every little girl dreams of being President someday."

"Mmmm." She licks her lips. "With all those people to dance attendance."

We chuckle and my tension dissolves in the talk of my prospects. "I may have dreamed it, but I did not come to Washington expecting it. I have my pet projects, I understand what I can do."

"Democracy is messy, but it's better than anything else out there."

"Right. One woman, one vote. Works for me."

"So do your looks, Carly. Your voice. Your humor. Nothing wrong with letting the party bask in the glow of that. You've been elected five times now, preparing for your sixth. It is time to move up."

"What if I don't want to?"

The turquoise eyes darken to a grim navy. "Why in heaven's name not?"

"I'm not perfect. I'm divorced and a Catholic. One strike against me as a woman and the other a strike against me in a state where Protestants and evangelicals are on the rise in numbers."

"You're human. At least you declare a religion, and divorce these days is not a sign of failure so much as intelligence."

I'm chuckling with her and say, "I want to do what I can, stay in the House."

"Why would you hide?"

"I don't call it that."

She puts her glass down. It's empty again, and I'm marveling at her capacity for alcohol, when she retorts, "What do you call it?"

"Prudent. Wise. I like where I am, what I do."

"So do your constituents, obviously. That kind of success comes from a keen mind, a sharp intellect. That needs to be used for your country."

Confused, I ponder what it is my party *really* wants that I've got lots of, but I reply with the only answer I have right at the moment. "I do use it for my country."

She folds her hands. "It is healthy to have fear. No great man ever won high office without a bit of reflection."

I am not a man, however.

She looks at me, and I know she has read my mind. "Precisely why we need you, my dear. So few women take the reins of power."

"Others are ahead of me. Most are more talented." I see my opening to go where I want with this conversation, even though my advancement was not the topic I'd originally planned to use to pave the way.

She narrows her eyes at me in consideration of my stance.

I rush into the void with names. "Lou Rawlings. Mirinda Pace. Dee Kurlander."

"Lou is doing nicely in the primaries. But she still needs to win at least two more. We will see what we can do to help her out. But she is getting on in age and if things don't go her way especially in June in California, she may be too old four years from now to start the process all over again."

I know Lou wants our party's nomination for the White House. If she got it, she would be the first woman to do so and she would need considerable support from all of us in the party to win the presidency.

Patricia picks lint from her skirt. "As for Dee, she has made a few mistakes. Policy mistakes. She may never be able to recover."

"But Mirinda . . ." Mirinda Pace, my Rayburn next-door neighbor, represents Los Angeles, a bling-bling powerhouse of a district. She has assets I could not or would not ever acquire. She follows party lines on all votes in all ways. She's about five years younger than I, always coiffed, manicured, and perhaps even surgically enhanced to sultry movie-star perfection. Latino, from a family of Mexican immigrants, she put herself through community college waitressing when she met her husband, a millionaire from his family's ice-cream business. By the time Matthew Pace won his seat in the House, he and Mirinda had four children and another on the way. Who knows what did it, some whispered she'd worn him out in bed, but four months after he was sworn in, Pace, age fifty, had a stroke one night. Boom, he was a goner. Mirinda took his seat two weeks later by appointment from the governor. Cameras love her, so does *People* magazine and the Hollywood crowd, to say nothing of the fact that she is so hot that she is many a man's big wet dream.

"No." Patricia is shaking her head. "Mirinda will never work."

Without a wish to display any ignorance, I wait for the explanation.

"She has too much baggage."

I know of none. I frown and Patricia sees it as the question it is.

"She has financial problems. She may have inappropriately used PAC funds. Not too many know. Yet. But that kind of thing cannot stay hidden too long."

My mouth goes dry. The similarity to Alistair's problem makes me swallow, hard.

Patricia knits her brows together, a tough go because of her Botox shots, I'm sure. "Surprised, right? Well, it's worse. If she doesn't get investigated for misappropriation of monies, she still has to overcome a bigger problem. She is conflicted about her role."

I nod. "I empathize with her on that."

"But you do not exhibit any of your concerns in your work. She does. With five children and no mate, Mirinda Pace runs like a bunny to keep up with those children and still do her legislative work." Patricia is so matter-of-fact about this, she strikes me as nigh unto heartless.

I try to examine my own behavior but make a note to do that when I have more minutes and no conversation going with a party leader. Instead, I recall how Mirinda and I serve on one subcommittee together and that I knew she missed more meetings and, worse, more floor votes than she should have. I shift in my chair, cross my legs, and recall that she and Alistair often argued about that. I walked in on one row they had about two weeks ago. I caught the tail end with Alistair seething as she called him a few nasty names, all of them in Spanish. More to myself than Patricia I say, "She has a wild temper."

"And that's not all. Her staff needs more supervision to produce better information for her. Her questions in committee to those giving testimony show it. My god, they are rudimentary, if not silly."

I say nothing, but don't have to. Our eyes meet and she knows I agree with her.

"Mirinda is also a minority," Patricia elaborates.

"Soon to be a majority," I point out.

"Not soon enough for her. Plus, we concentrate on one minority advancement at a time. This streamlines the process of making democracy truly egalitarian." Patricia zeroes in on my nervousness, smiles, and says, "You must not worry about this. Just let it happen."

"I have so little free time now, to think of adding more responsibility is daunting." Inside, the little girl I mentioned who played at being President was jumping up and down yelling like a cheerleader, *Yeah, let's go, come on, let's go!*

"A common complaint." Patricia lifts a brow. "Of women."

"And I lack a loving wife to help me."

My hostess's sculpted lips curve up in delight. "You don't need one, my dear. You have a housekeeper. Albeit part time. Make her full-time."

Hunh. Like Mr. Jones, Patricia knows an awful lot about me that my bios never list.

"You have other assets, too—a daughter who adores you."

That is public knowledge and I smile.

"A chimp named Abe who hangs on your every word."

I grin.

"A mother who would kill for you."

Ain't that the truth.

"A wit, a whiskey voice, a body, a brain. With all of us behind you, you can learn, soar, stumble, we won't let you fall."

This conversation is bringing me so much more than I

bargained for that my heart is racing and my mind is doing the Mexican hat dance. Hanging on to my common sense by a thin thread, I arrive at the other subject of my visit. "Is someone supporting me now?"

She dons a face of innocence that a child could envy. "What do you mean?"

"Have you all gotten your heads together and decided that I need assistance now with this murder investigation?"

"I think we should probably leave the investigation to the police, don't you?"

"I do." I am lying through my eyeteeth. "But I refer to private assistance."

"Interesting. Such as?"

"Such as . . . a man."

Her perfectly plucked brows rise in merriment, but I see she is weighing the prospect of danger in this topic. "Really. Has someone sent you a man, my dear?"

I cannot help but shake my head and suppress a grin. "Patricia. Help me. Level with me."

She asks for details.

I give her the rundown on his arrival over my garden wall, his suit, his gun, his James Bond rhetoric, and his Michael Corleone mind. I leave out last night's chase and his rescue, but add how he followed me home from the Harlans' and my new phone. She's loving the hell out of this story, and I have the distinct impression I am providing better entertainment than the five newspapers she reputedly reads each morning.

At my conclusion, she assures me that "such services do exist." She does not say, *But you knew that before you came here*—however, that's her implication.

"He shows up in odd places at odd times. It's unnerving to be . . ." I search for a word to replace *stalked,* but go for, "shadowed."

"And you worry that he is employed by some firm that does not have your best interests at heart." She puts a finger across her lips and examines my face for a very long minute. "Has he hurt you?"

I shake my head.

"Threatened you?"

No.

"Offered you what, precisely?"

"His protection. His detective skills."

"And what is your assessment of the quality of those?"

I inhale. "So far, so good."

"You need to test them."

I agree. "He has done his homework on me, and brought me information that was unique. I did check it with other sources and it seems to be accurate. But I worry, if I use him and he comes from a source that I cannot or should not be aligned with, and word gets out . . . then I won't have my House seat"—I wave a hand—"let alone anything else."

Patricia is not worried one iota. "Always let a man work for you," she advises, and I think she must be smokin' ganja, she's so nonchalant. "Makes them bristle with testosterone." She wiggles her shoulders a bit and she's got me laughing with her.

But then I stop and add, "There is more that concerns me, Patricia. He works, he says, for an entity—one he claims is privately owned. He says he is not privy to who hired the service. Is that possible?"

"Possible, yes. Probable?" She tilts her head. "It is rather odd."

"I asked Tommy Iverson if he hired him." I shake my head, bite my lower lip. "He takes no responsibility." I rivet her with my eyes, nail her with my need to learn the truth. "Do you know if he would, if he *did* do this?"

She holds my gaze. "He could. I don't understand why he wouldn't confirm it if it were so. I mean, what would be the harm?" Her brows draw together. "Such services are often used by many of us. I understand the importance of confidentiality, but most contracts such as this are drawn by obvious clients for obvious reasons."

"I worry about the reasons for this one. Politics I understand. Skulduggery I can learn to understand. But murder—and anything shady connected to it—gives me the willies."

She purses her lips in thought. The chill creeps back into my bones, and my heart begins to ice over as she opens her mouth and says, "We've looked at you too long and hard, Carly, to let anything happen to you now. We've vetted you every which way from the Rockin' O to Q Street. Use this man, talk to him, share what you can, learn what he has to offer."

I wait. This is more information than I came for—and I am honored and scared out of my boots.

Patricia Tipton gives me what she can. "Let me make a few inquiries."

I climb in my car and don my sunglasses. Before visiting Patricia, I traded in my Taurus this morning for a Ford Escape. It's not an Excursion, but it is slightly larger and makes me feel safer. In Texas, bigger is better. Always.

Grateful I see no one—not even Jones—following me on this bright sunny Sunday, I turn over the ignition and pull out of my parking space in front of Patricia's home, taking O Street at a crawl. Thrilled I made the reservation to go riding, I am wound tighter than a two-bit watch.

I hit Wisconsin and drift north with traffic. When I get to Q Street, though, I take one look down the lane, see a cluster of people near my sidewalk, and say, "Forget it, folks. She's not in yet." When the light changes, I gun the engine through the break in traffic and head for the stables out in Darnestown, where I often ride a horse named Jack.

Holding my thinking until I have the wind in my face, I punch on the radio and hit the tuner till I get a country and western station I can kick back with. Strains of "All My Ex's Live in Texas" fill the air and I begin doing my rendition stopped at a red light. I'm having as good a time as a suspect in a murder case can, charmed by the lyrics, cultivating any serenity possible, knowing what I know. I check in the rearview mirror for signs of lunacy in my eyes. That's when I see him.

Jones. In a black Hummer adorned with all the bells and whistles.

What does he have, a change of car for every occasion? And does he have answers to last night's mysteries already?

I groan. Not sure I'm capable of processing yet more pieces of puzzles.

At a red light, I stare back at him. He's brooding, chewing on a toothpick. Could he know what Patricia Tipton just shared with me? That I—little ol' Ms. Wagner here—have a shot at bigger and better things?

Bah. Humbug. He couldn't know that. Hell, until a few minutes ago, I hadn't even known that.

Alistair had never hinted at it.

William Preston Scott never had, either.

Why not?

Were they saving it for some special occasion? Ah, pardon me, Carly, but we have had a party meeting and you have been chosen to be the one we advance. Don't mind, do you? Care to give us your thanks, would you? Good, good.

Damn self-congratulatory, back-slapping bastards.

Why shouldn't I know that I'm the subject of their discussions?

Why shouldn't you expect that you would be, Carly, girl? Sooner or later, this had to come. You've been in office long enough for them to notice you are no maverick policymaker. No chick with baggage.

The word makes me think of Mirinda again, her baggage— and my need to learn just how deep her rifts with Alistair ran.

Half an hour later, I'm feeling pretty chipper as I pull into the gravel drive and stop my rental by the clubhouse. I open my door and climb out.

Jones pretends to get something from his back seat. He's dressed in . . . what else? . . . black. Today it's a long-sleeved polo and Dockers. I glance around, find no one anywhere around. I greet him with a nod. "Lovely day."

"We need to talk."

"Shoot."

Behind dark shades, his electric eyes sear mine. "Not here."

"Do you have answers for me?"

"Not the ones we expected."

Well, why should I think a murder investigation would be simple? Or so intrusive to every corner of my life? "How long will this take?"

He inclines his head toward our very public surroundings. "I am not concerned about length but quality."

Just like a man to downplay length. I'm smirking, but for the life of me, I am too consumed by other issues to go for the joke. "Okay. Let's get you a horse." I take a step, then turn back, eyeing his spotless vehicle. "You do ride, I reckon?"

"Yes, ma'am. Horses, Harleys, Humvees."

"I get it. Let's roll, Jones. One condition."

"Name it."

"Take those damn glasses off so I can see the whites of your eyes when you talk to me."

He peels them off his all-too-handsome face.

"Good. And no talking for at least the first thirty minutes on the trail."

"Yes, ma'am. But—"

"*What?*" I halt, pissed he has already objected to some fool thing.

He lifts those *GQ* lips in a crooked smile that could melt polar ice caps. "That's two requests."

"Live with it." I march off.

eleven

"Been a while since you've been in a saddle?" I ask Jones after we've galloped more than two miles and come to a wooded path where I've taken pity on him and slowed us to a walk.

Jones's eyes flare at my pointedness. "Yes, ma'am. But it's good for a man to get back in the habit."

I pull the reins and direct my stallion to lumber over to his favorite shady spot by a stream. "Last night you had a Volvo. Today it's a Hummer. What else have you got?"

"Whatever I need."

Surprised that I predicted this answer, I ask, "Why did you choose a Volvo last night?"

"Wanted to blend in with the Virginia countryside look."

I snort. "Why not a Mercedes, then?"

He shakes his head and climbs down from his mare. "Too conspicuous."

"Didn't know you were going to need lots of horsepower, did you?" I chide, recalling my nemesis on the parkway.

"Oh, you have no idea what I've put under that Volvo's hood."

Yet, the fact that today he's driving a Hummer with—what?—at least fifteen hundred pounds more heft to it makes me feel safer. I swing my leg over Jack's rump and jump down. "And

I suppose black is not only the color of choice for cars but clothes, as well."

"For cars, it's camouflage. For clothes, it eliminates fashion faux pas."

"Among other things," I comment.

"Yeah, well, better get used to it, because after last night's track meet, I'm closing the surveillance distance."

Works for me. But I don't say that. Wouldn't want him to get too cocky that I'm going to keep him on. Strays bear many resemblances to in-laws: They're fun at the start, but after two days, they've overstayed their welcome.

So I keep my mouth suitably shut as we tether both horses to a small bush and let them drink. A few birds are chirping, adding tones to the crisp rippling of the stream over rocks.

Finally, he breaks the silence that I am loath to end. "Do you want to talk about your visit with the famous Mrs. Tipton?"

I jam my hands in my jeans pockets and stroll along the bank. "She was helpful. Enlightening."

He narrows his gaze into the distance and wiggles his nose. "She tell you anything enlightening about me?"

"No." I detect in his manner that he has no knowledge of a tie to her, so I feel relieved.

"She know anything about you talking with Iverson about me?"

I nod. "I told her I asked him."

"How about Sally Sonderberg?"

"No. Actually, we talked about a lot of women, but Sally was not among them." I halt and face him. "Why?"

His face goes taut with apprehension.

I'm not gonna like this. In fact, I'm gonna hate it. "Tell me."

"Sally Sonderberg is missing."

"Since when?" I ask, but I have a sneaky suspicion that I know.

"She hasn't been home since Friday morning."

"Oh, god." I rub the back of my neck.

"Her husband is frantic."

"Has he called the police to report it?"

"About one o'clock."

"And you heard it how?"

"As an all-points. Police band."

"I see. Bad for her image if he's gone ahead and done this and she isn't really missing. What if . . . ?" She was very upset Friday afternoon when we talked. Had that sparked some need for solitude? Had I said something that pushed her to this? "What if she just decided she needed to go away somewhere to think for a while or . . . ?"

"Her husband doesn't think so. He's worried."

I sink down to sit on a boulder. The heat warms my fanny but not my heart. "She's been working very hard. And she has young children—and her husband has conflicts with his law partners. Money's an issue. She could've gone to a hotel for a weekend away." But if that were so, wouldn't she have told her husband, not left him hanging?

Jones obviously follows the same logic, because he's silent. Instead, he picks up a handful of pebbles and starts throwing them in the stream. After a few of those, he says, "Ma'am, there's more you need to know."

As my eyes meet his, my guilt gives way to an uglier fear for what he is about to tell me. "What?"

"The Sonderbergs own a black Excursion."

My eyes drift closed. "And?"

"It's gone, too."

I spot Jordan from far down the gangway of the airline. Youth is a wonderful commodity. She's waving to me, chipper as only a twelve-year-old can be after an eighteen-hour flight. Me, I'd look like I'd been hit by a cyclone. I know, because I've done a couple of congressional fact-finding trips and I always need a few days afterward to recuperate from jet lag and jammed eighteen-hour schedules.

"Mom." She hugs me, and I hang on a bit longer than she, finally pulling back and examining her doe-brown eyes and her clear porcelain complexion.

I tuck her long mahogany curls behind her ears and cup her cheeks. "You look terrific. You slept, I guess?"

"Yep. No one next to me from Narita to Houston, so I lived like a princess." She fixes her backpack over one arm. "I am dying for a real greasy American burger, though. Think we can?"

"Hey, the world is yours, sugar." I grin and loop my arm around her waist. At twelve, she is almost as tall as I am—and actually looks a lot like I did at her age, only I had a mop head of Irish red corkscrews and boobs. "Pick whatever you want. We'll go eat while they unload the luggage."

We head for a restaurant, where she orders the 'shroom burger with everything and I opt for the crab cake dinner. We eat, she recounting the sights and sounds and delicacies of Japan while I try to avoid checking too often on Jones, sitting in a booth across the room, nursing a Coke and a sandwich.

"I loved the soba. Ever had soba?"

"No, what is that?"

"Noodles. And guess what, you slurp them. It's am-a-zing! It's okay to make noise when you snorkel them up!" She goes on like that, with stories of sushi and sukiyaki with raw egg and a fish that can kill you if the chef doesn't fillet it the right way.

And her cell phone does the electronic version of some rapper song. She digs it out of her backpack and flips it open. "Yeah? Heyyyy. Right." Her eyes find mine. "Dunno. Haven't talked about it yet. I know I said that in Houston, but lemme ask and call you back, okay? The service was wicked, I bet. You're all right, though, yeah? Yeah. Me, too. Later." She flips it closed, and picks up a French fry. "That was Zack."

I nod, knowing I should've bet the ranch on it. "And?"

"I called him when I landed in Houston and we talked."

I lean back. "How is he?"

"Okay." She nibbles at the fry and watches me. "I need to go see him."

"I know. Soon, right?"

"Tonight?"

This I figured, too. I nod. "As long as his aunt will let us come."

"Zack asked already. She's good with it." Her eyes widen. "And you are?"

"You bet." The timing for this would always be crap. But the two of us had to get through it and the sooner, the better. "Shall we drop over on the way home?" Alistair and Zack's home was in Potomac, off River Road and a straight shot off the Beltway north—and an easy shot back to Georgetown. We might get home by ten. "No time like the present."

"God, Mom, thanks. I told Zack you wouldn't be evil about this. I know you found his dad in your office and all, but"—her eyes twitch—"you didn't kill him."

"No, Jordan. I did not kill him." I try to smile, but my heart's definitely sore over all this sadness and death. "Finish up and let's get your suitcase and go see him."

Zack, unlike my daughter, looks like hell. Though one day he will become the spitting image of his dad with ladykiller looks, tonight he is a gangly, disheveled twelve-year-old in mourning. So much so, he has decided to remove all the body-piercing rings, including the ear studs. That, I conclude, was to attend the funeral parlor viewing earlier this evening.

A stark study of grief, he's got hollowed-out eyes, dark circles, and unruly inky hair that definitely needs a trim. With a wan smile for me and a hug for Jordan, he greets us at the front door and swings it wide for us to come in.

The foyer of Alistair's mansion is a black and white Italian marbled affair that he had owned since before I'd come to town. Back in the day, probably in the eighties when he first bought it, the price tag must have been dirt cheap. Today, you couldn't touch a Potomac River Road estate of this grandeur for less than four or five million. What astonished me about the news that Alistair had money problems was the very fact that he could have sold this puppy in a heartbeat and made out like a bandit. I mean, what did a widower and his only child need with three acres of prime real estate in horse country of the nation's capital?

"Come on in." Zack beckons us. "Meet my aunt."

Zack's aunt, Alistair's sister, appears to be a sweet little lady of modest dress, much older than her brother. At seventy or so, Sarah Mae—as she urges me to call her—resembles Alistair in an eerie way that makes me uneasy in my easy chair.

"We need to talk, Mom," Jordan says to me, asking with her eyes if it's all right for them to leave.

I look at Sarah Mae. "I think that's okay, if it is with you, Sarah Mae."

"Yes, run along. That's fine. I want to talk to your mother anyway."

Is that right. Of all the conversations I have sought out in the last few days, this is not one on my list.

Her demeanor changes as soon as the two children close the double doors on us. Sarah Mae suddenly grows ten feet taller and fills with the authority of an Amazon warrior woman on a mission. I know this look. Sadie acquires it often. I am told I can, too.

"Congresswoman Wagner—" she begins and I put up a hand to have her call me Carly. "Carly. I will not beat around the bush. The detective has been here a couple of times and talked to me and I do know that, according to what he said, you are not a person I should be talking to. But I am talking to you. I will. I have talked with Zack and he has told me he doesn't believe you could have harmed his father. I trust that boy's judgment. Even if Detective Brown does not."

That gives me a poke up the ol' keester, I tell ya, and I sit up straighter. "Thank you, Sarah Mae. Zack's assessment is sound.

I would never have hurt his father. I wish we could find the culprit who did, but my hands are tied, you see."

"Oh, I do. And I am not interested in talking about Alistair's murder. Whoever did it, they'll find him. I want to talk to you about something else." She folds her hands in her ample lap. "Now, I want you to know that I have never lived in Washington, Carly. Only visited. Even after Molly died and Alistair said he would never remarry. No, siree, I told him I would not live here, much as I love Zachary. But I do not care for Washington. I always told Alistair that. Always. He was a good congressman, did his job well, and we were always very proud of him. Always." She's nodding. "But I am here to tell you that I am not proud of what he became."

Stunned at her frankness, I rush to uphold Alistair's reputation without being dishonest. "He was a good leader in the House, Sarah Mae. He was—"

"I know, I know." She puts up a finger to wave it back and forth. "But he was not doing what he should have been—and doing what he should not have been."

Does she really want to go there with this subject, with me? Something's stuck in her craw and whatever it is, it really got her ticker going before I got here, that's what I bet. So I try to take the power out of her head of steam and say, "As a man of influence here, he may have appeared to do things that—"

She glares at me. "Carly, do you know that he was in debt?"

I stumble to form a truthful response. "Not in debt, no."

"Alistair's attorney was here this morning with the will. Everything goes to Zachary. But let me tell you, it is a worthless piece of paper."

"Sarah Mae, this is really none of my business."

"I gather you care for Zachary."

"Yes, I do. I've known him most of his life and he and Jordan are—"

"There is nothing for this young man, his only child, to go to college on. Nothing!"

I am speechless.

"Now, I ask you, how can a man who proposes to save the people in his district—and the people of this country—not have provided a damn red cent for his sweet son to go to school on?"

"Well, Sarah Mae, I am certain that there must be something. Life insurance and—"

"Some. His government insurance. But it is not enough for me to pay off the credit card bills, let alone the mortgage on this mammoth big place."

My mouth must be hanging open.

"Yes," she confirms. "Disgraceful, isn't it?"

"But . . . but Alistair's been in this house for more than twenty years, and he must have paid off—"

"No, he didn't," she sputters. "He kept taking second mortgages and refinancing for larger sums. And now he has left me with this enormous house to sell and that poor child to come to live with me. And what do I have? I'm a widow, Carly. I am seventy-four years old, with high blood pressure and diabetes, and I live on a fixed income. Where am I going to get the wherewithal to raise this young man and do right by him, I ask you?"

Appalled that this is true of Alistair, who dearly loved his only child, I'm more frightened by the way Sarah Mae's face is now beet red. "You know, Sarah Mae, you're looking a little flushed. Are you . . ." In need of your medication? "Do you want a drink or . . ." Where the hell is the housekeeper or the governess—what was her name? Barbara! Barbara, Barbara, wherefore art thou? "Let's get Barbara to bring you—"

"No, I gave her the evening off. She's an idiot, if there ever was one. Be glad when she packs her bags. And don't you worry about me, I'm clear as a bell, Carly. Clear as a bell."

Good. I think.

"I want to know from you how someone can get into this kind of a scrape, being a congressman for all these years."

I lick my lips. "Truly, Sarah Mae, I have no knowledge of Alistair's finances."

"How do you do it?"

"Well, I . . . just pay my bills."

"Where's your house?"

"Georgetown."

She knits her brows. "That's where John and Jackie Kennedy lived. Hoity-toity, isn't it?"

"Well, yes, you could say so."

She eyes me skeptically. "How do you afford it?"

"I come from a long line of frugal people. In Texas, for a hundred-and-fifty-odd years, we farmed rocks and dust for a living. When we made any money at all, we learned to pay the creditors, buy more land and more cattle, and just keep on going back to the savings bank with our pennies."

She's not real satisfied with that.

So I elaborate. "I was a barrel-racing champion when I was a teenager. I won so many purses that it mounted up. My mother insisted I put it in the bank and I used some of it to pay for my freshman year of college."

"Didn't you finish school?"

"Oh, I did. I did. But my freshman year, I competed in the Miss Texas Pageant and won. That sum equaled enough for my next three years and then some. When I finaled in the Miss America contest, I earned even more . . . and I put it in the bank and later into the stock market. Plus, too, my first husband was a generous man and left me well set when he died." Lord, Sarah Mae now knows as much about my finances as Patricia Tipton and the party leaders. Nothing in this town is sacred.

That takes some of the wind out of her sails. She looks shrunken and tired. "Do you know anyone named James Hollister?"

D.C. is filled with so many people whose names you must remember at a moment's notice. This one draws a blank. "No."

"Never heard of him?"

I shake my head. "No." Do I dare ask why?

"Alistair would write checks every month to this person.

From a separate checking account. In a Montana bank. I found the checkbook and the stubs in his desk drawer in his office across the hall there this afternoon. In a locked drawer, I should say. I found a file filled with the canceled checks, too. Each one is for thousands of dollars. One thousand. Three. Four. Never the same amounts. Always an even thousand, no odd dollars or cents. The account seems to be solely for the purpose of writing checks to this Hollister. There are no others."

The hair on my arms is standing up and my brain is doing somersaults to keep up with the logic here, if indeed there is any. "I don't understand why you are telling me this, Sarah Mae. Or why you would ask me."

She cocks her head. "No?"

"No."

"Zachary thought you would know."

Bewildered, I turn my head toward the door where he disappeared with my daughter. I look at his aunt again. "Did he say why?"

"No."

"Do you mind if I ask him?"

Zachary refuses to discuss this James Hollister in front of his aunt. His shakes his head once more and looks at the carpet. "No, ma'am. I'll talk to Ms. Wagner about this."

He's standing in the living room, holding hands with Jordan. The sight of them like that touches me in a way that is endearing and startling. Are they more than friends? Do they do more than hold hands? Or is this merely the mutual bonding of children nowadays?

Exasperated, Sarah Mae struggles up from her chair. "I'll leave you, then. You tell her everything, now, you hear, Zachary? She can't help you if you hold back, my dear."

"Yes, ma'am," he whispers, and watches her go, while he chews on his lower lip.

"Why don't you two sit down while we talk?" I suggest, to put him more at ease. "Unless you want Jordan to leave, Zack." "No!" He's alarmed. "No, I mean—can she stay? I want her to."

"All right." Whatever this is, I gather Jordan knows some, maybe all, of Zack's story. So I just pray I have the courage to hear it—or that I'm being overly dramatic about nothing at all.

The two of them sit side by side on the sofa, their two hands so tightly bound that I can see the whites of their knuckles. I decide to lead the way because children who are scared are tender creatures, best strengthened by gentle direction.

I lean forward and give Zack a small smile. "Zack, your aunt told me the name of a man whom you told her I might know."

He nods and looks at me under thick black lashes. "Yes, ma'am." He fiddles with the crease in his trousers. "James Hollister. Aunt Sarah found checks in Dad's office today and they were all to this guy."

"Zack. Look at me. I don't know who he is."

"No?" He looks crestfallen and confused. He licks his lips, moves his shoulders, agitated. "But you gotta."

I try to be kind, diplomatic. "Honest, Zack, if I knew who this was, I'd tell you. I want to ease your mind, sweetie, and—"

Zack springs up from the sofa and walks around it. "He called here. A lot. Dad would take the calls. Right away. All the time. Sometimes, after this guy would call, he and Dad would meet at night. Dad would go out. He'd say it was business, he had to go, you know the drill. And off he'd go. Zoom. No matter what I had going on, Scouts or basketball practice."

"And why would you think I would know who Hollister was?"

"Because one night last week, Hollister called and I heard them talking, laughing. Dad always took the calls in his office, but this one time, he didn't know I'd come in from practice and he had left the door open. And they were talking about you."

"Me?"

"Yeah. How they would like to get you in on their deal."

I sit back, stumped. Hands on the armrests, I gaze at this boy. "Any idea what kind of deal this was?"

Now he looks sheepish. "Maybe."

"Why maybe?" I press.

He's not real happy about having to spill the beans here. I'm patient and quiet.

Jordan smacks her hands on her knees and demands, "Zack, tell her. You've got to."

"I followed him that night."

This is not what I expected as an explanation, but I'd take the circuitous route Zack wanted if it landed us at our destination. "How?"

"On my bike. I always figured he didn't go far. He couldn't, because he'd be back in an hour or so. That night, he didn't know I was in, so he couldn't know I'd been out, following him."

"And where did he go, Zack?"

"Up River Road, past Travilah. To this road—dirt, really, that goes down to the river. It was . . . um . . . very dark and I had to turn off my headlight or they would've seen me. And when I saw how many there were, I just got so scared, I turned around and went back."

And I was scared, too. For what he'd seen. And not. What Jordan knew about this. And what none of us really knew about it.

"What did you see, Zack?"

"Lots of cars parked off the road. Lights out. Some with the doors open. Others with them closed and then one or two people got out and left the doors open. A few people, maybe five or six standing around, smoking cigarettes and weed. Maybe doin' other stuff."

What was this? A meeting. A secret meeting? A group of druggies? Sounded like one of those old hush-hush societies like the Ku Klux Klan—and I certainly knew Alistair's view on civil rights would never let him join an organization like that. But there were other nut-jobs out there in this complicated world. None of them, however, did I want any part of, let alone to be included in their "deal."

"I need to know more, Zack. Your father went . . . drove into this group of cars?"

Zack nods.

"And he met this James Hollister?"

"Well, I guess so, I mean that's what it sounded like they were planning."

"But you never saw him?"

"Well, I don't know. I saw a lot of men. But I only knew my dad."

"And what did he do?"

"Yeah, tell her, Zack," Jordan urges, like she's a cheerleader at a game. "Just do it."

"Got out of his car and climbed into the back seat of one that had its back door open."

Jesus! What the hell was Alistair doing? Giving information to someone he had to meet on a dirt road in the suburbs? That smacked of—good god—party disloyalty. Worse, it could be international. Espionage, like the Navy mole in the Pentagon during the nineties who had fed top-secret intel to the Russians—and planted his documents beneath a telephone post on Darnestown Road.

I clutch my arms, a bad case of the shivers forcing me to get a grip.

Alistair would not betray his country. That was not who he was, at core. No, logic said—my instinctive knowledge of him said—that, clearly, Alistair wasn't just giving something, he was *paying* for something as well. Something this Hollister provided.

I find my voice. "And how long did he stay there?"

"I dunno. That's when I got really freaked, you know? So I just sneaked out of there and got back to River Road and pedaled home like a son of a bitch!"

Jordan and I give him a quick evil eye for the curse words, but then we're all three sitting there, glum and clueless. That's when I ask him, "How much of this did you tell to Detective Brown?"

"Nothing."

My gut says, *Terrific.* My mind says, *Be careful.* "Why not?"

Zack shrugs. "I was sad when he first came and talked to me. I didn't think about any of this stuff. Not at first."

"And when you did?" I egg him on.

He fixes me with a flat stare of truth. "I didn't want to get my dad in trouble."

I nod, a small smile of compassion for a child afraid and protective of his father. "I understand." *Good for you,* I want to add, but don't, lest this conversation sometime, somewhere wind up recounted by Zack to the detective both of us wished we'd never met. I inhale, searching for a center of peace in the eye of this conflict raging inside me, but like an alcoholic who tells himself he'll have just one more drink and then he'll quit, I succumb and ask, "Could you find this place again?"

"Sure. I . . . I think so."

"Mom." Jordan is outraged. "You're not gonna go there?"

"No, course not, sugar." But if I want to learn who James Hollister is—or what vice he's into—there are only a few ways. And asking people only invites more prevarication than I have time or patience for. "But I need to be able to find this Hollister, don't I, Zack, to see why your father was paying him so much money? And we don't want the police to know because that might be messy." Then Alistair's reputation is sullied even more than it already is. Plus, I have to know why in the world Alistair thought I was a good candidate for this "deal," don't I?

"I could show you now, if you want."

Zack's invitation cuts my reverie. "Now? But . . ." I'm thinking about this place, whatever it is, weighing the dangers, carrying two children in a car I don't own, with a bodyguard of dubious origin behind me. "Not a good idea."

"We could, it'd be safe," he offers.

"How do you know?"

"Dad only went out to meet Hollister on Tuesdays and Wednesdays. It's Sunday night."

Still and all, meetings might happen on other nights as well, not necessarily those that Alistair attended. I sit there, wooden. Churning information, weighing odds. Feeling the clock running down on my ability to find Alistair's killer.

I rise. "Show me. Jordan, you stay here."

She jumps up. "Mo-om!" It's a groan.

"Stay. Here."

She sits.

Zack gets permission and a jacket, and within minutes we are in the car, headed north on River. Behind us, at a discreet distance, is Jones.

I drive, cognizant of my toy gun and cell phone, courtesy of the man behind me who is, I am certain, wondering where in tarnation we're headed. Why, depending on what we find here, I might never explain to him.

Zack and I take the winding lane at a reasonable forty miles per hour while my mind and heart are filled with sad trepidation that whatever Alistair was doing may have depleted his bank account and driven him to bankruptcy.

The question remaining is, what was Alistair buying with his money and his soul?

twelve

Zack points me left off River onto a lane that is dirt. A few small houses dot the terrain. A small farm, too, sits off to the right.

"They raise llamas," Zack tells me, apropos of nothing because he's so spooked.

We're bumping over rocks.

"Turn right in here," he says suddenly, and I lean forward because I can't see for the overgrowth. "No. There." He points, and I see the path he wants me to take. We scrape by the tree limbs, with me grimacing. If the Taurus had alignment damage, this Escape is going to need a paint job. This rental company will never let me take a vehicle of theirs again. I'm smirking with sadistic satisfaction at this prospect when a clearing opens up.

Nothing is there. No cars. No lights. No people. Nothing.

Just the sound of the Potomac, rushing southward on our left.

"What is this?" I ask him, unaware I'm speaking aloud.

"The towpath is just down that way. One of the old locks is there, too."

"This is the C&O Canal land?"

Zack bobs his head. "I ride my bike up here all the time. But in the daytime, you know. The towpath down there is really good."

The Chesapeake and Ohio Canal had been dug back in the

1800s to haul goods and travelers by horse-drawn barge upriver against the current, and downriver safely during floods. In service until the early twentieth century, the canal today is managed by the National Park Service. Hundreds of tourists each year take barge trips up the canal to listen to park rangers recount the history of this marvel of early American commerce. Others stroll along the canal or bike along it. Zack had found delight here.

And anguish.

"Do you want to get out?" he asks me, because I guess I seem stuck here.

I look around. If Jones has followed me in off River Road, he has either turned off his lights or stayed well back of us so Zack doesn't see him.

Emboldened by the knowledge that Jones is close, I say, "Sure. Give me my purse, will you?" He hands it over and I dig for my two presents from Jones. The gun is so small, I can smother it with my palm and surreptitiously stick it in my left jean jacket pocket. The phone resembles a thin business card holder, so I have less challenge putting it in my right. "Stay here. Lock the door behind me."

I climb out and check out the site. Nothing special about it, except that it is a clearing. A natural one, sequestered by the natural canopy of trees and brush, so lush it serves well as a rendezvous. Probably not patrolled, either, not by a Park Service whose budget has been sheared for years of funds to employ night-watch rangers.

I stroll around the clearing, then head down toward the towpath and the river. The night sounds of the forest make me flex my shoulders. But no one is around. Only falling leaves, the crunch of a small wood creature skittering away from the smell of a predator like me—and the whispers of the wind through the branches.

My vision slowly becomes accustomed to the maw of night and I feel marginally safer, though I'm foolish to trust my senses totally. I whip out Jones's sleek silver phone, flip it open, and instantly I hear him murmur, "Where are you?"

"On the towpath." I step gingerly toward the ridge, gazing across the twenty-foot expanse of river that fills the canal.

"Want to tell me why we're here?"

"Me to know. You to find out."

He curses under his breath. "You sure you have no visitors following you?"

"Just the one I'm talking to," I tell him, seeing nothing moving anywhere in the umber shades surrounding me. I stroll along the path, pushing aside vines and tree limbs.

"All right. I'll play that way. But here's one for you to consider. . . ."

"What?" Up toward my left, I spot a cabin and decide to check it out.

"My lab finished the paint analysis and model year for the Excursion. They're posting the list of all Excursion owners to my cell phone as we speak."

I step around the cabin, noting footsteps near the door. Getting a faceful of spiderweb, I claw away the strands from my eyes and mouth as I ask him, "Mmm, okay, and how many are there?" Praying for a two or three seems pretty lame, but I do it anyway.

A total of two hundred and thirty-four of them in the greater Washington metro area."

"Swell." I decide to trudge back up the hill toward the Escape and Zack. "I assume Sally Sonderberg is among them."

"Me to know. You to find out."

"Ha, ha." I'm about to emerge from the shadows into a clearing where Zack will be able to see me and I don't want him asking me who I'm talking to. But I have to figure a way to see this list. Tonight. "Fax me that list at home."

"Can't. Proprietary intel. Want no traces."

"What? How about this phone, then?" It has no face, only two little screws, undetectable as the speaker and audio, but I'm hoping it's got powers that Jones hadn't tutored me in. "Send it as e-mail."

"Incompatible."

Frustrated, I'm trying not to wake the forest creatures with my hissy fit. "I need to see that list. Now."

"In the flesh, ma'am. Only in the flesh. Just tell me where and when."

As the numbers flip to 2:49 on my bedroom clock radio, I fling back the comforter and pad the floor with my toes searching for my slippers. Sleep is an illusion when my brain wants to churn clues and possibilities and dead ends. This detective business is not as easy as it looks, especially me doing it with what feels like two hands tied behind my back.

I head for my kitchen and make myself some instant cocoa in the dim rays of the night-light. I settle into my favorite chair and acknowledge the first source of my distress.

My conscience bothers me. I can't get beyond it. For one thing, I fibbed to my daughter tonight, telling her on the way home from our visit with Zack that I needed to stop at an all-night drugstore on Wisconsin and buy aspirin for a headache, just so I could view Jones's list. After I saw it, I definitely needed more aspirin, that's for sure. Of two hundred and thirty-four Excursion owners in the four area counties and the District, the only ones that jumped out at me were Sally Sonderberg and her hubbie. Since she is missing in action, reason says I should put my money on her as my only candidate for Saturday Night Stalker.

Here tonight in my own home, I feel temporarily barricaded from her or anyone else who might try to hurt me and mine. I have my Capitol Police at the front door and on the roof. Jones, alone or in concert who knows with who, out there doing his thing.

But I'm not safe. Not from myself.

I did do something else tonight I'm proud of—but it makes me ashamed of myself in other ways. When I dropped Zack off at home, I advised him and his aunt to volunteer everything they know to Detective Brown. Neither of them was very happy about it, but they agreed that when next the detective came to call, they would reveal what they know. Zack, sweet guy that he is, loves his daddy so much he wants to look out for his reputation. But he can't hang on to that for too much longer without incurring the wrath of the law.

Yes, I hated to tell them that. No, I didn't want them to do it. I'd rather they saved themselves the painful revelations—and the notoriety that brings in its wake.

Conflicted as I am to do the same myself and tell Detective Brown everything I know, my rationale is the same as Zack's: I am protecting someone's reputation. Mine. Fear of retribution from the police for failure to cooperate weighs against fear of self-loathing for lack of integrity. My obfuscation is, at base, indefensible. A sin, as we say in the Catholic Church, of omission.

I cannot hide from the need to observe the law. Not for others. Not for myself.

"You can't outrun your conscience." I can hear my granddaddy warning my mother one night after my father went missing—while I eavesdropped from the stairs. They sat in our kitchen, big and wide with wild bobcats' and boars' heads mounted on the walls like silent sentinels to the old judge's advice. "Come clean, Sadie. Tell 'em what your marriage was like. Tell 'em the nasty stuff about Ted's affairs. *All* his affairs with gamblin' and women. Cuz if you don't, sure as shootin', lots o' other folks will—and their versions'll be none too sympathetic."

Lord knows if he suspected she'd killed my father. But ever after, they circled around each other like two one-footed dancers. For certain, whatever she told Sheriff Hernandez to get him off her back was sufficient, because the law stopped sniffin' around her as prime suspect. To his long-admiring public, my granddaddy was a happy man, too, because his sterling reputation was saved. He ran twice more for county judge before he died and won both elections by eighty-percent-plus majorities. When we buried him, half the county turned out to pay their respects to Judge "Big John" Casey.

I could hope for the same results.

If I could summon the gumption to share all I knew.

And what precisely is most of that but half conjecture, half fact? Among those of us who serve here in a town of diplomacy and politesse, fact is a movable feast and few ever feel too full when nibbling is the preferred way to dine.

But as a representative of government, just like Big John, I have an ineluctable responsibility not only to encourage others to observe the law, but a higher obligation to do it myself.

I rise from my chair and head into my little office. I turn on the desk lamp, pick up a pen and yellow legal pad, then settle into my easy chair to write. In my head, the gruff bass voice of Big John Casey is supplanted by that of some now-nameless long-forgotten investigator of the Watergate affair: What did I know and when did I know it?

The next morning, I back out of the garage by seven, my house-keeper Ming ensconced with her buckets and mops inside while Jordan continues to sleep off her trip home.

I feel like I've been hauled through a barbed-wire fence, but I've wielded a deft hand to my puffy eyes with the help of Estée Lauder and her various pals. Staying up 'til four doodling charts of clues has done nothing to brighten my tendency to dark circles—but feeling a bit more whole gives me the edge to ac-complish my mission.

Grounded, I've opted for black today, in mourning for Alistair, for what he was publicly and officially, for what he had become privately. More, I'm in mourning for Zack, too. I know what it is to question the culpability of a parent—and to never learn an-swers to your most horrific questions about them.

Zack's impending revelations have me hurrying toward accomplishing my own agenda. Because now, knowing what I do about Alistair going to clandestine meetings up River Road past Lock Number 22, I feel compelled to share with Brown some of what I know—and some of what I suspect. I won't mention Alistair's meetings. No, that would only get Zack and Sarah Mae in a passel of trouble for withholding information in a capital murder. Because if the meetings contributed to Alistair's financial problems, then according to Scott and Dez, they might contribute to someone's motivation to kill him. I will dance around that to get at the other issues biting away at me like a horde of fire ants. With little time remaining to do the right thing for Zack, his father, and me and mine, I must interview today all those folks whose names Harry gave me and learn who had the biggest motive to kill him by stabbing him. A personal and—given the intimacy of the attack on his genitals—a grizzly way to kill a man.

I pick up my regular cell phone from my passenger seat and punch in the direct-dial code for Detective Brown, facilitating my visit to him for this bright Monday morning. Wanting to make certain he is in his office when I get there—and not waste any of my very limited time—I head east across town. "Detective, good morning. Congresswoman Wagner here." I use my title whenever it buys me the respect—and the clout—I need to gain the upper hand.

"Yes, ma'am." He's curt but thick-tongued, sounding like he just rolled out of the sack. "What can I help you with?" He is surprised—and guarded.

My tactic to catch him unaware is to give him limited time to cook his suspicions to high boil. "I'd like to come visit with you about a few things. Now."

"Now?" He must be stroking his chin on that one. "All right, come on over. I'll fit you in."

How did I know?

Within fifteen minutes, I park, climb the stairs to his not-so-pretty-in-green office, and sit in the same chair I occupied a few short days ago.

"Thank you for seeing me on short notice."

He sits across from me, taking in my severe dress, my pearls, my tired face. He looks bone-tired as he clasps his hands in his lap and tilts back in his chair. "Not a problem. What is it you want to talk about?"

"Where you are with your investigation."

He cocks a brow. "We're moving along." He waits.

"You released Congressman Dunhill's body for burial, so I presume you have all the results of the autopsy."

"You'd be right about that."

Good. Because some of my conclusions are based on what you must know—and what I can only deduce might be accurate. I take a deep breath and start with my most inconsequential point. "When do you think I might have my car back?"

"Maybe tomorrow. Late."

"After the congressman's funeral, then." I nod. "Thank you. I look forward to that." *Did you find any glass?* I want to ask, but do it only with my unwavering gaze.

"Why did you change rental cars?" he asks, foiling my hope for a statement that might give me absolution from his suspicions.

I suspected that his men on my house would tell him of my trade. I tell him, god help me, part of the truth. "I hated the Taurus. Too small. Too light."

"According to the rental company, you had given it a rough ride. Shocks seemed strained. Wheel block, too. Where did you go, that you had such a problem?"

"To dinner with some friends out in the Virginia countryside. I came home along GW Parkway and didn't see the construction signs until I had to hit the brakes and wound up in the median. We Texans drive too fast. It's a hard habit to break." I sit serene.

He matches me. "My detail on your house tells me all's been quiet on your street. No one else has tried to break in."

Except for Jones. "A few reporters come and go, but many lose interest as each day passes." *Like you, I hope.*

He searches my eyes and just waits.

Okay, I came to deliver. Here goes. "Last time I was here you asked me about my lipstick. I gave you mine. I also went looking for anyone else who might wear the same color."

Now, that surprises him, and his weary eyes blink a couple of times. "You asked around?"

"Not really. This information just fell in my lap."

He frowns. "And what did you learn?"

"My receptionist Rayanne wears the same color as I do. According to what I know, she was not in the building at the time that Alistair was murdered. So she couldn't have drunk from that glass that was broken into my carpet."

Now he scowls. His chair jerks forward and he pulls open a desk drawer to reach inside and extract a notebook. Flipping it open, he grabs a pen and leans back while he takes notes.

"Now, I don't know if you've finished that analysis on that trace of lipstick. . . ." I check his attitude which borders on *none of your business.* "But so far, she's the only one I've found who likes the same brand and color I do."

Rather than wait for the tongue-lashing I figure I'm more than eligible for, I charge on. "Regarding the number of glasses in my cabinet in my inner office, I always had six. I did not drink from any of them that day, so all of them must have been there when I poured a drink for Alistair. I truly cannot recall if I locked the cabinet after he left me. If the broken glass you found in my shoe came from my office, then there should be fingerprints on the cabinet of the person who opened it. Fingerprints other than mine. If there are six glasses in my cabinet, then the glass came from some other office." I take a breath to calm my pounding heart. "Sound reasonable?"

He doesn't say yes, he doesn't say no, just looks up when he's finished jotting notes.

My eyes lock on his. Next subject. "You know Congresswoman Sally Sonderberg is missing."

"I do."

"And I know she is on your list of those who stayed late Monday night."

"Do you? Interesting. No one is supposed to be talking about this case except to me. So. Can I ask how you learned that?"

I do not move my gaze from his. "People communicate in our business. Often. About a lot of subjects."

"You to her?" Only his eyebrows rise with his question.

"Last week, yes." The less I say about Sally's conversation and mine, the better, because I can't remember it verbatim and don't want to misstate what I know. Instead of waiting for his reaction, I give him food for thought. Little bits he might not be privy to without an enormous investment of time into interrogations and digging into financial records. "She has troubles, Detective. Quite a few of them. I wonder if you learned that."

He sits forward. His chair squeaks. "No. I didn't. Was she disturbed about legislation?" he asks sarcastically.

I shake my head slowly. "She has family problems. Financial issues. Living in a pricey town with all the trappings of a high-profile job are getting to her and her husband."

"Why share this with me?"

I'm interested in saving my own hide—and self-respect—what else? "I'm concerned that she left town for a little R&R after this discussion we had. I'm worried about her. Any ideas where she may have gone?"

A ghost of a smile crosses his lips. "I should be asking you that question, since you're the one who had the conversation with her that, according to you, tripped her wire."

Getting anything out of him was like pulling taffy in a blizzard. "I have no clues where she might have gone."

"But you wanted me to know you and she had talked."

Cooperation is my name—and my game—this morning. "Yes. And what I learned about her challenges."

"Just so I have other folks to investigate besides you?"

I choose not to honor that with an answer. I inhale, gathering force. "There's more."

He falls back in his chair. "I figured."

"I was told that one of the people who met Alistair at the restaurant he dined at Monday night left after talking with him, crying." Oh, this guy is so good, he does not blink an eyelash when I say this. "She had been seeing him privately."

"Really?" Appreciation spreads across his broad features, even if it doesn't squash all his anger. "Do you have a name for this person?"

"I do." I give him Krystal Vaughn's name and the fact that according to my sources, she drove home after seeing Alistair at La Colline. "I have no idea if that is true or not, nor do I know if she is on your list of those who were in the building at the time Alistair was attacked."

Brown does not write any of this down, which tells me he already knows this. Was his source his own force's officer who is Krystal's lover? Whoever it was who told him, I am pleased because I know what he knows.

Now I go for the gold. "I've been thinking about the murder."

"Is that right."

Okay, so he's still not happy with me. But he soon will be. I purse my lips and pick an imaginary piece of lint from my skirt. "That morning when I walked into my office, I didn't see any glass, broken or otherwise. I don't recall crunching any into the carpet, either."

"Would you have, discovering a dead body like that?"

"I definitely would have, Detective. I was very lucid that morning. I usually am in the mornings. I had had a good night's sleep, short though it may have been."

He leans forward, his elbows on his thighs, and stares at me. "You're not put off by the sight of a dead man?"

"I've seen death all my life, Detective. Mostly animals. A few men and women. Accidental, on purpose, and natural. Doesn't matter how it comes, death is never pretty. Alistair's was ugly. It made me heartsick to think of it, then and now." I fold my hands in my lap and cross my legs. "Whoever cleaned up a broken glass, I think, did a good job."

He's bobbing his head, acknowledging my insight. "There were few shards left."

"So you have to ask yourself how they could have done that unless they had a vacuum—and there is none is my office— or they had some means to pick up the pieces, carefully and painstakingly, just so they wouldn't leave traces of their own blood from any cuts. My conclusion is that they had something that allowed them to do it rather quickly—and safely."

His eyes go dark. "Such as?"

"I'm just conjecturing here, but it could be any number of things, like . . . gloves. But who would think to keep gloves handy? That is, if they even knew they were going to kill some- one on the spur of the moment like that? Doesn't make sense. So, how about a handkerchief? Lots of folks—men and women— carry handkerchiefs. Or a scarf? A tie? But whatever it was had to be handy, apparent in the chaos of just having killed some- one. So whatever they used to clean up the glass had to be avail- able, don't you think?" I don't wait for an answer, but plow on. "Whatever they used had to be either on them or in my office already. Something they found easily in plain sight—and maybe in the open desk drawer. Something that wouldn't injure them when they picked up the little pieces of glass. Like . . . tweez- ers?"

He blinks, stunned. "Did you have a pair of tweezers in your desk drawer?"

"Absolutely. A girl keeps a couple of pairs in different places so she can make certain her eyebrows are always well-kept." I stare at him. "Mine were silver. Only I used them. They had, I do believe, only my fingerprints on them."

He brushes one hand across his mouth. "Keep talking."

I lick my lips. "The murderer also had to have a bag or something to carry all that glass in and get it away from the scene of the crime. Easily, of course. Now, while I sat there working Monday night, the cleaning crew came through. Ask them, if you haven't already. The maid emptied my trash and put a new liner in. Did my trash can have a liner in it that morning, Detective? I don't know. I scoured my memory and I can't recall looking at my trash can that morning. If there was no trash liner there, my thinking is, the murderer dumped the glass in the bag that was there."

Respect begins to dawn in his gaze. "Of course. And then?"

I inhale, getting bolder. "If I were he, I'd want to get it out of the building, as far away as possible. Surreptitiously. Perhaps even . . . tuck it in my briefcase."

He says, "Or your purse," and I feel we haven't gone too far from me as his star suspect . . . yet.

I mash my lips together. "I'd have to do more work there at the scene, too, before I left Alistair."

Brown's handsome face fills with more admiration, though on balance, he begrudges it to me still. "Like what?"

"I work here, so my fingerprints are on file. I know that anyone who works in Congress has been fingerprinted, their prints used for all sorts of ID and clearances. If I'm the murderer, I also know that the murder weapon is going to have my fingerprints on it."

One black brow arches up like an arrow. "Must have."

"Mmmm"—I'm savoring this discussion now—"must have." I uncross my legs and recross them, adjust my skirt to demur draping, then refold my hands. "I have got to do one of two things. Either wipe the weapon off and hope I do a thorough job when I leave, or just take it with me, too." I skewer him with my stare. "For my money, I'm gonna take it with me because I'd rather be safe than sorry."

"Unless you're not thinking straight."

"And I make a strategic mistake."

"So what will you do?" He pursues my line of thinking.

"Well, that depends on what we have as evidence." I tilt my head at him. "Are there fingerprints on my letter opener?"

He stares at me. "You tell me."

"Mine *should* be on there. Only mine. Why? Most of my mail is already opened for me by my receptionist. Only personal mail comes directly to me—but that is rare, so rare I cannot recall when I last used the thing."

"Go on."

"My other thought is that when I hold the opener to slit envelopes, I do it blade up with my right hand. If I were going to attack someone, wouldn't I instinctively grasp the opener blade down? And wouldn't my fingerprints be on the opener, in that case, in the reverse?"

He has no answer.

That's fine, because I'm not done. "There was blood on the letter opener. I've thought about this, relived that scene over and over, and I recall seeing blood on the tip only." I lock eyes with him. "Detective, I told you I have seen death in many forms. I have killed animals with a gun, and used knives to gut boar and deer and fish. I know death can come quickly or slowly as the animal bleeds out, depending on what organs the knife pierced. I don't know what organs of Alistair's were pierced, and not the rate of death, but I did see some blood on his chest and zipper and some at the base of his penis. This means to me he was still alive when he was emasculated. So logic begs me to ask the question: Why did he remain in that chair while someone did that to him?"

"You are right, ma'am," Brown concedes. "The autopsy showed that Dunhill was close to death when his penis was severed. He had suffered a massive heart attack the minute the weapon pierced his left lung."

I sit back, heartsick for Alistair's suffering. I swallow hard. "A heart attack. Poor man. I suppose I would have one, too, if some-one attacked me with a knife."

Brown does not say a word.

I lean forward, measure out my words slowly. "But it was not a knife, was it?"

This time it is a question, and he knows it. But to answer would violate his own secure method of investigation.

I venture forward in the silence. "I would say the attack was not premeditated. Killing with a knife is an intimate crime of personal rage. And whatever was available would have been the weapon of choice. Unless the murderer brought a knife with him into my office, he could not have used a knife against Alistair because I have no knife anywhere in my office—not anywhere in any of my desk drawers." We each ponder that for one heart-beat. "But I did have a letter opener. And while it might have been sharp enough to kill, it certainly was not sharp enough to emasculate. And when I saw it in Alistair's hand that next morn-ing, it didn't have a lot of blood on it—meaning not enough to do either crime. So let me tell you what was in my office, what was in my center desk drawer and what was big enough and sharp enough to accomplish both attacks on Alistair."

Only his lips move when he murmurs, "What?"

"Scissors. I ask you, Detective, have you found a pair of scis-sors in my desk drawer?"

thirteen

Jimmy Jeff Holden can't see me. I have a suspicion that statement translates to *won't see me.*

Aaron has just delivered that not-so-good news to me as he hovers over my desk. "I told his receptionist we would consider it a very special courtesy to you, because you are so overwhelmed with this investigation." He throws open his arms, palms up in surrender. "No admittance."

"All right, we'll just live with it," I tell him. "For now."

My first reaction is to have Aaron substitute a visit with Jimmy Jeff for one with Mirinda.

The day is still young, not even ten yet. And no return call from Detective Brown, who promised to let me know if he wanted to see me again today. I had left him with a complete list of every item that had been in my center desk drawer, as well as the side drawers. That included a good pair of tweezers and a hefty pair of scissors. He hadn't been so forthcoming as to reveal if both items were in his possession, but that didn't matter to me as much as my contribution to his wealth of knowledge. Why hadn't he asked me before now for this info, I had asked him. Ah. He hadn't proceeded that far, he'd replied.

So, definitely timing seemed to be everything . . . except among forensics teams, where time stood still instead.

Aaron has paused at my door, examining me. "Is there something else you'd like me to do?"

Should I have him request a meeting with Mirinda? I let that idea simmer a bit. But, as Jones would say, my Second Mind isn't quite ready for that encounter. My rational mind says the reason is I don't want to tangle with her, like I did the other day on the floor. She wears war paint more often than not, and I don't care for myself too much after I've wrestled with someone like that. No, sir. In those encounters, my Second Mind gives way to my Second Nature, which is to fight fire with fire. But I know I will see her late this afternoon at a reception sponsored by Holly Ireland's group, Senior Citizens United and AARP, so I go with that as a more natural way to connect with her to ask probing questions.

"No, thank you, Aaron."

He leaves me and I can tell by his slack shoulders he feels like he's failed me with Jimmy Jeff Holden. Unusual for him to be so downhearted, but hey, more people than I have taken a beating during this past week. He closes my office door behind him and I sit there a moment, then dig for my cell phone and call home.

Jordan answers. "Oh, hi, Mom. What's up?"

I can hear Ming running the vacuum in the background as I ask, "You're up?"

"Yep. Having some eggs. Ming made 'em for me."

"I wanted to tell you that I'll try to leave here around three so that you and I can go to the viewing at the funeral home at five. Be ready. Wear something dark, maybe your navy suit you got for Easter."

"Euuw. I hate that."

"Well, you don't have anything black."

"Yeah. Who's fault is that?"

Not liking her tone, I don't like her recrimination, either. Both are new traits. Thanks, Len, for inspiring—or maybe even teaching—such things. "Just wear your suit and we'll talk about the lack of black at a later time. Let me talk to Ming, please."

She doesn't say yes or no or sure, but passes the phone over. I'm nagged by this new irritability in her and hope it does not endure.

"Fine, fine." Ming always begins in Mandarin when she speaks, then quickly converts. "Tai-tai Wagna. You want me, miss?" Ming came from Beijing two years ago to study American history at George Washington University. She came toting her very good knowledge of English, Chinese singsong tones and all.

"Ming, I want to talk to you soon in person. I meant to ask you this morning if you could stay until I get home today. Can you?"

"Hun hao, good, yes, miss. I brought books today. Not much clean. House not dirty today."

"Okay." I have to broach the subject of her working for me full-time, don't I? I mean, if I am being taken seriously for advancement—and my time will be more precious—I need to explore if I can hire Ming for more hours, à la Patricia Tipton's suggestion. "Thank you, Ming. See you later."

We say goodbye and I sit there a second before reaching in my briefcase for the teensy-weensy cell phone to Jones. I flip it open and within the space of a heartbeat, he answers.

I ask, "Any luck on any of the employers or home addresses to go with that list of Excursion owners?"

"Yep. Got 'em about an hour ago."

"Anything interesting?"

"A few."

I sit up straighter in my chair. "Like what?"

"One is a brand-new reporter for CBS news."

That makes my flesh crawl. "Look into that one, although I have no idea why he would want to drive me off the road. Are there any others?"

"Two live on Capitol Hill. One's the owner of a gourmet shop in Union Station. The other works for Senator Sam Lyman of Mississippi. He's Lyman's press secretary."

That strikes me cold.

"Any reason why Lyman would be unfriendly to you?" Jones asks.

"None." I'd gotten to know Lyman well only recently as the two of us chaired a party committee to develop a program to increase voter registration among poorer citizens in the Deep South.

"Think. Be sure. Because if you're not—"

"Lyman is a friend of mine." And he is a man who wants to be a better friend of mine, personally. I know it, approve of it, reciprocate the feeling if only I had more time—or more of an itch to be romantically involved. Yes, I like Lyman's politics, his style, his divorced marital status—and his reputation, public and private. But maybe I am too quick to defend him—and for little reason other than I had spent forty minutes with him one-on-one and found he tripped my hormone meter.

"Ma'am, that may be true," Jones is telling me, "but I'm reluctant to pass on an investigation into Lyman's aide because of your approval of his boss."

"I hear you. Look at him—and Lyman, too, if it seems warranted." Looking at Lyman was not hard to do. For his constituents and for me. His looks went toward a fortyish Robert Redford, a WASPish contrast to the muscular dark brew of Eur-Asian-African that Jones personified. "We want to be safe, not sorry."

I note I just used the term "we."

Unhappy with myself for accepting Jones to the extent I have, I concede I'm more unhappy about Sam Lyman's press aide showing up on this list. The fact that a member of his staff owns an Excursion kills a lot of my burgeoning enthusiasm for him. Could Sam—would Sam—be involved with this murder? There'd been no hint he or any of his staff had contact with Alistair on a regular basis, let alone last Monday. More inconceivable would be the thought that Sam would send his press aide to do me in on Saturday night.

Logic, Carly, please, logic. Clearly, I do not know everything about everyone who works in Washington. And if I am to do myself any good in this investigation as well as save my own sanity, instead of casting my net wider, I need to be focusing on working with what I know and who I know had a connection to Alistair.

I drop my head in my hand. "All right. Let me know if you find any correlation among any of these people with Alistair."

"Will do."

I slowly fold the phone closed in my hand when Aaron knocks once and enters. He's flushed, but he draws up short, spotting the phone still in my palm. I stare at him, displeased he has entered so summarily to find me clutching it. But he is unperturbed and asks what it is. "A private phone," I say.

His brow wrinkles. "New," he states, but it's a question, too.

Without an explanation I decide he should never have, I drop it in my briefcase. "What did you want?"

"A new development. Over in Rayburn." His expression broadens. He's excited. Holding in a secret.

"What?" It better be good. I should be getting back to studying those Air Force base closings that are high on my list of long-delayed tasks.

"Sally Sonderberg is back."

Oh, brother. Had Jones known this? If he had, he would have said.

"She's about to give a statement to some of the media now over in the Rayburn radio-TV studio, and her receptionist just called here to ask if you could come visit with her in an hour."

No, I was not going to her. I had already done that and paid a price in lost sleep and some measure of guilt that I may have contributed to the cause of her disappearance. She might not care to look subservient or summoned, but for just as compelling professional reasons, I couldn't care about her image more than mine. Besides, I had seniority. "She should come here. Thank you, Aaron." I dismiss him with no more courtesy than that, irritated with his efficiency and his presumption to knock only once before entering. Yes, he has done it before on countless occasions, but today is not the day to interrupt me, is it, with Jones's gizmo in my hand?

That subject pales compared to my anticipation of learning why Sally Sonderberg went away the way she did and why, now that she's back, she asks to see me.

My study of Air Force stats has me listing my strategic arguments against closure of bases when Aaron knocks, twice this time, and waits for me to bid him to enter. I remove my reading glasses, fold my hands in my lap, and tell him to come in.

"Ma'am, can you receive Congresswoman Sonderberg now or would you like me to have her wait?"

"Close the door."

He does.

"What did she say in her press conference?" I ask in a low tone, needing the headline to navigate this discussion with her.

He lowers his voice. "She regretted the chaos of this weekend. She had gone to Harpers Ferry for a working vacation at Hilltop House. Her husband had failed to receive her voice mail that she was going and she was so incommunicado that she didn't watch the news. She came back home earlier this morning and had her press secretary call this conference just a few minutes ago."

I raise my brows. The timing explains why Jones might not know about this before Aaron and I did here. And as for Harper's Ferry as a plausible locale from which to withdraw from the world, it could be a drive of an hour and a half or so. I had been to Harpers Ferry for an ecology group's forum two years ago, and we had stayed in this same hotel that Sally supposedly did. Could she have registered there, then driven down here, pushed me to the median, and returned to her hotel and room without anyone there the wiser? From what I recall, a desk receptionist does not man the lobby around the clock. It was possible. "Intriguing."

"Yes, ma'am.

I note Aaron's increased courtesy and without a reprieve of a smile, I nod. "Send her in."

He steps to the door, swings it wide, turns, and finds her beyond my line of vision. "Please, ma'am, do come in."

She is well inside before I rise. I don't walk around my desk, but reach across it to shake her hand. "Hello, Sally. How are you?"

"Better now than when we met the other day."

I motion for her to take the chair in front of me. "Good. I'm very glad to hear that." My words are in many ways truthful, but I reserve the right to change my attitude. For now, my posture is unbending, my tone cool. Let her come to me all the way to explain herself. If she is the one who tried to mow me down Saturday night, well, I need to know that quickly. Warmth will only imbue her with the notion that she can lie to me with impunity. I needed to make her sweat a few bullets.

Frankly, she appears to have already done that. She's pale, more pale than her usual plaster, her platinum hair severely pulled back in a bun, her only color the red lipstick. She's quiet, too, worn through with some kind of worry.

She brushes her skirt, looks me in the eye, and says, "I came to say thank you."

I don't speak but give her one of those blinks that imply, *Really, I can't imagine why.*

"Your visit—our talk—made me reflect on what it is I really want here, anywhere."

Again, I widen my eyes to ask for clarification.

She looks around a bit, noting the stark confines of my temporary quarters. When she finds my gaze again, she appears to be girding herself to say her piece, but she seems also more self-conscious, less confident. "I've decided I cannot do this any longer. When the next filing period comes around, I won't be submitting my papers. I will resign."

Now she has my unvarnished sympathy and reaction. "Sally,

I am sorry to hear that. Is that what you said to the media?" I'll kill Aaron if he failed to inform me of that before she walked in here.

"No."

I inhale, sit back.

"I could not do that today. That's for another time. You are the first to know that and it is in confidence, if you will please keep it that way. I need to tell everyone, beginning with Scott and Iverson. Today, I just wanted to quell the rumors. Stop the speculation about where I was this weekend, what I'd done."

Which was what?

She brushes her skirt again, blinking back a few tears, then, once more composed, she lifts clear eyes to mine. "I love politics. But I cannot be all things to all people. I'm not that strong."

I want to object, encourage her to persist, but I question the wisdom of selling such a difficult job to someone who has tried it and decided she can't handle it. Instead I say, "Strength is not necessarily the main characteristic."

"Probably not," she agrees with gruff remorse. "But I did some soul-searching up there on that hilltop." She rolls her lips inward, but clears her throat and says, "I cannot fail at my marriage. I love this man, I have for more than twenty years from when we were freshmen in college together. My parents had a shitty marriage and it's only by sheer willpower that I can say I turned out fairly normally. I don't want to lose my husband to this job—and I certainly don't want to lose my two children to it, either."

The comparisons flood me with remorse. My parents' marriage failed. My own to Len did, too. My daughter is growing up between Len and me, and if the last few days were the enduring example, they showed that Jordan has been bounced about among his interests, mine—and her own. Never good to be a ping-pong ball. "I understand, Sally."

"I know you do. You are going through hell here this past week, with all the rumors about whether you may have killed

Alistair—and so you don't need my angst to add to your pile of concerns. But I feel responsible for contributing any additional anxiety to your situation."

I freeze. "How so?"

"Last week, I failed to tell you something that will . . . interest you." She stills, gathering courage, I think. She weaves back a strand of hair that has escaped her bun. "Did you know that Alistair had odd ways of persuading people to vote within party lines?"

I have gone to stone in my chair. "No." And what has this to do with his meetings out on River Road, his financial problems, and his penchant to hook up with women anytime? "Odd in what way?"

"He told me he knew about Jerry's and my financial problems. He said he wanted to help us. Help me. He said that if I went with him to meet a few people, he could ease my burdens. Those were his words, 'ease your burdens.'" She swallows so hard I can hear it. "I told him I couldn't."

"Good for you."

She bares her teeth, shakes her head. "He would not take no for an answer. Came back again and again to make the same offer."

There had been hints that Alistair was losing his touch as whip, but this added to the evidence that he was losing his political savvy along with his money and home—and maybe his mind.

I choose my words carefully. "Look, Sally, I know this is not easy for you to tell me. And much of it does need to be told to Detective Brown."

Her blue eyes pool with tears. "I can't, Carly. I can't. I . . . am . . . so . . . afraid." She breaks down. "I told Alistair over and over I couldn't. I was afraid, Carly, of whatever Alistair was into."

"And you obviously had good reason to be."

She sits back. "But you don't know what that is?" Is she relieved?

"No," I tell her honestly. "I may know as much as you, at this

point." But now, because all Alistair's sins came to rest in my office a week ago tonight, it behooves me to uncover all the facts
of whatever this was. "Did he ever explain who the people were
he wanted you to meet?"

"No."

"How were they supposed to help you, then?"

She shrugs. "I had the unpleasant feeling it was something . . .
illegal. That they would give me money for whatever I was to
give. I was afraid, Carly, it was government information. Classified documents."

Right. "Did Alistair ever say when you could meet them?"

"Often."

"No, I mean"—I lick my lips—"a certain day or . . . ?"

"Weeknights. 'It'd be so easy,' he'd say. 'Quick.'" She clutches
both her elbows.

I feel the same chill she does. "Any certain place?"

"Somewhere close. Up in Maryland."

My heart drops through the floor. *Oh, Alistair. When this comes
out, how many will you drag down with you?*

Whatever he'd been doing up off River Road had been an
addiction that had killed him. His crime included his attempt to
corrupt other government servants, like a dedicated, struggling
young representative like Sally Sonderberg. How many others
had his addiction touched, turned, and ruined?

And which one of them had killed him for it?

fourteen

As if she were the bride at her wedding reception, Holly Ireland greets guests at the door of the reception room at the Hyatt Regency. She's donned some shapeless yellow caftan to do it in, and to contrast her bland attire, she's commandeered a butler who's a twentysomething Chippendale type holding a tray of every assorted mixed drink you could wish for. He himself is terrific eye candy.

Good god, what is the matter with me, that I now examine anything in pants? Am I lonely, horny, beginning menopause—or just plain stupid? Maybe all of the above.

"Gin and tonic, Carly?" Holly asks, able in private to avoid my title and use my given name because she once served in Congress herself.

"Thank you, no, Holly." I smile perfunctorily at her and her waiter. "Diet Coke will be good. It's too early in the day for alcohol." And too relaxing when I've got more plowing to do tonight than five farmers in a rock forest.

She sidles closer and leans over to ask, "Are you going to the funeral home tonight?"

"Yes. Taking my daughter."

"I read that she is buddies with Alistair's son."

"Really?" I try to appear accepting, but actually the amount of column inches devoted to Jordan's and Zack's friendship increased today, so Aaron told me. That irritates me, and to have Holly bring it up just adds salt to my wound. "Well, I came for a few minutes only."

"And I'm so glad you did. I want to introduce you to our vice president of government relations." Translated, that means her chief lobbyist in charge of corralling House and Senate votes for their way of thinking. Because I tend to vote for bills that provide funding for the extension and improvement of benefits to seniors, I am here more as moral support than as someone who truly needs to be convinced.

"Thanks, Holly. Maybe another time." In my few minutes here, I've got to find Mirinda Pace and engineer a conversation with her that not only looks natural, but brings me some knowledge of whether she and Alistair met last Monday night and what she knew about what he did afterward. "I just wanted to show my support for the defeat of this attempt to put more restrictions on Medicaid."

"Well, just let me try to find him quickly, okay?" She takes my elbow and instructs the waiter to take over.

Since she's intent on steering us through the crowd, I figure I'll let her because it looks so nonchalant. We're weaving our way past her staff when I see Sam Lyman across a crowded room. He turns around just at the right moment when I pass and our eyes lock. "Carly," he croons in a molasses baritone that makes you want to shuck your clothes and get all hot and sweaty.

"Hi, Senator." I put my hand out and he grasps it, pulling me toward him.

"Let me introduce you," he says, and does the gentlemanly thing, getting Holly in on the act with the man he's been chewing the fat with—and, from what I see, eagerly wants to dump, with our help.

In a matter of minutes, Sam's body language has maneuvered Holly and his friend out of our conversation. "You have no drink." He raises his hand to summon a waiter and I interrupt him.

"None needed. I'm here only for a few minutes."

"I'm delighted to see you." He smiles and his laugh lines bring out the charm in his handsome face. "I've been worried about you."

Really? Have you shown that? Called? Written? I try to smile, kicking myself. *God, Carly, why are you ticked off when the guy is just trying to be nice?* "Thanks, Sam. I'm fine." More like scared to death, for myself and nameless others. But, "Fine, really." I smile more broadly.

"They've been rough on you."

"The press? Well, not as bad as they might've if they truly thought I might be guilty."

"What's the current word on the investigation?"

"Ah. Well. You know as much as I do."

He looks contrite. "Sorry I asked. They told you to say nothing. So, don't. As an old district attorney, I know the ropes."

Oh, yeah? Well, how about this one, then? "Totally different subject here, Sam, but help me with something, will you?"

"Anything."

"What do you think of your press secretary?"

He does a big double-take. "Can I ask why?"

"I need to know, Sam. That has got to be enough reason, now and always. Simple question. Tell me about him."

"Good guy. Known him for three years. Known of his work back in Hattiesburg for over ten. Excellent writer. What? Are you trying to steal him from me?"

"How is he ethically?"

"Solid gold."

"You'd swear on your mother?"

He puts his hand up. "Honest to God."

What more can I do than that with what little provocation I have to ask in the first place? "Good." I smile and put my hand to his arm. "Forgive me, but I have got to find someone here and have a little talk."

"All right, but wait." He grabs my wrist. "Why don't we have dinner sometime?"

Here is a man who could light my fire—and might even, if I were to be prudent and wise, save me from the nunnery I've seemed to be auditioning for the past few years. My gut reaction to Jones—unacceptable as he is as a bodyguard, let alone a companion, public or secret—has shown me that living the cloistered life might be bad for living a balanced life. Maybe lack of a loving mate was what had gotten to Alistair, too. A lack of love and affection. Not a normal way to live for anyone. So I grin at Sam. "After all this is over with Alistair, yes. I'd like that."

"Good. We'll do it."

"Great." I give his arm a little squeeze. "I must find someone before I leave. See you soon."

"That's a promise."

I drift away, noting Sally Sonderberg in close communion with William Scott. Is she telling him about her decision not to run again, I wonder for a minute? If she is, this is a terribly public place to break such news. I dismiss the subject as none of my business and focus on what is.

I work my way toward the window that offers a panorama of part of the city when through the milling crowd I catch a glimpse of dark-haired, salmon-suited Mirinda Pace. She is talking with Holly, who looks like pale ale compared to her.

"Ah, hi, Carly." Holly looks relieved that I've joined them. "Maybe you could help me explain the reasons why we need to see the long-term-care requirements in this Medicaid bill reworded."

"Reworded" is Holly's diplomatic code to imply that the bill needs to be killed. I know the cry of the wounded when I hear it. "Sure. Hi, Mirinda. How are you?" *How do I segue to Alistair?* I'm thinking.

"Good." Mirinda nods and takes a drink of what looks like scotch. Straight. Neat. The way Alistair drank his. "I told Holly I would stay only a few minutes. My son has a soccer game I've got to get to."

"I'm here for a short spell, too." I focus on her mouth, covered in a shade of lipstick I swear is the same as mine. Neither the shade of her lipstick nor the way she drinks her scotch proves she killed him, I remind myself as I force myself to smile. "I'm going to Alistair's viewing later and have to stop to pick up my daughter."

"That's tough duty," she confides in what is the first sign I've ever seen that she is real or caring or even sensitive to the challenges of being a mother—or a human being, for that matter.

Using facts that Patricia Tipton gave me about Mirinda, I go down the single-motherhood road. "Jordan has always known my job was this. That's a help."

"She's always known you did it alone, too." She sounds like she's lamenting it. "That's a help."

Is she complaining that her children resent her attention to the job? Let's see. "Children tend to rise to the occasion, I've found."

"Does your ex-husband help with her?"

"She and he went on a trip to Japan last week." But does he go to her dance recitals or show up for family night at Girl Scouts? Not on your life. Doesn't fit into his lifestyle. "He takes her once a month on weekends and sometimes when I am campaigning."

"Well, that's some relief. I've got five and it's a real chore, I tell you."

"How about a housekeeper? Nannies?"

"Yes. I have them all." She signals a waiter to take her now-empty glass and refuses the refill he offers. "I never seem to be happy with any of them. I often wish I could just bring my mother here. Tried it once, but she hated Washington. Too Anglo, too uppity, too impersonal."

"I understand," I commiserate and wish I didn't have her on my list of suspects for murder. "Mine hates it too. Although she loves politics. Only the homegrown type."

She laughs and for the first time, I note how strained she looks, around the eyes and mouth. "I have got to run. Thanks, Holly."

Holly appears to be okay with Mirinda's departure. "We'll talk another time. Maybe we could all three do lunch next week?"

Not my job to help convince someone else to support a bill she doesn't care for. But I figure I better say yes just to have a venue to meet Mirinda on safe ground and hope for an opportunity to discuss her relationship with Alistair. "Sounds good. I've got to go, too. Goodbye, Holly. Thanks. Mirinda?" I indicate I will follow her through the crowd to the elevator.

We make our way across the room and, thankfully, when the elevator opens, we get in alone. As the doors swish closed, I inhale and go for the gold. "I hate doing this."

"What's that?" she asks, facing forward, totally uninterested.

"Paying my respects to Alistair."

She doesn't say a word, and after a long minute I turn to look at her.

In profile, she is a study in stone. Eyes straight ahead, jaw clenched, she speaks just above a whisper. "He deserves no respect."

The doors open and she steps off.

I stand there much too long, suddenly catching the closing doors with an outstretched hand.

Clearly, there was no love lost between Mirinda Pace and Alistair Dunhill. Not even in death would Mirinda say something good of him. I knew they had fought, knew she supported his demands to comply with the party stance. Was she unhappy with what she'd done?

And if so, just how unhappy?

Jordan has some kind of burr up her behind. Has had since I picked her up at home a few minutes ago. I've endured her cold shoulder, but that's at an end, now that I have a public face to present inside this funeral home.

One way I have dealt with my multitudinous tasks is to deal

with issues as they arise, especially any that bear on Jordan's health and welfare. Tonight, that means confronting her in her snit.

I pull into the parking lot off Wisconsin and kill the engine of the Escape. Photographers fill the sidewalk, taking pictures of anyone entering. We are sure to be on their list. So as Jordan pulls up the door latch to get out, I put a hand to her arm. "Tell me what's bugging you before we go in."

"Nothing."

"Wrong answer. Try again."

"I hate this suit." She pulls at the lapel. At home a few minutes ago, she'd already complained loudly to me about her fifth-grade class school photo the *Post* and *Times* ran today alongside the story detailing her friendship with Zack.

"Noted. But you can't wear jeans to a funeral parlor." She had lobbied for that, too, minutes ago, though it was halfhearted because she knew she would not win.

"Who says?"

"Me. And I'm in charge."

She crosses her arms and stares straight ahead.

"If you want to see Zack tonight, you'd better tell me what the problem is now."

"Or what?"

"Or I am not going in there . . . and neither are you."

She scoffs. "You have to."

"No, I don't."

"It's your *obligation*." She makes the last word sound repulsive to her. The tone and the thought are both new for her—and distressing to me.

Containing my anger, I turn my head and watch the traffic go past. "My first obligation is to you as your mother. And I can't address what I don't know about. So what is your problem?"

"I overheard you talking with Ming at home. You want her to move in full-time? How come you never talked with me about that?"

I sigh. Ah, I see. "You are right. I did not discuss it with you first."

That cools her jets a little. She fiddles with her watch. "I just felt . . . I dunno, left out that you would ask her that."

"Should I retract the offer?"

Jordan faces me, mouth open. "You'd do that?"

"Of course I would. If you don't want her to live with us. If you don't like her."

"No, I really do like her! Honest. I just . . . well, I just got creamed that you did that and didn't ask me." She licks her lips. "Sorry."

I reach across and take her hands in one of mine. "I'm sorry, too."

"Can I ask you something?" She's still looking out the windshield.

"Sure. What?"

"Why do we need her full-time?" She swallows like she's going to cry. "I mean, I thought we did okay, ya know? And I thought, well, if you think I need someone to keep track of me, I mean, that's not really true."

Wow. I really had not had the extensive conversation I needed to have here with her, had I? I had gone off half cocked, reacting instead of acting. Thinking only subconsciously about Patricia's and Scott's statements, I had not rationally decided if I truly wanted what they offered . . . and if it was good for the one person in my life I loved totally. "You are right, Jordan. I am not certain if I need her full-time. Not for you, certainly. You and I have done well together, between school and carpools." Then, to give him his due, I add, "And your father takes you for visits."

"Yeah, well, count him out, would you, from now on."

"Well, Jordan, really I don't think I can. I mean, he is—"

"My father? Yeah, riiight, Mom." She grabs the door handle and yanks.

"Jordan? You can't just leave this discussion."

"Hey, Mom, this is not the time or place for this, is it?"

Who is the parent here? I'm proud and miffed. "You are absolutely right. Let's go."

We're out of the car, walking to the huge white building and its wide front doors when I inhale. I guess it's a big one, because Jordan turns to look at me with big doe eyes and says, "Sorry. I know this must be real tough, Mom, to look normal and sad he's dead and play the representative when lots of people wonder if you killed him."

Astonished at her honesty, I stare at her. "How old are you?"

She gives me a huge grin. "Du-uh."

I nod and wince at what I have to do inside this building. "You are right. It is a real big job. I hope I do well."

She mashes her lips together. "I know you will."

"Thanks, sweetie." I put my arm around her waist—and she puts hers around mine. We walk in together and that's the way the photographers shoot us and the way a lot of people see us as we enter the receiving line, where only Sarah Mae and Zack stand. Beside them lies a huge gold closed casket draped with the American flag.

Tonight's event is a reception, with Sarah Mae and Zack receiving invited guests at the door.

As Jordan and I wait in line, I acknowledge a few people ahead of us whom I know well in the House. Aaron had told me the event was by invitation only. Alistair's staff was to attend and all of Minority Leader William Scott's as well, plus a few chosen members of the House and Senate who were close friends or colleagues of Alistair. Sarah Mae and Zack together had chosen tonight's invitation list, along with Alistair's chief of staff.

I wonder if I will see the elusive Krystal Vaughn, Alistair's ex-receptionist, and figure that probably she was not invited this evening. As the line shortens, I note a lack of both Sally Sonderberg and Mirinda Pace. Neither of them worked well with

Alistair or admired him, and so it makes sense that neither would attend.

Coming upon Zack and Sarah Mae, we all say hello and hug, while I try not to focus on Zack and Jordan holding hands the entire time Sarah Mae and I talk. Finally, I break away, Jordan in tow, and we work our way to the back of the room, where Tommy Iverson and his wife Glenna stand somberly chatting with Louise Rawlings and William Scott. We adults say hello and I introduce Jordan to them, after which she shakes hands.

Lou talks with Jordan for a few minutes, living up in every way to her white-haired grandmotherly image as she asks Jordan about her trip to Japan.

I'm chomping at the bit to be able to discuss the conflict of interpretation of "my protection." But with Jordan and Glenna Iverson there, I must remain mute on the subject of a man who, according to many, was not hired, it seems, by anyone I know. We discuss nothing of any import, until Jordan asks if she can please sit with Zack for the short service an Army chaplain has just announced.

"Certainly, go ahead, sweetie," I tell her, and turn to find Detective Brown standing at the back of the room. Our eyes lock and he nods hello. What is he doing here? Looking for suspects? I glance around. If he is, none of them here is on my most likely list. Am I totally off base—or is he?

"Carly?" Tommy Iverson asks, leaning over and indicating a row of chairs for us to sit together. "No protocol in force tonight. Shall we sit here?"

I file in next to Lou, who is next to William Scott, then Tommy Iverson with his wife on the end. Reluctant to let this one brief opportunity to discuss Jones escape me, I lean over to Lou and say, "Whoever authorized my protection, I want them to know I am grateful."

Lou smiles, her grandmotherly wrinkles making her seem like such a down-home kinda gal. She pats my hand. "We've all seen to it that the reporters who came to ask about you got a right nice earful."

I sigh. She is still stonewalling me about who hired Jones.

Tommy confirms that by saying nothing at all, just laying a finger across his mouth and saying, "Shhh."

The Army chaplain begins a eulogy that recounts how he met and served with his lifelong friend, Alistair F. Dunhill, decades ago when they were drafted and sent to basic training at Fort Dix, New Jersey, headed for the hell that was Vietnam.

"Alistair told me then he wasn't certain if the war was justified, but he thought it was his public duty to fight his country's battles, if called upon to serve. He did serve, honorably, and for many years to come, for his country. He thought it was his duty to fight for the good of his men, the good of his mission, and the good of his country. Even now, as many Americans still fight to forget the Vietnam conflict, Alistair's devotion to his family, his constituents, his party, and his country serve as a shining example of devotion without question. That such a distinguished career ended abruptly and violently is a tragedy that I am certain Alistair would trust that the American system of justice will correct."

Mute, we glide out of there, all of us, adrift, numb, without closure on what went wrong, that a man who once gave so selflessly had lost himself completely in the process.

fifteen

Jordan and I are about to climb into our Escape and Detective Brown catches up with us.

"Can I talk with you a minute, please, ma'am?"

"Detective, you can, but I'd prefer it to be someplace not so
public and out of the view of those photographers." I tilt my head
in the direction of the five or so still stalking attendees from the
sidewalk. I let him mull that while I ask Jordan to wait in the
car.

"My thought, too. Let's go back inside the building a minute,"
Brown says, and turns on his heel to lead the way.

Fearing the photographers will get a negative shot of me following Brown like a puppy, I am thrilled when he waits for me
to walk beside him and even opens the door for me. We enter
and he leads me to a small anteroom, then slides the parlor doors
shut. Voice low, he gives me a ghost of a smile. "I just wanted to
say thank you for giving me that list of your desk contents this
morning."

"You are welcome. Whatever I can do to help, I will."

"We asked our forensics team to let us know if anything on
your list might have been the weapon that created the stab wound
piercing Alistair's lung."

"And?"

"Scissors," he announces. "Big ones. Sound like a good bet."

"Great." Cautioning myself that it might be too early to cele-
brate that I am cleared of this murder, I refrain from appearing
anything other than measured and wise. "Glad I could help.
Problem is . . ."

He presses his lips together and nods. "Yeah . . ."

And we both say together, "Where are they now?"

"Any clues?" I ask him, but then shake my head and apologize. "Sorry. I know you can't answer that."

He narrows his eyes at me. "Then let me ask you . . ."

"What?"

"Have you thought any more about why Alistair would be in
your chair in your inner office?"

"Oh, yes. Often." I put my purse down on a table and cross
my arms. After what Sally Sonderberg told me—and what I
question about Alistair's dealings with people in that clearing
near the C&O Canal—I wonder if he was enticing people to do
something, then trying to blackmail them for it. For what, about
what, God only knows, cuz I sure don't. "He was looking for
something. Don't know what."

Brown relaxes against the wall, arms crossing, a large, dark,
handsome man, troubled and confounded. "Let's not play games
any longer, shall we? I know you've been asking questions, trying
to find out who did this—and much as I hate to say it, your thinking, like your list, has been a help. I also suspect that you have probably found out some things that I can't . . . or won't . . . ever."

I stare at him, neither confirming nor denying his assumption.

He continues. "While I might be grateful if your efforts help
to flush the person who did this, I am not quite there yet."

I swallow and consider the toe of my shoe. "I hear you."

"Plus, you have to know that if you hide anything from me
that contributes to a delay or an obstruction in this investigation,
I will prosecute you to the best of my ability."

I bite my lip. "I understand."

He exhales. Comes away from the wall. "You can have your
Tahoe back tomorrow," he says, totally surprising me.

"Thank you very much." Wow. I could kiss him. "Lord, do I hate these tiny cars." I shrug. "What can I say, we like our cars big in Texas."

His shoulders shake with one moment of mirth.

I grin. "No glass, right?"

He smiles now, and his chiseled features take on their extraordinarily appealing humanity. "No glass."

I frown. "I don't know when I'll be able to come get it. The funeral is at ten, but I have no idea how long it will be—and I have my daughter to take care of, what with her friendship with Congressman Dunhill's son, so I—"

"No rush. Whenever you're ready."

"Okay. Thanks." Instinctively, I walk over and put out my hand.

He considers it a minute, then grasps it. Warm and strong, his grip is a comfort after a week of tension, terror, and sorrow. "Promise me something, ma'am?"

"Absolutely. What?"

"Don't do anything foolish."

I open my mouth and clamp it shut.

"This is still an open case and you cannot and should not try to investigate it yourself for any reason. Do you hear me?" His deep chocolate eyes hold mine.

I nod, unhappy with what I must say. "Yes, sir, I do."

"A murderer is still out there, thinking they can or maybe even should get away with this. Many times a person like that thinks they can do anything to protect themselves. Even strike again."

"I understand."

"I'm not kidding."

I try to look contrite and sincere and wonder if he has any idea what Alistair might have been doing out off River Road on Tuesday and Wednesday nights. "Thank you," I tell him, getting vibes he knows nothing about those rendezvous.

"You can thank me by going home and doing nothing more."

Well, for sure, the other thing he needs to know is that I am not about to take his advice.

Washington Cathedral reminds me of Westminster Abbey. Airy, medieval, wooden choir, and marble everywhere. Understanding why medieval architects built their houses of worship to reach into the heavens, I have always felt inspired by these structures. Calmed by them.

This morning, as I walk down the aisle to take my assigned seat near others in my delegation, I feel just the opposite.

I haven't heard from Jones since late last night when he and I talked on the phone about the list of Excursion owners, and I wonder where he is. Spotting him last in his Volvo trailing Jordan and me as we left the funeral parlor last night, I wonder just how many people he can command to do his bidding. I have called him twice to ask for updates and what I've gotten is his report of "not a complete list yet," punctuated with a few grunts and unh-huh's. Acquiring from him the addresses and occupations of all those Excursion owners will give me a good handle on who might have tried to run me off the road—and who had reason to. I did inform him that as far as I can detect from my conversation with Sally Sonderberg yesterday, she has no reason to be among those suspects. He said he was still checking out her actions in Harpers Ferry over the weekend—and I should not assume anything until we had more evidence.

Meanwhile, most of my day will be devoted to attending the funeral service with the rest of official Washington. The usher shows me to my pew, and thankful for great fortune, I notice that Jimmy Jeff Holden has arrived before me. He sits alone, without his wife, and because I have given in to Jordan's request to sit with Zack up front, I am alone with Jimmy Jeff. We have opportunity and, more importantly, privacy.

With small talk, I strike up a conversation with him. We're

reading the order of service and commenting on the skills of the organist when I launch into the issues I need to discuss with him. "What do you think of Detective Brown?"

Jimmy Jeff is shocked. Now, you must realize that Texan men, when shocked, never blink, swear, sweat, or gulp. They smile. Like someone stuck a pole up their behind. "Brown? Why, I think he's a nice young man."

Which, of course, tells me nada. "I thought he was efficient, but clearly he's not doing too well or he would have found the murderer by now." I fold my arms, doing my smug impression.

"Alistair had made so many enemies, it's no wonder he died the way he did."

"How did that happen, Jimmy Jeff? I mean"—I shake my head, never having monitored this change in Alistair's methods—"we all know his job was to whip votes, maintain ranks. We'll never regain a majority if we can't maintain some discipline."

"You believe that?" he asks, incredulous.

And I am surprised he is. "Yes. Why don't you?"

"You are a prime example of the new free thinker and you can't see that all the discipline of party political lines these last few years has chafed the herd something fierce? I am here to tell you we are seeing the equal and opposite reaction. We're headed in the splinter direction."

Well, now, that is a unique concept . . . and he might just be on to something. And I suppose I am one of those mavericks that Alistair had trouble keeping in the confines of the party structure. But I could not be too objectionable, could I, or they wouldn't consider putting me up on a pedestal and running me by the American people for bigger things.

"I think there's room for movement within a party," I tell him firmly.

"You do and I do. Lots of others do. But for some reason Alistair didn't. Or couldn't."

"Any idea why?" I press.

"Something in his private life snapped. He had money problems. Real, deep money problems. In debt."

"Did he gamble?"

"Maybe. It was some kind of vice. Women."

How in hell could you gamble with women as the stakes? "I don't understand that."

"Me neither. But he did love sex." He shifts in his suit. "I feel real funny talking about this in church, I gotta tell ya."

"Did he ever . . . um . . . approach you to do something you might not have wanted to?"

"Ha! You mean go cattin' with him?" he asks so loud that he stuns himself—and he ducks his head, looking sheepish for his next words. "Sure. He wanted company."

"Could you easily refuse him?" I am, you see, making the assumption that Jimmy Jeff, as a god-fearing, good-living man, would say no to temptation.

Jimmy Jeff's watery gray eyes examine mine. "Easily if you knew in your heart that you didn't want it, didn't need it, or had it waitin' at home for you." He shrugs. "If not, he'd come back again and again, needlin' you."

I swallow and go for broke. "Do you know of anyone he asked and got accepted?"

He gets real quiet. Looks straight ahead. "Not for me to say."

I bite my lower lip, recognizing he's not gonna reveal any name to me, even if he knows one or just suspects. "I understand. Thanks. I had to ask. I just . . ." I have to play the card that makes such delicate inquiries legitimate. Otherwise, I look like a nosey broad with big *cojones*. "I have to ask. They still think I might have had a reason to hurt him."

He reaches over to pat my hand. "Not one of us thinks bad of you, Carly."

But I have to think well of me. And think well of my government and my country—and what sticks in my craw is that I have an obligation to learn what it was Alistair was doing. Not just to clear my own name. Not just to put finality to an investigation.

My investigation. But I have to figure out if what Alistair was doing threatened the national security of the country. Or the integrity of the Congress or the Senate, or perhaps even some other branch of government. It grieves me. No, no, it sickens me to even speculate on what Alistair was doing . . . and how it impacts him, us, and the rest of the country.

And that is the crux of my dilemma, isn't it? I am speculating.

And until I go out to River Road and find out who and what people do out there, none of us will be safe or sound or happy or absolved.

Especially me.

sixteen

The rain that began while we were in the cathedral has continued through the day and into a dreary night. In the chilling drizzle, the atmosphere feels more like December than mid-April. My body is as frozen as my feet and hands as I drive north on River Road toward Travilah in a search for truth that makes me shiver in my boots.

I've worked myself into a dead calm, though. Knowing, believing what I am about to do is right, I have left Jordan with Sarah Mae and Zack for the night. She asked. It seemed appropriate. I did not want to leave her home alone and I did not want to rely on the police detail. After all, what comfort and companionship Jordan could provide to Zack would be an added boon to him in his loss—plus it would give me the opportunity to investigate without worrying about her.

Knowing what Jones would say if he knew where I was going—even if he did not know why—I have created a diversion. I've asked Sarah Mae if I could borrow her rental car in the Dunhills' garage to run an errand. She readily agreed, wanting to do something for me, after I complained about an uncontrollable shimmy in the rental I purposely had not traded for my available Tahoe. There is no shimmy, of course, but Jordan had left the room and hadn't heard me complain about the nonexistent problem. I hope I'll be back before anyone is the wiser.

As I zoom up River at a cool fifty-five in Sarah Mae's really ugly gray four-door sedan, I'm relieved I see no one behind me. I've dressed for the occasion in jeans, black turtleneck, boots, and a short raincoat. I've donned a hat. Low brim pulled down to let my eyes peep out. I've brought gloves. A flashlight. Jones's gifts of gun and phone. Plus my own SIG-Sauer. A girl can never have too many guns.

One I tucked in my coat pocket. That's Jones's. The other I have slid between the driver's seat and the center gearshift panel. Let us have a moment of silent prayer that I need neither one.

As I turn off River onto the dirt road that leads me to the clearing, the drizzle becomes a steady drum upon my roof. Tinny. It sounds tinny. I mash my mouth in distaste. Did I say that in Texas we like cars and trucks and wagons and horses that have some heft, some solid integrity to them?

Yeah. Well, that is not what I am driving tonight.

And if I feel a bit touchy, if I sound a bit touched, we'll all understand why.

I bounce and jounce down that road, come to the clearing, check that it appears to be just the one I need, and push on through the undergrowth to get to the second clearing.

Only it is not a clearing tonight. No, sir. No, ma'am.

Tonight we have a congregation of . . . well, let's count them . . . eight vehicles. All manufacturers, all years. Yet all have four doors. That had been one element of the vehicles that Zack had noted in his description of those he found here—ones that had their back doors open. None of them is a black Excursion.

I pull into an opening in the circle with the other cars, turn off my lights, kill my engine, and sit, blood pressure mounting, hands sweating. For maybe ten minutes, I remain there, watching nothing move. Only the tattoo of the rain on my roof provides counterpoint rhythm to my thudding heart.

Another vehicle sways down the lane, lights going to dim as it nears. I look around. Opposite me, one set of back doors open and a man backs out, butt first. In the rain, you'd think he'd move quickly. But no, he strolls, *strolls* to the shelter of a tree in plain view right in front of all of us. Worse, he leaves the door open. I can't make out his face. Too dark. Too many shadows. And without a moon, no chance exists I'm gonna glimpse what he looks like.

I cross my arms to stop the sudden wild trembling in my limbs.

Get a grip, Carly. You'll be no good to anyone if you can't be in control.

I swallow. Try to take a deep breath from my dan-tien. Find my center. Call upon my *chi*. My force.

Two, three more minutes drift by and another back door opens—the SUV to the left of me—and a man shimmies out. As if on cue, the first man leaves the canopy of trees and enters the back door of the second. The second man enters the car the first one left.

Ten minutes go past.

I hear the back door of the car to my right. A man emerges, fanny first, just as before. And just as before, in a few more minutes, another man appears from yet a fourth vehicle and the two exchange.

What are they doing?

Now, as another group of men emerges, it is clear that all eyes are trained on my car and the latecomer. One man approaches my car and reaches the back door.

"It's open," I croak, and he lifts the handle, pulls it wide, and gets in the back seat. I turn, facing him, examining a face, a handsome face, an ordinary face, a white one, a wet one, a middle-aged one. One I do not know. "Hello," I say, and he swipes a hand down his face, wiping it of raindrops.

His eyes grow wide, alarmed. "What the hell are you doing?"

"Why?" I ask. I can't very well come out and ask him the same thing, can I? No. He'll run before I have any answers—and he may even alert the others that there's a stranger in the crowd.

"We're not supposed to talk," he explains.

"No one told me," I say because it's true.

"And you're supposed to be back here." He points to the seat, miffed.

"I am? No one told me that, either."

He blusters. "Wow, no one told you too much, did they?"

I shake my head. "What should I do?"

"Get back here."

"Right."

His eyes run down my torso. "Without any of that."

"What?"

He goes stark still. His eyes narrow. "Clothes."

God. What do I do?

I swallow. "You mean . . . ?"

"Yeah. What did you think, we were gonna strip you?"

"Well, I wasn't sure. I mean, I haven't ever done this before, you know."

He is definitely suspicious now, and cautiously looks to the right and left. "Who told you to come here?"

"A friend."

"From Alexandria?"

I figure what have I got to lose by saying, "Yes."

"When?" he persists.

Breathe. Think. Try huffy as a diversion to keep him talking. "I don't like the way you're talking."

He crooks a couple of fingers and gives me a *come here* sign.

All right, I can do this. I lift my handle.

He grabs my shoulder. "No! Do not get out by the front door!"

"Why not?" Am I sounding as serene as I think I am?

"Not our code."

"Code. I see. I had no idea there was a code. So, tell me if I get in the back seat what should I do next?"

"You mean after you take your pants off?"

Ah, yes. I clench my teeth together because now, no breathing, no focus exercises can keep me from harm. I know what they do here.

"Yes. After I take my pants off."

He snorts. "You spread your legs. We have our event and then you get a new partner."

My thighs are automatically clenching. "Until I've had everyone."

"Yeah. That's right. And everyone has had everyone else."

"I had no idea it was that many."

He arches a brow. Under any other circumstances, I might have thought he was nice-looking. Baby-faced, even. A man I might work beside. But not a man I'd get under. Ever. "You like bareback or covered?" He pulls from his jacket pocket a square foil little packet. A condom.

"Covered." I nod, probably too much. "Definitely."

"Good."

Thinking fast is something we do real well in Texas, especially when confronted by a critter with evil on its mind. What springs to my mind makes me wonder about my sanity—and intelligence. "Ever have an audience on any of these?"

He falls back in his seat, shocked, and then a grin spreads on his face. "Only once before for me, but if that's what floats your boat, I can get another one to join us."

I lick my lips. "Oh, I don't know. . . . I rather hoped we could have, well, a group. Do you always do it just in cars, or can we"—I look around, wave a hand—"find a bigger space?" Wow, am I nuts. Can I do this, inspire as many as . . . what? . . . four men to join together and go somewhere while I hold two guns on them and call for backup? And how do I ensure the others . . . the women . . . or I assume they are . . . won't gang up on me?

"We have a cabin. Private property. Over there. We can walk." He points through the trees.

And I want to drop to the floor and escape through the exhaust system, like a ghost. "That easy, huh?"

Damn, he looks like I gave him candy for Christmas. "Done deal. Anything you want. Let me go give the word and then we can all go together."

Okay, smart girl, now what? I finger Jones's gun in my pocket. "Tell you what, why don't you get your buddies here and all of you go get ready. I'll be right behind you."

He frowns. "I don't know about that. I think it'd be better if you came now."

"I'd like to be anonymous as possible, you know. That's part of my thing."

"Yeah. I hear what you're saying. Okay. Let me get the others. They're almost done anyway, I think. New hostess. They're gonna really like this." He leans over the seat and points through the woods. I catch a whiff of far too many perfumes rising from his skin—and my stomach turns. "There's a path in there. You can't see it from here, but it's there. Just stay on it. Need a flashlight?"

"No, I'm good." I hoist my light to show him.

He gets a lecherous grin going. "Yeah. I bet you are." His eyes travel down my chest. "I can tell you got great goods."

He smiles.

I can't.

"Let's wait till the guys are done with their rounds."

I ask, "Does every man have every partner one time?"

"At least. Sometimes we get a request to stay, but usually it's five, ten minutes. We're fast. Good. Efficient."

"No foreplay, right?"

"Hell, no. That's not what this is about." He's laughing. "Doggin' is all about getting it up, getting it in, and riding till you're done, then moving on."

"Dogging." Rough, raw, impersonal sex. "A crude name for it, don't you think?"

"Baby, you can call it whatever you want." He leans forward and reaches out a hand to cup my cheek, but I withdraw. "Oh, oh. Okay, I get it. You are a no-touch brand. Works for me."

The impersonality, the terminology make my independent soul rise up and want to bite his head off. But I tip my head toward the cabin. "I'm eager to get going. How long do you think the others will be?"

"Let me check." He gets out, stands in the clearing, and in a minute he's joined by three other men. He says a few words and they turn in unison for the dark of the woods.

I place my SIG in my left pocket, open my door, and watch them turn for the woods. I'm hoping they're headed for the small cabin I spied night before last when I walked around. I worry about the remaining cars and their occupants, wonder if any have weapons. I just have to see if I know any of these men, if any of this makes any sense.

The rain picks up. The ground is sodden mossy mess as I traipse through the brush, following these men, silent in their dedication to their goals. The flashlight one of them holds offers sufficient light for the path that I don't turn on my own. They arrive at the door of the cabin, and one thrusts it open and leaves it open. Through the door and the small window I can tell the man with the flashlight has upended it, sitting it somewhere to offer some kind of light.

A plan, Carly. What is your plan?

I reach the door.

I step inside.

I wonder if these men have ever been as objectified as they have done with the partners they meet here.

Let's see.

"Hi, boys," I croon, and kick the door closed with my heel. I hear the thud, the latch clink down, and the four of them shift one foot to the other. "How are you?"

"Real good," says one, crossing his arms, lifting his chin. "What you got under that jacket?"

I grin—and I'm pretty sure it must be nasty. "Me to know. You to find out." I take a step to the left. "Does this place have lights?"

The one who'd climbed in my car objects. "Thought you wanted anonymity."

"Oh, I do," I croon in my best *come to mama* voice. "I just need it on for one little minute."

He looks askance at me, suspicious once more of my change in temperament. "Why?"

I finger Jones's gun in my right hand, my SIG in my left. "I need to see the goods first."

"Not," objects the first guy, "part of the code."

"You want a new experience?" I ask, bold as brass, wagering my life that the thrill of the risk is what these dudes crave more than anything else in their miserable existences. "I'm capable. I'm smart and I'm definitely gonna give it to you." I narrow my gaze in what I hope is seduction but I know underneath is hatred. "Take your coats off, boys. Shoes next. Then your shirts." I give them a five-alarm-fire smile. "Then your trousers. Give it a bit of class and . . . whaddaya say, let's see the wares."

"You gotta be jokin'," hoots the first man.

"I dunno," says another. "Works for me." He starts to strip, shoes, shirt, then flips the button on his jeans. "I got nothing to hide."

"Me neither," says the fourth, and zips down his fly so fast I have to swallow back shock at what I'm looking at.

Oh, Mother, save me. Every man shucks every stitch. Even in the shadows of this cabin, I can now see things that, well, are best reserved for bedrooms and nicer language than I am capable of under these circumstances. I am being treated to flabby abs, paunches like the Pillsbury Doughboy, very hairy legs, bad choices of argyle or white socks, and, you guessed it, no underwear. We have—from left to right—long, ultra-long, stubby, and balloon-shaped accoutrements.

My eyes dart about the cabin. It's used to store fishing and hunting gear, and I don't find enough line to tie them up—and no weapons that they can use to deter me, other than their four-to-one advantage.

"I like to be watched," I tell them. Creating a scenario as I go, hoping my mind does me proud—and saves my girlish hide here. "Sit down, please. On the floor."

But the first man who objected now gets up a head of steam. "No." He steps forward. "Your turn."

I hold my ground.

He keeps on coming. "In this cell, men are in charge."

"New code." I put my fingers on the triggers. "Mine."

He steps too near and the air is filled with the sound of my SIG cocking.

He rushes me and I pull out both weapons, SIG trained on his pals, toy gun poking Mr. Ballsy in the chest.

"Breathe," I warn him, "and you are a dead man."

He flows backward and just when I think he's gonna be a good boy, he hauls off and tries to deck me.

I duck.

He misses.

His three other buddies run toward me and I fire. That's enough to wing one and halt the other two. But only for a second. Next thing I know, they've got my left arm pinned to the floor— while the first guy wrestles Jones's little gift from my hand.

He's looking at it, grinning like a fool, wondering what in the hell he's got his hands on, when he tries to fire.

Well, we know, don't we, that he gets no action.

That's when the door bangs open behind me and I hear a voice I haven't heard up close and in person for more than two days.

"Okay, gentlemen," says Jones, weapons like his gift to me in each hand, "time to cool down here." He slants his eyes down at me, checks me out, then orders them to step backward toward the far wall. He's checking out what God gave the assembled men before him and his electric eyes are dancing. "Interesting packages." His expression drains to the steel of disgust. "Too bad they're all going to be covered for years to come."

I rise, dust myself off, and stand next to him. "What's the best way to take them in?"

Eyes on our prizes, Jones says, "The usual way. Brown is right behind me with a detail."

"You called him?"

He smiles crookedly. "We met on the way in." He throws me a look. "You okay?"

I nod, coming back to normal enough to begin to shiver.

"You go ahead down to the clearing. Brown's got someone you need to see."

Expectation makes me eager. "Who?"

Infuriating as he is, Jones gives me no answer.

I hurry through the overgrowth, pushing aside vines and branches, hearing the sounds of police radios and then, in the clearing, seeing six cruisers surrounding the circle of cars. In one knot of officers and women, I find Detective Brown in plain clothes talking quietly with someone whose face is turned from me. But as I come to stand next to him, I ask myself if I expected to find her here. If my Second Mind knew she would be here, I did not want to acknowledge it.

But she is. And as I come abreast of her and Brown, I look at her with sorrow and outrage. She gazes back at me, ashamed and teary-eyed. From the state of her attire, she has recently dressed, and hurriedly. I am not surprised. She was in one of these cars. She was one of these participants. She was one person to be condemned for what she destroyed in herself and would cause to be questioned about our government and its representatives.

I stare at her. Glare at her. And walk away.

Mirinda Pace would never have my pity.

Only my scorn.

seventeen

The dust 'n cleanup on Alistair's murder was one of those events I wanted to skip town for. But couldn't. With all the earmarks of sleaze and political repercussions, the case brought out revelations that made me cringe. I approached reading the newspapers the following morning and the next with a vow not to read any longer than my angst meter could tolerate.

That was not too far.

I had most of the answers I needed and none of them were too pretty.

Mirinda, from what Detective Brown reveals to me now as I sit in his office, sang like the proverbial canary.

Lonely and roiled by the demands of her job and her children, Mirinda sought relief in sexual encounters with numerous partners. What began as an escape became an enticing risk, then an addiction. One that escalated into other sexual escapades. Brown does not tell me how she learned about dogging—I don't ask Brown and frankly do not want to know—but she began attending sessions more than a year ago.

Happening upon Alistair one night in one of the cells, as this group of people called their clusters, Mirinda had been shocked. One of the keys of this type of sexual activity is the expectation, real or implied, that no one knows anyone else, won't recognize them—or if they do, won't reveal any identities. Alistair, the more established member of the cell, had used his knowledge of her involvement to complement his lagging political expertise by blackmailing her professionally. He had required her to vote along straight party lines.

She had balked at first—or so she says—but, not seeing any way out, had complied. Over time she strained at his bit and began to quarrel with him. He demanded compliance. She felt trapped by him as well as by her own addiction to the perversion. Meanwhile, Alistair, feeling his oats, attempted to expand his network, trying to recruit others, especially women.

Brown outlines how Alistair met his death at Mirinda's hands. "Last Monday night, Pace and Dunhill met in her office. They argued about policy and his blackmail of her. She was angry and followed him into your office. He was rummaging through your desk. She says he was trying to find something incriminating to persuade you to follow his lead on a few votes."

"My god. He really had lost his marbles." I think of something more disastrous. "Did Mirinda tell you how he got into my office?"

"No idea. She didn't see him do it. Do you have an idea?"

"None. He had to have a key, though."

"Right. That's an issue we need to solve for."

My mind is awhirl with conjecture. Who would have given Alistair a key to my office? And why? "So then what happened with Mirinda? She followed him into my office and . . ."

"They fought. He had helped himself to some more scotch, and in the argument the glass fell and broke, she hit him in the eye—"

"And the lipstick on the glass?"

"We analyzed it. Compared our sample to the color and make of the sample you gave me. It's the same shade, same make. But it took us a while to learn if it was yours or not, because we had such a very small sample. We determined that it had oxidized to the point that it must have been on the glass days before the murder."

"So it was mine. Wow. I guess my talents as a dishwasher need improvement." I'm feeling pretty ugly about that, but ask him to continue with Mirinda's tale.

"Yeah, well, they argued, she hit him, and turns out she cut his eyelid with one of her rings. He went for her, she retaliated—having seen your open drawer and the set of big scissors, she stabbed him. He fell into your chair, where he clutched his chest and she used the scissors to emasculate him and show him what she truly thought of him."

I am heartbroken to hear the details of these two people's downfall. "She must have truly hated him, to have not only stabbed him but disfigured him."

Brown smacks his lips. "She was objectifying him, as he had her."

"What a waste of good people. How does that happen?" I ask rhetorically, knowing the answer is long and complicated.

"Some people know how to say no." Brown sits upright in his chair. "Krystal Vaughn was one—and she refused to go with him. Instead, she wanted a more open approach to their relationship. She demanded Dunhill date her. When he pressed her to join his group, she decided to get out completely. The police officer she is dating encouraged her to tell us all this and your investigation of her activities helped us clear her—and look elsewhere into his activities."

I shake my head. "I could never figure out if that story about her telling Alistair good-bye because she wanted to get married was true or not, but I figured you had more ability to learn that than I did. Especially since she supposedly was engaged to one of your men."

"We checked that out thoroughly. Especially because one of our men was involved. But in the end, Vaughn's involvement with Dunhill was a dead end," Brown says. "We had a lot of dead ends in this case. Beginning with no murder weapon."

My mouth drops open.

"Oh, yeah, I knew for a while that your letter opener could not have been the weapon. The blood was purposely put on there."

I cringe. "Don't tell me Mirinda dipped it in Alistair's wound."

"No. But we could tell from forensics that the tip of the opener had been smeared with blood. Placed on the tip by a cotton fabric. None of your clothes matched the cotton fibers. We suspected a handkerchief, usual cotton variety. But we couldn't find any match."

"So Mirinda tried to frame me." Bile, strong as the color of Brown's walls, flows through me.

"Yes, ma'am, she did. And just like you deduced, she took everything she could with her from the scene."

Had I been right about what I thought was the weapon? "Scissors?"

"Scissors. Glass, trash. Tweezers from your drawer. Everything. She was good. Because I had little hope that search warrants of every office and home of those who remained late at Rayburn that night might bring me anything useful, I had to look for other clues to who had killed him."

"And that's why you tolerated my own investigation."

He lifts both brows. "I would never say that."

I smile at him.

He gets a sweet glint in his eye. "Tuesday night when I went to see Dunhill's sister and his son, I realized you knew quite a bit more than I anticipated."

Ah. "So that's how you knew where I'd gone. I'm glad Zack told you."

"Do they teach you to be hardheaded in Texas?"

I grin. "Yes, sir. Survival is based on it."

He is dead serious. "That was very foolhardy of you to go there."

I inhale. "I know. But I was worried. No, make that terrified about what Alistair was into, going there. I was inclined to think it was espionage. I suspected him of a lot of sexual peccadilloes, but I had no idea that his rendezvous off River Road were connected to any sexual shenanigans. I hope that your investigation will prove that that was all it ever was." I cross my arms. "I'd hate to think Alistair jeopardized the welfare of the country for a few minutes of . . . well, you get my drift."

"I understand your concern. And we certainly will dig long and hard to find those answers. Explain to me why you thought it might be espionage."

"Secretive meetings. Scheduled in a private place on certain days. It just felt . . ." I roll my shoulders. "Spooky. Certainly not sexy."

"I hear you. But then how did you reconcile that with what Dunhill's sister and his son told you about the checks Dunhill wrote to James Hollister?"

Brown's knowledge of that makes me breathe more easily. "I couldn't. So many threads, and none of them wove with the others." I bite my lip. "I read in the paper that one of the four men at the cabin was Hollister."

"Works at NIH."

"Anything classified?"

He shakes his head once. No.

"Thank god for that."

Brown looks pained. "Hollister saw an opportunity when he recognized Dunhill and used it to blackmail him."

"What an awful mess."

Brown sits forward in his chair. "I expect there will be a congressional inquiry."

"Yes. I had a meeting with the House leadership of both parties yesterday." Behind closed doors, I had told them what I knew and when and how I had learned it. "They were so stunned by what they heard that they said they would talk among themselves about it, but they predicted that the House Ethics Committee would want to do an inquiry. They indicated they'd begin now with an investigation, but wanted your opinion on that because they didn't want to interfere with your prosecution of Mirinda."

"I'll work with them on that."

"I told them I would, too."

He grins again, definitely a more pleasing way to view this man. "So I'll be seeing more of you."

"Right. But not as often."

"My loss," he says, with an acceptance of me that lights up his stunning features—and my appreciation for his professional behavior.

"Thanks."

"One question."

"Sure." I pick up my purse. "What?"

"How'd you get your bodyguard?"

I roll my eyes. "Good question. He's a present."

"Jones"—he raises his brows—"is a present?" He whistles softly. "Pretty expensive present."

"You know about him?" I feel my pulse race, finally about to learn something from a source I never expected.

"Saw his investigator's license the other night. He's legit."

My mouth waters in anticipation. "Who does he work for?"

"Far as I can tell, he's freelance."

Damn. "Meaning he doesn't have an employer?"

"Meaning," Brown corrects me, "he can work for anyone. We have so many investigation companies in this town, you could fall over one on every street corner."

"Any one in particular you like as his employer?"

"Dunno. VentureX. Wayland and Harborough. Macinverny. Pick one. They're all good. Top dollar. All operate like ghosts."

Shoot, just my luck, I grumble to myself. "Thanks."

"If I were younger and had the training, I'd apply. But I was your average grunt in Desert Storm."

"Nothing average about you, Detective. You solved this case."

"With your help, ma'am. Only with your help."

We walk toward the stairs.

He says, "The one I feel most sorry for in this is Dunhill's son."

That sadness I understand in so many ways. One, because I like Zack tremendously and am proud of how he conducted himself in this case, and another, because his burden in many ways is shared by his best friend. "Do you have children, Detective?"

"No. I'm a widower. No kids. Wish I did have, now and then."

"Zack is really a sweet boy. It's a very painful thing, to know that he will grow up with such a burden."

"'The evil men do lives after them,'" Brown quotes a famous line.

"'The good is oft interred with their bones,'" I complete it. And we smile sadly at each other for a second, commiserating over the idea that what good Alistair did was now lost to his friends and colleagues, perhaps forevermore.

I break the silence. "I have to ask you something before I go."

Brown frowns. "What?"

I want to laugh. He thinks I'm going to tell him something more about this case he does not know. "Far be it from me to be presumptuous—"

He gets a hoot out of that one. "Yeah, right. But what?"

"Do criminal psychologists say that interrogations of suspects are easier if everything in sight is bile green?" My eyes dance around the room.

His face crumbles into pieces of laughter and feigned indignation. "What? You don't like my decorating scheme?"

"The only reason it might work is if it truly is a setup to make suspects spit up the truth."

He tips his head toward the exit. "Go home, ma'am."

"Happy to." I shake his hand.

"Stay away from trouble."

"I'll try."

I've asked Aaron to set up a media conference outside in a free press area at the southeast corner of the Capitol. Because the weather has blossomed into a balmy seventy-degree spring these past two days, I figure the cameras will capture a pleasant picture of the congresswoman vindicated against the backdrop of the Capitol Dome. Afterward, I'll be able to walk into the sunshine, in more ways than one.

I've purposely maintained a very low profile for the past nine days since the crime, and I want to say my piece, get it over and done with, and then leave, forever, this tawdry, sad murder behind me. I have hailed a cab from Capitol Police headquarters and I'm grateful when I climb out onto Independence Street that I haven't had the kamikaze taxi driver who gave me last week's wild ride.

I say hello to Aaron and my press aide and step in back of the microphones. We have a full battery out there, maybe fifty or so with every imaginable type of equipment. I have never seen so many reporters and photographers in any of my previous conferences and wonder just how many people around the world will want to see this.

"Good morning, ladies and gentlemen, and thank you for coming. I am pleased this morning to tell you that the Capitol Police have officially informed me that the investigation into Congressman Alistair Dunhill's death is largely concluded. While the accused is behind bars and many facts are still to be fully revealed, we mourn a man who was taken from us brutally. In any society, acts of violence are always despicable. In a democracy, justice is the means by which we seek and support to serve every man, woman, and child equally and fairly. We all will watch with reverence the accused's prosecution and the determination of her guilt or innocence by a jury of her equals. As for me, I thank you for your courtesy and your kindness to me and to my family during this difficult period. I return now to my office and continue the work that the people of my district elected me to do. Thank you."

I step away and as I do, my press aide and Aaron walk to the mikes. The clamor of question fills the air, but I am walking back to Rayburn.

"Ma'am! Ma'am!"

I grind my teeth. I know who it is. And I just keep walking.

"Ma'am, wait, please."

I exhale. Turn. "Mr. Gonzales, I am not taking any questions. It has been a long and tiring week for me."

"I know, ma'am, but I'm your hometown reporter."

San Antonio is not my hometown, and only a tiny bit of it sits in my district, but I know how many people read the paper in my district. "Let's walk, Mr. Gonzales." I step out and he has to hustle to keep up with me. Good.

"Were you surprised it was Congresswoman Pace who killed Dunhill?"

"I can't discuss the case with you, Mr. Gonzales."

"Aw, come on, ma'am. We all figure it was you who did a lot of the spadework for the police."

I don't want that coming out. "I don't know why you think that, Mr. Gonzales."

"You and I both know, ma'am, that what comes and goes in these buildings is often a secret known only to God."

"Evidently not, Mr. Gonzales. My mother used to say the truth will out. It did here."

"Okay, okay. I'll work with the accepted line here. So tell me, what are you going to do now that the murder's solved? Going to Texas soon?"

"Next weekend."

"Yeah. Where are you going?"

"Ask my receptionist to give you my schedule." We're trying to cross the street and finally the traffic breaks. He's still jotting in his notebook, but I take the opportunity and hurry across.

"What else you gonna do? Rest? Read? Plant some petunias?"

I pivot in the middle of the street—and one car swerves around me while the driver leans on the horn. I stare at Mickey G. "Petunias?"

"Yeah, I . . . mean . . . uh . . . yeah. You like petunias, don't you?"

You little pest. "I hate petunias, Gonzales. Loathe them." Note, please, I am still standing between the yellow lines in the street. "Why would you think I like petunias?"

He has no answer.

I do. "The only time I have ever had petunias in my home was last Tuesday, Gonzales. The same day that someone was in my home, snooping around. And whoever it was took a tour of my shed, my journal, my trash can, and my oatmeal. I know this because they didn't hang up the shed key the right way—and they messed up the order of trash in my kitchen can. More than that, they disturbed my chimp."

I'm the one in the middle of the road, but it is Mickey G. who is sweating bullets. But I'm lovin' it. "Whoever that was in my home saw the flat of petunias that my receptionist mistakenly bought for me. They better not come back, Gonzales, because what they might not know is that I am an expert marksman. And I own two guns." I raise my right hand and shift it to the right just once. "Good-bye. Let's not meet again too soon anywhere."

Being able to work in my own office again has its charms, but I'm exhausted and decide to go home early. There is no floor business scheduled for late today, Jordan is visiting Zack and helping him pack, and me, I just want to go home, crawl in my tub, and pour in some bubble bath.

There's no police detail on my house and I have my Tahoe back, so I figure I might be getting back to normal here. No, I haven't heard from Jones today. He's still working that Excursion list—and I'm still mentally working the logic of who might have tried to run me off the road Saturday night. I've got a big zero, going back and forth between who knew I was going to the Harlans' and who might have been able to follow me there without Jones seeing them do it.

Both Jones and I have told Detective Brown about this, but no one has a clue so far who might have done it. Until we learn, Jones and Brown said yesterday, we have no final conclusion to the attempt to kill me.

I gulped on that idea yesterday—and I gulp on it now. But hey, as I draw my bathwater, I keep my SIG handy, sticking it in my wicker basket of bubble stuff. Jones's peashooter is still in my purse in the kitchen, where I have kept it since Tuesday night, in the expectation that when I see him again, I can return it to him and call our little relationship a day.

I have just stripped, climbed into my cloud of happiness, sunk up to my armpits, and closed my eyes when I hear someone walk into my bathroom. I'm figuring it's Jones, impertinent cuss that he is. But no. Not him at all.

It's a woman.

And of all people I suspected, she was not it.

"Do you have a razor over there?" Sally Sonderberg asks me, and her voice is as shaky as her hand with a gun in it.

"Why? Do you want to shave your legs?"

Her mouth is moving, trembling. This is good for me. Bad for her—and bad for her aim if she decides to get trigger-happy. "Not funny."

"Neither is what you're contemplating." I lift my chin toward her gun. A revolver. Not good news for me. All she has to do is pull her trigger. For me to fire my SIG, I have to chamber a round first—and by then I am gone to the angels.

She glances around my bathroom, opens my medicine cabinet, and paws through my aspirin and Neosporin. "You've gotta have some."

"Look, Sally—"

"Stay in there and no talking!" She wipes a wild tear from her eye.

"Okay, okay." I sink back down. "But I think if you're gonna kill me, it's gotta be a little obvious to the police who did it." Am I nuts? Provoking her is no way to treat a would-be assassin.

"What do you mean?" Her face is all screwed up in anger.

"I mean that they're looking for whoever it was attacked me the other night. This is only going to make those charges worse. Really, Sally, think."

"I have!"

"No, I mean, think what this will do to your family—"

"He doesn't care about me."

The husband, I assume. "Sure he does, Sally. Didn't he stand by you when you ran for office? Didn't he move here with you? He must love you—"

"No! No! He won't care! He never did. He married me because I was pregnant and he didn't want a scandal. He doesn't love me."

Oh, brother. A low tide grounds all boats. I get up on my knees and, thankfully, in the interest of modesty, my bubbles are big and not popping out all over . . . too fast.

I reach out to her with the hand nearest my basket. "Sally, listen to me. You have two children who need you. Love you. Think what it will mean to them if they have to go through life thinking their mother hurt someone else." I refuse to say "killed" someone else. Been there, heard that too often this past week. "Would you want them to grow up motherless?" Hell, they might anyway, depending on what she had done. "Just put the gun down and we can work this out."

She walks forward. She's listening to me, heeding me. "Alistair wouldn't stop hounding me."

"I know. I understand. He was a sick man, Sally."

"He made me do things I didn't want to do."

Ah, hell. It's gonna take more than bubbles to make me feel better anytime soon. "Sally, you—"

"Don't you get it?" she yells at me. "I did it with him."

I close my eyes and, yes, I know that is not smart, but I am crushed at her revelation. "Sally, was that a crime?" I don't know if she means that she had sex with him in one of those hideous cells or if she just had sex with him one-on-one. Either way, none of it is gratifying to know.

"I ruined my marriage." She can barely talk now for the sobs . . . and as she doubles over, in back of her I see the man who has appeared like my guardian angel at the weirdest times and places in the last nine days.

He steps up in back of her, silent as the first night he came over my garden wall, and in three swift moves, he pins her to him, wrenches her arms in back of her, and forces her face first down to the floor.

One hand to her wrists, he straddles her and casually whips out a phone that looks like an upgrade to the one he gave me. He plugs in a number, waits while he grins at me, and says, "Brown? Yeah. She's here. Carly's bathroom. No. We're fine." Jones beams at me. "Yeah, lookin' real good here. Come and get Sonderberg."

As ever, I am shocked. "You knew she'd be here?"

"No. Came here and saw her car. I just cleared that she did stay at Hilltop House last Friday night, but no one could verify she stayed there all Saturday night. Then I found a gas station in Thurmont where she stopped and got gas at two-twenty A.M. The attendant remembered her. She was in the clear except for needing to guzzle some gas."

Sally struggles a bit to be free, but then breaks down in more tears.

Wishing I could climb out of this tub, but unable to get to my towel without showing my birthday suit to Jones and Sally, I sink farther in and settle my naked self. "What I want to know," I ask her, "is how did you know I was going to the Harlans'?"

Sally's face collapses in grief. "Rayanne."

My receptionist?

"She's one of Alistair's girls. She gave me your schedule, just like she gave him the key to your office so he could go through your desk and find things to blackmail you for."

I sit there, feeling like I've been sucker-punched. Wow. I need to get my Second Mind in shape, don't I? I missed any big instinct that said not to trust either woman. Time I start paying more attention, isn't it?

"Okay, enough of that," Jones barks. "Let's move you out so the lady can get dressed." He literally lifts Sally up with one elbow hooked under her waist. Then he frog-marches her out my bathroom door.

Ten minutes later I'm dressed in a T-shirt and jeans, with Brown and two of his men hauling Sally Sonderberg out my front door. Jones stands by my side.

Before Brown leaves I ask, "What are you going to charge her with?"

"Breaking and entering, for one thing. Attempted assault with a deadly weapon, for another. You are going to press charges, aren't you?"

I cringe at the idea I would contribute to Sally's problems. "Let me think about that."

Brown stares at me. "You can't save her from herself."

I bite my lip. "I know."

"Ma'am, she'll have to be brought up before the Ethics Committee as well. Whatever she did to cause her to come here will not go well with her."

"She had relations with Alistair."

His eyes close and he shakes his head. "How many more we gonna find?"

"I don't know, but I do hope none of them finds their way to my door."

"Me neither." Brown bids us both good-bye. "You sticking around?" he asks Jones.

"My employment ends at midnight."

"Really?" I plant both hands on my hips while Jones shuts my front door. "My own Cinderella man, huh?"

"Yep. I'm done here." He smiles. "Been a good run. We did all right together, you know."

"Yeah. I know." I turn on my heel and head for my kitchen and my purse.

He follows me. "Did you ever find out who hired me?"

I'm thinking I never got a call back from Patricia Tipton.

"No. Everyone in this town is shut down tighter than a June bug on a pile of cow manure."

He chuckles. "That's okay. The money spends, and that is my bottom line."

"Along with the job satisfaction of rounding up all the bad guys in town."

"Oh, yeah. That first." He considers me. "You're good, ya know. I hear word that you've come out of this smelling like a rose and headed for bigger things." He waggles his eyebrows.

"Bah. If I ever recover my sleep—and my sanity."

"You will." He leans over to Abe's cage. " 'Bye, buddy! Take care of your lady here." He saunters forward, shoves his hand out to shake.

I slap his gun into it.

He chuckles. "Okay, I get it. I'm on my way. Never fear." He pockets the gun, and puts his hand out once more.

This time I take it. "Thanks, Jones. Nice working with you."

"Same here, ma'am." He heads for the French doors.

"Ah, Jones. You can go out the front now, don't you think?"

"Old habits die hard."

"Ain't that the truth."

I stand there and watch him scramble up the wall, nimble as a ninja, gone like the wind.

I inhale. Close my eyes. Grateful this is done and over with before Jordan saw any of it. I flick the lock on my back door and pause.

Now I could think about normal things again. Like motherhood, and my job, and my district. And whether I wanted what my party was offering for my future.

Would any of that include a man? Love? Marriage?

One thing it would not include was sex without love.

I had loved a man. I could again. Given the right circumstances . . . and the right man. But he couldn't be an ordinary man. And he might not even be an extraordinary man to anyone but me.

Maybe, at some point in my future, I might find a man I could respect and love. And want to make love with. As an equal.

I smile and wander back into my bathroom to scrub my tub and pick up my towels.

That's when I notice the phone on my bath counter. Jones's gadget.

Well, I surely don't need that any longer. The same way I no longer need Jones.

I toss it in the trash can.

And damn if it doesn't give off a sizzle and pop, shrivel up in a silver ball, and just go *poof*!

Swell. My own personal Improvised Explosive Device.

So much for white-ops techno toys.

I won't need that again. The same way I won't ever need Jones.